MELTED INTO AIR

Fra   el's life has seen better days. A
the   of
an i   **2 2 OCT 2013**   of
Mat   es
falls   rd.
To   as
don **1 2 MA**   ge
left.

As   it,
'Ho **1 6 JUL 2009**   ng
with   dy
and **HADLOW LIBRARY**   a
plan **TEL 01732 851704**   to
Italy **ENGLAND**   nd
conf

MELTED INTO AIR

Sandi Toksvig

WINDSOR
PARAGON

First published 2006
by
Time Warner Books
This Large Print edition published 2006
by
BBC Audiobooks Ltd by arrangement with
Little, Brown Book Group

Hardcover ISBN 10: 1 4056 1547 8
           ISBN 13: 978 1 405 61547 1
Softcover ISBN 10: 1 4056 1548 6
           ISBN 13: 978 1 405 61548 8

British Library Cataloguing in Publication Data available

Printed and bound in Great Britain by
Antony Rowe Ltd., Chippenham, Wiltshire

To Peta

Our revels now are ended. These our actors,
As I foretold you, were all spirits and
Are melted into air, into thin air:
And, like the baseless fabric of this vision,
The cloud-capp'd towers, the gorgeous
    palaces,
The solemn temples, the great globe itself,
Yea, all which it inherit, shall dissolve
And, like this insubstantial pageant faded,
Leave not a rack behind. We are such stuff
As dreams are made on, and our little life
Is rounded with a sleep.

Prospero, *The Tempest*
(Act IV, Scene I)

CHAPTER ONE

Se non è vero, è ben trovato

Even if it's not true, it makes a good story

'We should have cancelled.' Gina Harper exhaled as if she could barely believe what she was seeing. 'Oh God, why didn't we cancel?'

'Don't be ridiculous. It's going really well.'

Frances Angel, theatrical impresario, stood in the wings of the small regional theatre and watched the understudy Macbeth try for the fourth time in as many minutes to remove his sword from its scabbard. Even Macduff, who was a stalwart old actor of the jobbing variety, was beginning to run out of reasons not to just run the King through with his steel and be done with it. He leant on the proscenium arch and feigned a fascination with a piece of debris in his teeth, which he began picking at with his dirk. In his day he had been a good character actor and in the circumstances he tried for a reasonable interpretation for his delay in dispatching the feckless royal. Perhaps, he thought, Macduff was a fastidious fellow who would not deign to take someone's life with defiled dentures. The house was fairly empty and the sound of Macbeth's plaintive panting, highlighted by the ping of steel on teeth, echoed round the gallery.

Gina and Frances had stood together in the wings of a hundred theatres. First as children in school plays, then as university students of drama and finally for twenty years as producers. Both were dark, fiery-looking women; there was more than a hint of the Mediterranean about them. Frances had more height. She was not exactly beautiful but she always made the most of herself. Slim and stylish but sensible—the three S's of Home Counties fashion. Gina had had children, and the inevitable effect of gravity had left her the chunkier of the two. They were both, however, immaculately dressed. There was a care in their own presentation that had once been represented by the work they produced on the stage, but that was some time ago. Lately, and inexplicably, every theatrical standard available had been allowed to slip, culminating in what was proving to be a unique evening of entertainment.

'I should have insisted. He doesn't know what he is doing,' repeated Gina.

'Nonsense,' countered Frances. 'He trained at RADA.'

'As a stage manager.'

'In which case you'd think he could deal with the bloody sword. It's a prop, isn't it?'

As if reminded of his erstwhile training, the King of Scotland at last managed to pull the sword from its holder. Sadly, in the excitement he forgot the weight of the thing. The three-foot-long weapon slashed up in the air and then flew from his hand in a great arc, shot past Gina and Frances and landed in the wings on the toe of the company manager. She let out a great yelp of pain, at which point Macduff, fed up with the whole business, simply plunged his knife, tooth detritus and all, into the hapless Macbeth, who wisely collapsed on the spot. Gina crossed herself and briefly closed her eyes. There was, to say the least, tepid

2

applause. A small class of GCSE students left to catch their coach none the wiser as to why Shakespeare might ever have been considered great.

Tim Allen, the theatre manager, was incandescent as they stood outside. The rain had stopped but the streets were drenched and the tyres of the ambulance services gave a farewell splash as its lights flashed away up the anonymous high street. The manager was a small nervous man in a hideous velvet tuxedo. He had bought it off the peg some years ago and, indeed, it was so ill-fitting there were places where one suspected the peg was still lurking.

'Now, Miss Angel, you and your sister—'

'Cousin, she's my cousin.'

'—have brought me many fine shows over the years, so I took this one on trust, but let me just be clear where we are at the moment. We now have no Macbeth.'

Frances put up her hand. 'Please, Mr Allen, we have no "Scottish king". You can't say words like "Macbeth" in front of a theatre. Don't you know that's bad luck?'

'Bad luck! Bad luck!' Mr Allen was apoplectic. 'We've just sent a member of the crew to hospital with a three-foot sword sticking out of her big toe. Isn't that bad enough?'

Gina, who had been on the phone, appeared out of the shadows. 'Right. Sorted. Mr Allen, I wonder if you might get the company together on stage?'

The manager shook his head and splashed back to the stage door, while Gina turned to face her cousin.

Frances tried to smile. 'Well, that wasn't too

3

bad.'

'Not too bad?' Gina was beside herself. 'Not too bad? What the hell is the matter with you, Frances? The company manager had to go to hospital.'

'Yes, well, I'm sure she won't *actually* lose the toe.'

Gina tried again.

'Frances, we have just allowed a production of Shakespeare to be performed in which the three witches were laughing so much one of them fell into the cauldron.'

'Three witches? I thought we'd agreed to make do with two? Kidding! I'm kidding. Anyway, it lightened the whole thing up considerably. I've always found it such a depressing play.'

'It's a set text. We had to . . .' Gina ran out of steam. 'Frances, this is enough. It has to stop. I will not put my name to any more of this nonsense. We used to have a very good reputation. You used to care about what we did.'

Frances, who knew she bore the brunt of the responsibility, tried a counter-attack. 'You're the bloody finance director. Look at the sodding margins. People don't want to go to the theatre any more. Certainly not to see straight plays. We are in a dying profession and it's not my fault.'

Gina shook her head. 'That's not true. They'll go if there is something decent to look at. No one wants to see Henry the Fifth leading a charge of soldiers consisting of two people in the wings banging a saucepan. I feel as though you're abandoning everything we've worked for over the years.'

Frances was tired and a flash of temper erupted.

'I am not abandoning anything. I have never abandoned anyone in my life. That is why there was a performance tonight. Not one of those people went away disappointed—OK, mildly surprised, perhaps, but I will not just turn my back and walk away when things go wrong. I'll make them work, whatever it takes. Don't you know that the show must go on, or did you skip that bit of theatrical lore because it doesn't suit you? And when did it all become *my* fault? Maybe things wouldn't have got like this if you didn't spend so much fucking time with your kids.'

Both women took a deep breath. 'Is that what you think?' asked Gina. 'That I've let you down?'

Frances shook her head. 'I'm sorry, no. Of course you must spend time with the girls. They're wonderful. It's just I feel like I'm on my own all the time and . . .'

Gina glanced at her cousin. The street light probably didn't help but she looked pale and drawn. 'You're right,' she conceded. 'I don't have the time I used to. I'm sorry.'

Frances smiled. 'Me too. I'm sorry too. I thought I could manage without you, but lately, I'm—'

'Miss Angel, Mrs Harper?' The theatre manager called out into the street. 'We're ready on stage.'

'So did you get someone to step in?' whispered Frances urgently to Gina as they made their way backstage.

Gina nodded.

'Excellent. Who?'

Gina gave a long and deeply felt sigh before she replied, 'Alistair.'

'You're kidding, right?' Frances stopped Gina in the wings. 'That was a joke?'

5

Gina stood silent, half on and half off the dimly lit stage. Frances grabbed her arm. 'Gina, why would you do that to me?'

Gina was also tired and had had enough. For the moment she couldn't recall why a theatrical business had ever seemed like a good idea. 'Oh, you're right, Frances,' she snapped. 'It's eleven o'clock in the middle of bloody nowhere. I'm sure I could have got Ian McKellen ready for tomorrow night. Alistair knows the part, he isn't working and, despite a catalogue of other unpleasant personal habits, he isn't a lush. All these things make him perfect to appear here, sober and with some idea of the lines, tomorrow night.'

'I make the artistic decisions,' fumed Frances. 'You do the bloody books. Since when have you decided to become the driver of the company?'

'Since our beloved lead actor, Mr Peter Durnley, fell off the wagon. Now get on stage and do what you do best.'

'And what the hell is that?'

'Make everyone happy.'

On stage the actors, cleansed of their make-up and all inclined to believe that they were emotionally drained, stood ghost-like in the dim light of a single safety lamp. Frances's hand automatically moved to touch the small gold cross she wore round her neck. Then she took a deep breath and stepped from the dark wings quietly applauding. While waiting, the company had all agreed that they were going to quit but they were unprepared for Frances's approach. She finished her soft applause, dropped her hands to her sides and nodded.

'Unbelievable,' she sighed and repeated the

6

word for good measure. 'Unbelievable. I've been working in the theatre for twenty years and I have never seen anything like it. I have never seen a more professional, more dedicated approach by any group of actors, bar none. God, you had a nightmare evening and yet your focus never wavered. Not once did one of you . . .' Frances swept her eyes around the assembled cast and looked in the face of each thespian '. . . fail either the play or the audience.' Frances swept her arm towards the empty seats as if to include the great burghers of the town. 'Now I know that things have been hellish since Peter Durnley was readmitted to rehab and could no longer give his king. Indeed you might wonder, with his history of alcoholism, why we gave Peter the job in the first place.'

'He was cheap,' muttered one of the witches.

Frances nodded. 'You might think that or you might think about what I regard as the family of theatre people.' Frances nodded towards the wings. 'You all know Gina Harper as the finance director of Angel Productions, the woman who makes the ghost walk on Thursdays.'

The company gave a little laugh at the old theatrical expression for getting paid. Frances had used it deliberately. It was like a Masonic signal to remind everyone that they belonged to the same club. 'Gina is in charge of finance but she is also my cousin,' she continued. 'Gina and I are family, and the bond that we share is the template we have tried to use in everything we do. We believe that when one of our family is in trouble we don't just let them go. We both wanted to help Peter just as we would reach out to help any one of you who might stumble in the future.'

The witch, who had recently had her first flirtation with cocaine, went quiet. Gina marvelled as she watched Frances hold everyone's attention.

'Sadly, Peter's demons proved too strong but how proud he will be when he knows that, despite everything, at least tonight the show went on. I know that John here . . .' Frances nodded towards the feckless understudy '. . . has given his all but, despite that, we know that the situation cannot continue. Nevertheless, John, thank you.'

Frances led a round of applause for the man who up until ten minutes ago the rest of the company had wanted to kill.

'Tomorrow morning the distinguished actor . . .' Frances took a small involuntary gasp of air before she continued '. . . the distinguished actor Alistair Barton will be joining the company. He has played the title role many times and I know you will enjoy working with him. Gina has agreed there will be an extra payment for everyone to rehearse Alistair into the production and I know you will all make him very welcome in this extraordinary and, may I say, very special company.'

Frances began to applaud again and, for reasons no one would ever be able to recall, the entire cast and the theatre manager joined in.

When at last everyone, even the fragile Mr Allen, had departed content, Frances and Gina got back in the car for the long drive back to London. Gina drove for a while without speaking until at last she said, 'Mama is worried about you. She says you have to stop.'

Frances gave a wry smile. 'Ah, the Aunt Emilia card. You haven't tried that in a long time.' She sighed. 'I'm just tired and it all seems rather

8

pointless. Like we're adults and still playing at shops. I can't remember what we used to see in it all.'

Gina looked at Frances out of the corner of her eye. They had grown up together. For thirty-five years they had shared secrets and successes and in all that time Frances had never been anything except single-minded about her chosen profession.

'Maybe we need to stop for a bit,' said Gina quietly. 'We've been doing this for a long time, Frances.'

Frances tried to pull herself together by doing a mock Groucho Marx. 'Why we've got a tour of *Oh! Calcutta!* out there that first went out as *Fanny by Gaslight*. We have things touring whose original cast included Henry Irving.'

'Very funny.' Gina pulled out into the fast lane and put her foot down. She was anxious to get back to her girls. 'You're probably right about the kids. I thought I could do it all and maybe I can't. But it's not just me. You need a rest, Frances. Forget the work. I'm your family, I've known you all my life and I don't like what I'm seeing.'

'OK, maybe letting that boy go on as Macbeth was a mistake. I had to make a quick decision. Who knew we'd hired a lead with a drink problem?'

'Everyone. It was front page of the *News of the World*. He was arrested for driving under the influence.'

'That happens to lots of people.'

'It was a fork-lift truck through the centre of Manchester. Forget him. I mean I don't like what I see in you. You need a change.'

'Change? I'm forty. The only change I have to

look forward to is the kind that brings you out in hot sweats at two in the morning.'

'Look, Frances, I know you don't want to talk about it but you need to stop for a minute. Your beloved Alistair—'

Frances held up her hand to stop Gina, but it was too late.

'Your beloved Alistair, much to no one's surprise, was a shit. He's an actor. They are all shits. You have a broken heart. Take a holiday. Go and have surprising sex on a beach in Barcelona. Or go to the Priory or Betty Ford or somewhere glamorous in one of those dusty states in America and dry out.'

'I don't need to dry out.'

Gina threw her hands up in exasperation. 'I know that.'

'Mind that truck.'

Gina gripped the wheel. 'Call yourself theatrical? Do you have any idea what publicly drying out could do for your credibility?'

'I'm a theatre producer. What the hell would I want with credibility?'

The two women paused for a moment and the silence was thick with things unsaid.

'Mama thinks you need to go home,' Gina said at last.

Frances sat looking out of the window.

'Home?' she said at last. 'To Bedford? No one *needs* to go to Bedford.'

'No.' Gina took her time. She knew she was treading on thin ice with her cousin. They had known each other all their lives, worked in partnership to build a successful production house, ever mindful to leave some things wrapped in neat tissue labelled 'The Past'. Until now. 'To Montecastello. Go and sort things out in your head. She thinks maybe you'll learn something in Italy.'

Frances gave a short laugh. 'What's to learn? Millinery comes from Milan, jeans are from Genoa and apparently there's a reason why Michelangelo's David had such a gleam in his eye.'

'Go and face up to what happened,' persisted Gina.

'Nothing happened,' snapped Frances, 'there was an accident, that's all.' The car went silent.

The rain beat down on the car windscreen and the rhythm of the wipers lulled Frances into a reverie. Italy. The land of her birth. She tried to picture it but there were only fragments left. A stone wall, a cypress tree, a puppy. Her puppy? Someone else's? A puppy, yes, but no people. She tried to imagine her parents but could only conjure up generic peasants. They had not been poor. The house had stood on the outer reaches of the town looking across acres of the Umbrian countryside. Sunflowers. There had been sunflowers. Frances could see herself running with the puppy. *Cucciolo.* How strange. *Cucciolo* was the Italian word for puppy. What a funny thing to remember. Neither Frances nor Gina spoke Italian. Aunt Emilia had insisted on English. She wanted the girls to fit in, to make good. A determined and vigorous woman, both girls had got their business heads from her.

Now Aunt Emilia was in her seventies and was slipping slowly into the twilight of dementia. More and more she lapsed into Italian when the girls spoke to her, which made both her daughter and her niece regret their lack of the old language.

Frances was five when she had left Montecastello and had soon forgotten her native language. She was only five. She had a red polka-dot dress. The town had been in the grip of panic and her parents had spirited her away. They had feared for her life, for their own lives. Frances knew that, and in their fear they had sent her to the safety of Aunt Emilia in Britain. She had flown wide-eyed and frightened with a brown label attached to her woollen coat. Aunt Emilia had been there with little Gina. Gina was three. In her mind's eye Frances could see Gina aged three but, try as she might, no image of her mother or father rose up. Her parents had been due to follow on. They stayed to pack up the house. They would come after her, but then there had been the accident and Aunt Emilia had closed the door to Montecastello. Frances's parents were dead. She was too young to return for the funeral. Aunt Emilia loved her. She and Gina would be her family now. None of them had ever returned home to conclude the story. How odd to think of doing it now.

Gina reached out and touched Frances's hand. 'Sweetheart, I know that Alistair broke your heart but—'

'Please, let's not give the man that much DIY capability.' Frances smiled. 'So you think now, when I feel like a waste of space, would be a good time to pop back to the past and give myself a good kicking? Is that it?'

Gina shook her head. 'I think you need to put some things in order. Maybe if you sort out the past, then you can move on. It's not too late to make a new life, maybe have kids—'

'I am not going to have kids. What the hell is the

matter with you?' Frances's rare bursts of temper seemed to bring out a genetic predisposition to wave her hands when she spoke. Now she gesticulated wildly. 'Who the hell wants kids? OK, you did, but that will do. I have a nice couple of nieces, thank you very much. Don't come crying to me when they pack up and leave. Look, I've let things slip a little lately but I know nothing about Italy. I left Montecastello when I was five, for God's sake. Everyone is dead now.'

'Mama says Maria is still there. Quite the centre of the village, in fact.'

Frances took a deep breath. 'I can't.'

Gina paused before she spoke. 'Frances, I know you are afraid of Father Benito—'

'I am not afraid of anyone. Gina, leave it,' warned her cousin, but Gina was on a roll.

'I'm sure the old priest must be long gone,' she continued. 'It's been thirty-five years.'

'Yeah, well, I don't like the sun,' snapped Frances. 'We don't even take shows to the south coast. I don't know anyone. Where would I stay?'

'At Sophia Fratelli's house.'

Frances felt a chill. 'She's dead. Sophia is dead.'

'I know. The family sold the house to an English woman. It's a summer school now that runs art courses.'

'An art school? What the hell do I know about art?' exploded Frances.

'After tonight's performance probably nothing,' agreed Gina, 'but you'll meet other people. It will give you something to focus on.'

Frances stared at her insistent cousin. 'You've already booked this, haven't you?'

Gina nodded.

13

Frances shook her head. 'I have almost no Italian left, what the hell would I do?'

'Learn to paint. Find yourself.'

'Ah, therapy speak, my favourite. Nobody goes to *find* themselves in Italy any more.'

'They do if that's where they got lost.'

'Who the hell says I'm lost?' flashed Frances, furious at the way she was being pushed.

Gina smiled. 'Honey, you're so lost no one is even bothering with a search party. Trust me, we drank the brandy and gave away the St Bernard.'

CHAPTER TWO

Love is the whole history of a woman's life. It is but an episode in a man's.

Germaine de Staël
Woman of letters (1766–1817)

Frances awoke, startled and trembling. Instinctively she reached for Alistair but he wasn't there. He hadn't been there for over a year, yet somehow she still kept to her side of the bed. His space on the right lay empty and available. Each night she would try to move a little closer to occupying the whole bed but in the morning, once again, she was tucked protectively as far to the left as possible. She had been dreaming. She was running and stumbling away from . . . away from what? The priest? Father Benito? Had that been him in her dream? Did she even remember what he looked like any more? The black suit, the white

14

collar . . . they all looked like that. Frances lay back on her pillow and tried to calm herself. Had he really been so frightening that her parents had given up their only child? Had there really been so much danger that Frances had had to leave the country? Why hadn't she asked these questions before? Aunt Emilia had told her to get on with a new life. To look forward and not back, but that accident . . . what the hell had happened? She shook her head and got up to shower.

Tired and thick-headed, Frances took the train back to the theatre where she would oversee the rehearsals with Alistair. The director had been called back from London but Frances wanted to make sure there were no more hiccups. She had let things slide long enough. At least that is what she told herself. The fact that it would be the first time she had seen Alistair since his departure was not the principal reason. It was time to pull herself together. She felt sure her unquenchable feelings for the man would no longer engulf her. Frances was a bright and organised woman. She was good at compartmentalising her energies and she knew that her wasted focus on her past lover was insane.

'Frances, you don't need to go,' Gina had said on the phone. 'I can take the kids and check everything is OK. Alistair was not kind to you. You don't need to deal with him.'

'He was never unkind to me.'

Gina's sigh echoed down the line. 'Of course not. That's far too strong a statement for the man. He wasn't unkind but then he never shifted himself to be kind either. That's much too active for him. Alistair can't see beyond himself. If we hadn't been desperate I wouldn't have called him.'

'I'll be fine,' insisted Frances. 'I'm over it.'

'Yeah,' agreed her cousin, 'and if you ever get pregnant the Pope will be happy to discuss the abortion option. Frances, you are one of the most together people I know. Before Alistair you kept every affair you had in neat little boxes labelled "Leisure" and only allowed them out on special occasions. That man blew your life apart. It's all right to have some trouble getting over him.'

The beginning of Frances and Alistair's affair had caused a great scandal. He had been living with an extremely famous but fading screen star when Frances had hired him for a one-man tour of Oscar Wilde. She had thought nothing of it when his agent had called her to arrange a meeting with her star before a matinée. There was a good chance of the piece transferring and Alistair wanted to talk to Frances about certain changes to the first act. They had met in the wings and in the middle of an intense discussion about the true nature of comedy they had both gone utterly silent. Frances felt an energy in the air that she had never experienced before. People have been crashing into love from the very beginning and it is always both absurd and splendid. A mix of symphonic emotion and reluctant zips. One moment Frances had been fine and in control and in the next her entire being was lost to the man in front of her. It was all so clichéd—her heart had pounded, she had almost gasped for air and her brain ceased to function properly. They had made love there and then in the wings, oblivious to the strong possibility of discovery. Alistair was a wonderful lover. He treated the act of lovemaking like any other performance. He gave his all with a great desire to

16

please but utterly confident of good reviews.

It had taken him a few weeks of secret trysts and frantic calls to Frances for him to leave his lover of the last five years. She was a woman well past her prime but she had once been a massive star with years of skilful tabloid manipulation. The story was played out across the front pages of the red tops for weeks, all somehow adding weight and importance to what should have been simply a transient sexual adventure. Suddenly the exchange of emotions and body fluids between Frances Angel and Alistair Barton mattered to everyone.

Once their relationship was established, he took her around town as a prize trophy. Frances had never been treated like that and, as anyone would, she loved it. She felt important and special and, along with everyone else, she fell for Alistair's charm. Everyone, that is, except Gina. From the beginning her cousin had been the only one who warned her to be careful.

'He's an actor,' she said. 'I don't doubt that he loves you, but not half as much as he loves himself. Be careful, Frances. This one lives life on the surface.'

'He loves me with all his heart,' declared Frances.

'Indeed, he does,' agreed her cousin, 'but we are not talking about a lot of capacity here.'

Frances had lasted longer than most with Alistair but she had, perhaps, made a fatal mistake. They had been having dinner in a favourite restaurant.

'It's my birthday soon,' she had begun.

'Indeed.' He had smiled and asked, 'And where are you taking me? How about a nice spa?'

Frances laughed. 'Alistair, it's *my* birthday. *You* are supposed to take *me* somewhere.'

He nodded and looked woebegone. 'Would that I could. Darling, I'm an actor. I could never afford to take you anywhere that you deserve. I would love to treat you but I would be mortified not to be able to do it properly. You wouldn't want to do that to me, would you?'

Suddenly and not surprisingly, the conversation was about him. Frances tried again. 'Actually what I want from you would cost nothing.' Alistair looked at her quizzically. 'I'm going to be forty and I think . . . I was thinking about . . . a baby.'

There had been a brief moment of silence broken only by the snap of a breadstick in Alistair's hand.

'A what?' he managed.

'A baby. I think I'd like to . . . that we should . . . have a . . . baby.' Somehow the wish had become immensely extravagant.

Alistair seemed genuinely amused. 'Not really?'

'Yes, really.'

'What, a human baby? A baby baby? One of those crying-in-the-night, grow-up-to-hate-you creatures?'

Frances was beginning to lose her nerve. 'Well, I don't think they hate you straight away. I think there's an interim period where you have to watch *Pingu* and answer a lot of questions, but yes, one of those.'

'Darling, you are sweet. What a funny idea.' Alistair poured some more wine and patted her hand. 'You'd be brilliant and it would be sweet. A dark little thing with an instinct for theatrics.'

Frances smiled back before Alistair sailed on.

18

He took a sip of wine and laughed again. 'Can you imagine me as a father? I mean I could play the part, of course, but not 24/7. It would be like being on some ghastly reality TV programme. You know, quite fun for a bit but I don't think it would take long for me to get voted off, if you know what I'm saying? You'd be marvellous, of course, but I'd be hopeless.' Alistair swept off on a splendid portrait of himself as the hapless father that was both hilarious and heartbreaking.

It was not mentioned again; then, a month or so later, without any further conversation, Alistair simply moved on. There was a younger, more driven woman in broadcasting who left her husband for him. She had a lovely home and a business zeal that suggested no desire to procreate. Frances did not doubt that, in as much as he analysed anything, Alistair honestly believed it would not take her long to recover. Sadly, however, human emotions come in many shades and he continued to have an absurd hold on her heart which even physical absence failed to wash away.

Now, seven years and seven months after their first encounter, Frances once again sat on a train heading for a meeting with her leading man. She had meant to go over some paperwork in the first-class carriage but instead she sat staring out of the window. It was May but nevertheless the flat countryside spread out grey and misty as they rattled through English towns each more nondescript than the last.

'Italy,' she said to herself. 'Italy.' How ridiculous to think that she might go to Italy. She knew no one. She couldn't possibly sleep in Sophia Fratelli's house. Sophia was dead but Maria . . . Maria was alive. Why wouldn't she be? Gina had said she was quite the centre of the village. Father Benito must be dead. He had seemed old then. Frances shook her head. She didn't need to return. Aunt Emilia had always said there was no point. Aunt Emilia would tell her to leave the past alone. Frances pressed speed dial for the old home number and heard it ringing in the hall of the rambling house. Her aunt still had the one phone on a telephone table by the front door. A conversation on the phone was an event for which Aunt Emilia still stood to attention. She would never understand mobile phones. When Frances's rang in the house, her aunt would always say, 'That is so clever. How do they know you are here?'

The phone rang for some time before at last Frances heard her aunt's slightly breathless answer, '*Pronto?*'

'Aunt Emilia, it's me, Frances.'

'Francesca,' sighed Aunt Emilia with immense pleasure and love but either the connection was poor or Aunt Emilia was having a bad day and the conversation went nowhere. The only English her aunt managed was to tell Frances that she had had macaroni for lunch.

*   *   *

The train was late and Alistair was already on stage when she arrived. He sat casually laughing with the rest of the cast, but as she walked on he looked up and smiled. It was a dazzling smile and so it should have been. He had spent thousands at the dentist's and many hours practising in front of the mirror. He was a man who wore charm like a second skin. His once full head of blond hair was a little thinner now but each piece had been carefully constructed into a golden halo. He was tall and lean with a lazy look that settled into a smile with ease. He stood and put his arms out but did not move towards her. He waited for Frances to come to his embrace. She walked forward slowly, embarrassed and uncertain.

'Darling girl,' he declared, as she accepted a soft kiss on each cheek. He smelt wonderful and in that moment Frances was lost once more. Her stomach did a bizarre involuntary flip-flop at his touch. If the world were run by pheromones then he would be king. Frances knew everyone was looking and she felt ridiculous. As if, at last, they had been caught together *in flagrante*.

'Right,' she declared, pulling away. 'Right,' she repeated, as if that would help everyone to focus.

The rehearsal went well. The director was an old-school type who didn't have a lot of time for discussions about motivation.

'But why am I going off with Lady M?' asked a young lad fresh from the RADA.

The director chewed on an unlit pipe before replying, 'Well, because I won't pay you if you don't.'

Alistair was good and managed to jolly the company through their paces with a nice mix of actor's anecdotes and some wonderful verse reading. Frances sat in the stalls, watching and making notes. She had always felt a certain magic in the theatre but now, for the first time, she was bored. This wasn't real life. She didn't care about the damn king or his woods or the absurd witches

21

and just wished they'd cut to the end. She had been doing this for too long. Alistair slipped into the red velvet seat beside her.

'How's it looking, chicken?'

Frances rubbed her eyes and realised she had no idea how it was going. 'Good, good.'

'Just good?'

'Excellent. You're excellent.'

Alistair shrugged his shoulders and slouched further down in his seat so that his head almost touched her shoulder.

'I knew you'd call,' he said quietly.

'I didn't,' replied Frances firmly. 'Gina did.'

'Whatever. We can't be out of each other's lives, you know that. Listen, have dinner with me tonight?'

Frances had enough objectivity to admire the force of the battle between her body screaming 'yes' and her mind, her sensible mind, knowing that 'no' was the only answer. Alistair leant towards her and for a brief moment she thought he was going to kiss her.

'Hold that thought,' he whispered, 'while I just deal with my mad wife.'

'You married her?' Frances spoke loudly enough to bring the entire rehearsal to a standstill.

Alistair smiled. 'Of course I married her. Wouldn't be much of a play if the king didn't have a queen.'

'Lady M. Right,' Frances managed.

He returned to his mad stage wife who, as it happened, was being played by an actress well known for not being the marrying kind. God almighty, it was all lunatic.

There was only the one day to rehearse Alistair

into the part, so everyone worked almost until the half-hour before curtain up. As they all raced off to prepare for the evening performance, Frances found herself once more alone with Alistair. He seemed surprised to find her still there and moved to stroke her cheek.

'What did I tell you, chicken? We just needed a few months before we'd be back working together. Who'd want to break up this great partnership?' For a moment nothing had changed. He was moving closer when his mobile phone rang.

'Hello? Oh hello, pickle. No, no, we just finished.' He moved away to take the call from his current lover. 'Well, I miss you too. Actually, you should come up. I think it's going to be rather an interesting piece. I feel the king has often been misunderstood so the route I'm taking, and the director agrees, is . . .' Alistair turned and winked at his old love.

Pickle. Chicken. Just different forms of food on the same menu. Frances turned and ran.

CHAPTER THREE

Meglio tardi, che mai

Better late than never

'All the world's a stage'—it was one of two things that Frances knew for sure. The other was that while the world might well provide an endless arena for performance, most of it suffers from terrible stage management. If one is to return anywhere it ought to be in triumph. The homecoming of the prodigal daughter should be a glorious return in a chariot of fire. Sadly, for Frances, it was in a clapped-out old Mercedes that railed and spluttered at the indignity of its last years being spent in the service of a local taxi firm. Of the three making the journey—the car, Frances and the driver, the latter was the most sanguine. He drove slowly through the evening penumbra sucking on a cigarette. He was in no hurry. The chances of collecting another fare from this distant Umbrian hilltop were nil. He knew that the narrow road wound up the tall, thin incline and gave up at the town gates. The climb was steep and once at the top, the exhausted road even lacked the energy to descend down the other side. Halfway between the great cities of Florence and Rome, no one passed through Montecastello. It was not on the way to anywhere.

Frances sat in the back swaying with each bend and steeling herself for the onslaught of something familiar. She did seem to recognise the scenery but then she had seen it in a hundred films and a million pieces of art. She looked out across the lush Tiber valley. After two thousand years of human occupation, the verdant valley was in neat order with vineyards, olive groves and sunflower fields carefully framed by rows of cypresses and umbrella pines. Here Etruscan, Roman, medieval and Renaissance men and women had each in turn toiled to bring order to nature.

The driver too spent more time on the view than safety might have suggested. His family had lived here for generations. From ox cart to Mercedes, the destiny of his people had been to haul others up and down the undulations of Italy. He watched the crimson sun set over those very inclines and, in the distance, the mountains of Lazio and Abruzzo. In the same light that had inspired some of the Western world's greatest art, the driver shook his head. 'Hills . . . mountains,' he muttered, 'put there by God to trouble my gearbox.' Without thinking, he brushed his finger across the small amulet of his name saint that he wore hidden under his lapel. He shouldn't criticise God. It was the natural state of things that a man should be poor and climbing a hilltop at someone else's behest.

At last the car drew to a shuddering halt. Frances practically fell out of the back door and energetically vomited beside a metal waste bin, a chipped and rusted green square, which hung on a medieval stone wall. *Montecastello pulito è più bello* the bin proclaimed in hand-painted yellow lettering—and it remained *bello* as she missed it entirely. She had arrived in this sanctuary of art, culture and miracles, needing perhaps art, possibly culture and certainly a small miracle. Instead she

25

had thrown up as soon as she hit the cobbled streets. It was hardly the entrance anyone with theatrical flair would have hoped for. She had no idea what had made her so unwell. Perhaps a combination of lousy airline wine, exhaustion and selecting every outer bend on a long mountainous route had taken its toll. Above her head, perched in a crevice, a grey pigeon with a mantle of purple trim eyed her with disdain. Yet another foreigner come to learn the history of civilisation, eat pasta and return home feeling vaguely dissatisfied with life. Like the migration of other, less settled birds, the tourists were beginning to flock to Italy for the first signs of summer and neither the pigeon nor the local populace were bothering with a welcome party.

Frances wiped her mouth with a hanky and stood up. 'I need my suitcase,' she muttered.

The driver, who did have a little English for work purposes, had obviously decided today was not a day for anything but his native tongue and failed to move. Frances gave a loud, dramatic sigh but it didn't help. The chauffeur remained motionless in his seat as he continued to smoke and left her to struggle with the boot of the car alone. The boot, too, thought there was no hurry and it was only after much banging and cursing that it finally agreed to pop open. There was a belch of stale air as Frances lifted her case out on to the ground.

'You have been utterly charming,' Frances declared with brilliant but utterly ineffectual British sarcasm. 'I would like to thank you for that scenic route. I particularly enjoyed the short detour across what I am fairly confident was

26

pavement in the last village.'

Her brilliance fell stony dead in the evening air. Both Frances and the driver had lost the will to maintain their fledgling relationship. She leant through the open car window and tossed paper money on to the passenger seat. At last the driver seemed to notice her. He smiled slowly as his eyes drifted up from the money to her breasts. Appalled, Frances drew herself up smartly, banged her head on the car door, turned, fell over her case, crashed on to the cobbled street and broke the heel on her left shoe. One might think that a driver whose passenger had suddenly disappeared from view might shift himself to find out why, but he merely looked down at the money on the seat beside him and he seemed to know instinctively when a contract between two people was concluded. He slammed his recalcitrant gearbox into action and drove off. The boot of the car banged open and shut in farewell as he roared back down the hill.

Frances sat on the narrow road and for a moment she rested her head on the wall behind. It was still warm from the day's sun and not a bad place to take a short interval in this comedy of errors. The town was still, with the aloof, dignified charm that belongs to a place twenty miles from the nearest railway station and whose main road runs out of breath just outside the city walls. Montecastello was a destination, not a thoroughfare, and it bore the distinction with pride. One thing was becoming clear—this was not the prelude to a great drama, just a mistake. She sat heel and heartbroken on some nameless street and cursed her cousin.

27

The trouble with self-pity is that it tends to run out of steam without the benefit of an audience. After a few moments of profound sorrow for herself, Frances looked around. It was only now that she noticed the castellated gateway that rose above her. The taxi had come to a halt where the road narrowed down to a lane fit only for human traffic. The stone entrance must at one time have been impressive but it had long ceased to keep the enemy at bay. Italian architects and masons have for centuries filled the world with breathtaking structures—part of the Kremlin in Moscow, the great Winter Palace in St Petersburg, the embellishment of the Capitol in Washington, churches, palaces, villas in Vienna, Madrid, Prague, Warsaw; architecture designed to please the onlooker more than serve a practical purpose—and the gate to the town followed in this noble line. Built of irregular honey-coloured blocks, it looked dignified from the front, but from behind, the holed walls and clumps of sprouting vegetation signified its role as merely a show of strength. In truth, it was like a stage set—impressive from the audience side only. From the gate a narrow lane rose up into the town lined with two-storey stone houses bearing red-brick trim round the doors and windows. Nothing was even or uniform as the houses leant uphill in bands of whatever rough material had been to hand. Along the centre of the cobbled lane a grey path zigzagged into the distance. On one corner a single Victorian-looking gas lamp provided the only illumination.

'*Donnaccia,*' muttered a voice as a man slipped past her and into the shadows of the next turning.

He was old and fat and wearing a large black cape. Frances wanted to ask directions but he was gone as quickly as he had appeared. Clearly she would have to wait for the Good Samaritan. She sighed again and then, because it sounded quite dramatic in the stone echo of the narrow street, she sighed once more. It had no effect. There was no one to hear.

Perhaps this was it. The bottoming-out of that roller-coaster of emotions that is suffered by the thwarted. Maybe, after more than a year of deep despair, she could climb back out of the pit of self-pity. Frances looked around her. Montecastello de Sanctis. The truth was, if she had truly wanted to calm her raging feelings then this was the last place she should have come.

In a vain attempt to orientate herself, she tried to look at her watch in the sepia light. It was then that she noticed the glass had smashed during her fall and a thin stream of blood was trickling down on to her hand. In the dark it looked like the chocolate syrup Hitchcock used as blood in *Psycho* to claim Janet Leigh's black-and-white death. Frances watched the liquid of her life flow gently across her pale skin and wondered how long it would take to slowly bleed to death on this quiet Italian road. Realising that without her watch she couldn't even time her demise, Frances decided to live a little longer. She picked herself up and retrieved her suitcase. The wheelie bag refused to play in the cobbled streets. Not wanting to bother with more sound effects, she picked it up and hobbled forward.

The first view Frances had of Montecastello disclosed a fair sample of the whole. There seemed to be no main part, no busy centre, just a congress of lanes, each one winding on from the other. She realised she hadn't bothered to ask the driver for further directions. The art school was in Sophia Fratelli's old house. She would not think about Sophia. Frances trudged upwards. Perhaps she might remember the way.

Despite its fame as a holy destination, Montecastello, celebrated home to the Miracle of the Innocents, still manages to be an intimate town of just 1500 souls, declared the brochure for the Gelosi Art School. *The residence programme provides the ideal combination of seclusion and community in a setting of truly inspirational beauty.*

The lanes, no more than ten feet wide at any point, snaked on past identical buildings of medieval charm, Roman foundations and no indication of their function. There were ground-floor windows defended by stout iron grilles, heavy wooden doors with iron studs ready to be barricaded in seconds, roofs flat enough to stand on while pouring boiling oil over assailants, and the odd hidden slit for arrows, crossbows or other darts of defence. The whole town was built with its fists up.

'Except no one can be arsed to invade,' declared the latest insurgent out loud. The sound of her own voice seemed invasive and any attempt at boldness swiftly disappeared. Was there something familiar about it all? Did she know that house, that street corner? Surely that was the road down to the school? Had she walked here with her mother? Frances felt as though she were shrinking; as if she was being sucked back into the past. She passed a poster advertising the fresh edition of *Corriere dell'*

Umbria, the local paper. *Bin Laden Sfugge All' Agguato in Umbria*, it yelled in bold print. What the hell did that mean? Was bin Laden hiding locally?

This time Frances kept her thoughts muted. 'I shouldn't be the least bit surprised,' she declared. 'No one would ever find him here.'

It was the first sign of madness—speaking to herself. It was very dark and Frances realised that she was childishly afraid. Father Benito said that it was in the dark that the spirits came out. She tried to think of other things. Where the hell were the happy locals who should be organising a chestnut or tomato festival for her benefit, or pressing grapes with their feet and slicing up mozzarella with an ancient penknife and a toothless grin? Where were the footsteps of the great travellers of the past—Byron, Goethe, Shelley, the Brownings, Chateaubriand, Mme de Staël—keepers of journals and thinkers of great thoughts who would help her find herself? Frances's irritation increased as she tripped in her broken shoe and fell against the wall.

'Chateau-fucking-briand.'

It was only then that she realised she had reached the top of the hill and was now going down the other side. Yet another stone building clung tenaciously to the land, but this one had a small grey plaque hung beside the wooden door. *I Gelosi Art School*. Below the plaque, embedded in the wall, there seemed to be an even older, smaller entrance, which had been bricked up. Relieved to have arrived, Frances stood for a moment to catch her breath.

'Come in, come in,' called a cheery voice as someone held the wooden door open. Frances

31

stepped inside and up two small steps into a large open hall. In the fading light and with the galloping drumbeat of an advancing headache, she no longer trusted any of her senses. She had no idea if it was a man or a woman. Most likely it was female, for the doorkeeper wore one of those vast, flowery, flowing dresses which on another occasion might host a summer fête. The outfit suggested womanhood but the hands and feet that protruded were enormous. Perhaps it was a man in drag. As for age, it was impossible to put a number to it. The doorkeeper might have been the same age as Frances but sported a chignon, which adds years to anyone.

'I'm Margaret Bertelli and you must be the Angel we've been expecting,' beamed and boomed the huge vision. 'I can't tell you what a pleasure it is to welcome you to our little home for the arts.'

Margaret might have looked like a madam but she spoke with the clipped confidence of a Mayfair *grande dame*. It was an odd combination. The hall was cavernous with a stone floor, and as they stepped further inside, a small brass bell began to ring. Like a Pavlovian experiment gone horribly awry, the tinkling of the bell released a howl from a room off the hall. With surprising speed, a tiny, eagle-faced woman of at least ninety hurtled across the stone entrance floor.

'*In fine, è per me, è per me,*' she called.

Margaret turned to Frances. 'You speak Italian?'

Frances couldn't tell if it was a question or a statement but then she realised she had both nodded and shaken her head in reply.

'*In fine, è per me, è per me,*' repeated the old

woman.

Margaret smiled. 'She says, "At last, it's for me, it's for me." She thinks you are her guest.' Margaret turned and spoke in heavily accented Italian, '*Cucciola, cucciola, avanti, avanti.*' She accompanied this command with the sort of hand gestures one might use on annoying livestock to shoo them away but the wizened old woman was having none of it.

She grabbed Frances by the arm. '*A che ora ci incontriamo?*' she asked.

'Sorry?' Frances replied.

Margaret gently took the old hand and removed it from Frances's sleeve. 'She wants to know what time you should meet,' she explained. 'She thinks you're someone else.'

Margaret rattled off a sentence in rapid Italian and the crone nodded. She had surprisingly bright eyes and retreated backwards, staring at Frances in an unnerving way.

'It's for me, it's for me,' she repeated over and over in Italian. The old woman shook her head and turned away. Her speed of entrance was replaced by a slow exit across the stone floor. As she inched her way to the other side of the hall, her slippers made a brushing sound on the stone like a slowly retreating steam train.

Margaret tutted and shrugged. 'She has, as they say, *un chiodo fisso in testa*—a nail fixed in her head—that someone is due to visit her.'

Margaret's English was perfect but she peppered her speech with dashes of Italian like a chef throwing in unmeasured seasonings at will. Even she, however, needed to draw breath and there was a slight pause as she headed for a large wooden desk which seemed to serve as reception. Frances tried to take in the entrance hall of the stone palazzo. It was like the set of a Feydeau play with many doors heading off in unknown directions. Stairs to the upper floor were immediately to the left and below them, a corridor led away with glass doors out to the garden. On the farthest side of the hall stood the reception desk, behind which was clearly an office. The rest of the space was given over to an eclectic selection of chairs and sofas and a large refectory dining table. Various oil paintings adorned the walls and a gigantic grandfather clock ticked steadily in a corner. It was the set of an English drawing room in the heart of an Italian palazzo. The actual age of the building was impossible to determine. Roman masonry mingled with the work of some medieval builder who had once stood there shaking his head and saying, 'Dear oh dear, who's done this then?'

At that moment Frances noticed the music. Instead of a light aria or Italian folk tune on the hidden sound system, someone had put on an album of show tunes. While Michael Crawford bemoaned his lot as a phantom, Margaret sat down, beamed at Frances and declared, 'Don't you just loathe Catherine de' Medici?'

'Sorry?'

Frances had been in Italy just a few hours and already she had turned into an English cliché, saying 'sorry' at every turn in the conversation.

'Catherine de' Medici.' Margaret's smile widened as she pointed down at Frances's broken heel. 'Italian of course, although she became queen of France. Tiny little thing, apparently. Anyway, she so wanted to make an impression on

34

the royal court that she invented the high-heel. Just imagine what an entrance she must have made in those shoes—it caused quite a stir. To be honest, I've loathed her ever since.'

Frances looked down at Margaret's own vast feet encased in acres of leather sandal and thought, uncharitably, that it was footwear surely only available by mail order.

Margaret leant forward and whispered confidentially, 'Don't worry about your appearance. I have to tell you that Italians are utterly indifferent to other people's personal appearance and idiosyncrasies. Frankly, you can be mad as a hatter and they just let you get on with it.'

Oddly, Frances didn't find this comforting. The truth was, she was finding it increasingly difficult to concentrate. She decided to go for the obvious.

'You're English,' she managed.

Margaret threw her hands in the air. 'I know. Thirty years in Italy and still the consonants of Chelsea haunt me.' Margaret stood up and came towards Frances. Although Frances was not particularly short, Margaret was inordinately tall and she towered over her. Stanislavski, the great teacher of theatre, said that there are three circles of performance that surround an actor—the public, the familiar and the intimate. Margaret might be English but she had learnt physical proximity from the Italians and she loomed into Frances's intimate space in a manner which, strictly speaking, should not occur until at least the second act.

'Miss Angel, you must see me as an inspiration. I too came to Italy heartbroken and desperate—'

'What makes you think . . . I am not—'

Margaret's speech was a monologue and did not require response. She swept on. 'And I found passion. Such passion that it tore me from the bosom of my life to live here—' Margaret threw her arms out and nearly knocked Frances on the ear '—in the land where *l'amore* pulsates from every pore.'

On the other side of the hall, the old woman had by now reached one of the many doors and begun pawing at the handle. Why the hell didn't someone open the thing for the old bat? Somewhere in the dark recesses of what had once been Frances's mind a little light glimmered.

'*Cucciolo* . . . that means puppy,' she blurted.

Margaret clapped her hands. '*Bene!* You do speak Italian!'

Frances shook her head. 'No, no . . . just that. I remembered *cucciolo* means puppy.'

Margaret gave a sharp laugh. 'The old woman, she is like a puppy. Always at my heels but you must ignore her. Some people they get left money, I got an old puppy. I'm afraid she came with the place and there's nothing we can do about it.'

Had Frances been thinking more clearly she might have wondered why the old woman had come as part and parcel of the Fratelli house, but she just stood there while Margaret took her passport and entered the details into a large leather register. Across the hall the old woman was still stuck by the door, but now she was joined by a rather dashing older man with brilliantined and probably dyed black hair that gleamed on his head like a cap of patent leather. He was immaculately dressed in blazer and cravat, grey flannels and a pair of spit-and-polish black shoes. He gave

36

Frances a curt nod and gently returned the ancient puppy to her room. No one said a word. Who were all these old people? The brochure had said the art school would look at many old masters but it hadn't mentioned living with them. Aware that Judy Garland was now singing about being born in a trunk, it took Frances a moment to realise that Margaret was speaking to her.

'Is there anything you require?'

'Yes . . . yes . . . yes . . .' There had to be something she wanted but Frances was by now completely confused so she settled on the English cure-all for bad situations. 'A cup of tea would be nice.'

'*Come vuole*—nothing is impossible. Follow me.' Margaret led the way out of the hall and up a rather grand staircase. 'Classes start in two or three days when everyone has settled in,' she announced. 'You won't be hungry now as it's too late but God willing there will be breakfast on the terrace in the morning.'

Along a corridor of plastered walls hung edge to edge with paintings by the alma mater—some good, some bad, some unspeakable—Margaret marched forward until she reached a door at the end.

'Here is your key. I do hope you will produce many fine works while you are with us. Good night then.'

'Sorry, Margaret, what does *donnaccia* mean?'

Margaret smiled as if it were the question every new guest plagued her with. 'Slut or hussy.'

'Marvellous.'

And then Margaret was gone, with no mention of the tea or anything else.

37

Frances put her key in the lock only to find the room was already open. Wooden shutters had been pulled closed for the night and the room was dimly lit by a lamp beside the bed. The main wall appeared to have a sundial on it, but as there was no sun it seemed pointless. Frances tossed her bag on to the bed and sat down beside it. She ran her hand across the smooth leather and slowly opened the zip. With little thought she began unpacking her belongings until her hand reached a small bundle tucked right at the bottom. She had not put it there and suspected the hand of her cousin. Bloody interfering family. Frances pulled out the bundle. A brightly coloured chiffon scarf was carefully wrapped around the contents. She unwound the scarf to reveal a small round tablet made of clay. It had once been painted the deep red of fresh prosciutto but over the years the paint had flaked and faded. The centre of the tablet was grey and unpainted and here, many years ago, a small child had placed a handprint. The lifeline of the imprint still stood out clearly. A testament to the uniqueness of each individual.

Sometimes an object can hold an entire history, and so it was with this small tablet. Frances remembered everything so clearly. She had been Francesca then and the teacher had been old. She taught every age and every subject in the small village school and had done for generations. If anyone knew anything in Montecastello it was because Signora Alienti had taught it to them. She was a curious blend of science, history and the arts all bound together with an unfailing belief in the divine.

'Today, *miei figli di Dio*, you will record who you

are at this moment for ever. Hold up the hand you write with.' Most of the children put up their right hands, but one or two, like Francesca, were left-handed and shot them above their heads, instantly marked out as different.

'The hand you write with is your *mano maggiore*, your major hand. Look at the lines that run across it. Here your character and destiny are laid out like a map for you to do the best you can with. Your major hand records what you will do with your life, and what you are doing now, while your minor hand reveals the skills, talents and qualities you were born with. The lines change depending on what happens to you and what you decide to do with your life. It is, if you like, your map of potentials, which is always changing. Each hand is entirely unique. Not one of you will have the same map of lines as another or, indeed, the same as any person who has ever lived. Not one of you will have exactly the same length of fingers in relation to the others. That is because the good Lord has made each of you like no other. He loves you individually and he wants each of you to lead lives of unique splendour. Your triumphs and tragedies will be entirely your own.'

The class looked at their hands in wonder and tried to see into the future. Their imaginations were gripped by the idea that their path might be mapped out upon their palms. The boys looked to see if they might make great footballers or maybe own a motorcycle, while the girls mostly looked for love and children. That afternoon Francesca rushed home to tell her mother of the great promise she was sure her palm betrayed. A map of life. A legacy of personality.

Thirty-five years later, Frances held the tablet in one hand and slowly placed her other over the tiny handprint. She wished, not for the first time, that they really had been able to see what lay ahead.

CHAPTER FOUR

The secret of getting things done is to act.

Dante Alighieri
Italian poet (1265–1321)

The next morning, when Frances awoke, the sun was filtering through the closed wooden shutters. Patterns of light waves rippled across the floor and shone on her face. She had slept deeply and now lay across the bed like a swimmer tossed from a rapidly rushing stream on to a fortuitous river bank. The image was appropriate for she felt seasick, which was odd. It was the first time in countless years that she had awoken with no timetable. No demanding clock had summoned her; no schedule awaited her immediate attention. Her watch remained shattered on the bedside table. She should have felt rested, but instead anxiety and nausea played through her system. She lay there for a few minutes not moving, like an accident victim checking for sensation in each of her limbs. Why had she come here? It was a mistake. Frances half rose from the bed and placed her bare feet on the floor. Her skin ached and the cold stone seemed to sting to the touch. She had no idea of the time, and for a brief moment could not even recall the day of the week. Untouched by the day's light, the sundial on the wall resolutely refused to work.

'Absurd. Who the hell would put a sundial inside? It's all bloody absurd.'

41

Instantly gripped with a desperate desire to depart, Frances scrabbled through her bag for her mobile phone. She punched in Gina's number, only to realise that an absence of beeps and squawks meant a dead battery. The wire of her phone charger had become intimately entangled with her hairdryer and it took every remaining ounce of patience to divorce them. Almost biting her lip with the effort to remain calm, Frances slipped off the bed and searched the room for a plug. None was immediately obvious and she began to examine the walls like a cat burglar seeking a hidden safe. At last she spied a socket on the wall behind the bed and with a final burst of determination she crawled beneath it with her charger. The socket was Italian. The plug was English. The two would never copulate. It was the proverbial straw that broke her camel's back. Frances lay under the bed amid the dust and beside some previous occupant's spectacles and for the first time in as long as she could remember she wanted to weep. She didn't, however, let vent. Frances was not given to open displays of her feelings, even when she was alone. It was partly because she suffered the British predilection for emotional constipation that she had taken so long to address her inner turmoil. After a while she calmed down and lay there breathing deeply. She was exhausted and needed air.

As if in response to her need, the door to her room flew open and her host of the night before filled the space.

'*Ciao, bella!* You wanted tea!' beamed Margaret, only twelve hours late and apparently not in the least surprised to find her guest under the bed rather than on it. 'Isn't tea the most marvellous elixir? However long I live in this glorious land, I shall always yearn for a decent cup of tea. I didn't know if you took sugar so I took the liberty of leaving it out.' Margaret plonked the cup on the bedside table and then plonked herself heavily on the bed. The springs sagged down around Frances's head. From her low vantage point Frances had a clear view of Margaret's plump ankles, which swung to and fro as she settled herself in for a chat.

'Now, I realise we didn't have a moment to talk last night so I thought we'd have a quick catch-up. You're bound to want to know a bit about the history of the place.'

'Actually, I thought I might have a bath and—'

Her uninvited guest swept on with her chosen specialist subject. 'Despite our remoteness, Montecastello really is a most gripping place,' declared Margaret with wild confidence. 'At first glance you might think nothing ever happened here, but not so. I don't know if you've heard of the Miracle of the Innocents?'

'Well, I'm—' From her below-bed view, Frances suddenly realised that up until then she had never seen someone else's foot quite so close. It really was a most remarkable construction. In fact, she felt, for a brief moment, as if she had never seen a foot before at all. The only light in the room filtered through the still closed shutters. It gave a slightly film noir lighting to the scene, which was strangely mesmerising.

'About thirty or possibly forty years ago—I can never remember dates. Indeed, I think it was a failure to grasp chronology which pre-empted a

43

career as a historian. *Che peccato!'* Margaret paused for a moment to consider this loss to the academic world before galloping on. As she clearly was not planning to go away, Frances thought perhaps it would be best to make an appearance. With some difficulty she crawled from beneath the bed and lay prostrate at Margaret's feet.

'You've the tiniest bit of fluff on your nose.' The interruption had clearly made Margaret thirsty. She picked up the cup of tea and began to drink. Frances brushed a hand across her nose, got to her feet and found there was nothing for it but to settle on the bed herself. She looked on with quiet regret as Margaret drank the tea.

'Anyway, there were these three little girls, Sophia, Maria and . . .' Margaret's grasp of names appeared as shaky as that of dates.

'Francesca,' murmured Frances, watching her tea disappear in great gulps.

Margaret turned to look at her guest. 'Indeed, you're right, Francesca. They were about five or six years old and huge friends. I had friends like that at school—Charlotte, Beatrice and . . .' She paused as if she half expected Frances to remember that too, but no help was forthcoming. Margaret sighed. 'Anyway, one day these three little Montecastellian minxes claimed that the Virgin Mary had come to visit them on the hillside by the little chapel. Well, the town, they're all Catholic, you know? Oh yes. The place is steeped in the stuff. They say no English woman can come here without being seduced by Italy and falling into "popery and filthy living".'

Popery and filthy living, was that what lay ahead? Frances did not want to hear the story. She

44

stared hard at the tessellated floor tiles.

Margaret continued without, it seemed, ever drawing breath. 'The town went quite doolally. Priests were called, meetings were held. Then one of the little girls, I forget which one, said it wasn't true ...'

Francesca. It had been Francesca.

'The families started fighting. Anyway, one night there was a fire in the chapel and in the morning . . . it was terrible.' Margaret was now relating the tale as if it occupied the central plot in some great theatrical piece. Frances looked at her own bare toes curled with tension.

'The bodies of Sophia and her parents were found right in the middle of the church. Panic all round and the little girl who had claimed it was a lie was spirited away, but Maria stayed and now she's quite the big Catholic cheese here. People come from miles around for her blessing. We're quite the cult. Don't you find it gripping? A sort of ecclesiastical soap opera.' Margaret expelled a great wave of air and got to her feet. 'Now then, do you need anything?'

The sardonic part of Frances wanted to suggest a cup of tea but too many images flooded her mind and she found she could not speak. She shook her head.

'Splendid. Well, I'm so glad we had this little chat. I do hope you will be happy with us.' Then Margaret, who was a well-meaning woman, enfolded Frances in her large embrace, pushed her back and smiled.

'How exciting. You come here with a *tabula rasa*—a clean slate. Isn't that thrilling?' And with that the exhausting woman departed.

Left alone, Frances was suddenly overwhelmed by a desperation to be outside. She moved to perform the minimum of ablutions at the small basin in the corner of her room. There was no sign of a bathroom and she couldn't face the corridor undressed.

'Popery and filthy living,' she muttered as she attempted to rinse the dust from her face and hands. 'Just popery to go then.' Her suit from the day before felt stiff with grime and brick residue. Frances looked around for a laundry bag but found none, so folded the clothes away in an empty wooden wardrobe. She pulled on some camel-coloured trousers and a crisp white blouse. Her trusty heels were a write-off and in deference to Italy, she put on some Gucci loafers. Exhausted by even this minimal amount of preparation, she glanced in a mirror and swept her hair into a ponytail. As a last-minute addition, she added her ever trusty string of pearls. She knew she looked terrible but perhaps the pearls would distract everyone.

Frances was a handsome woman who personified the clothing instruction 'smart casual'. Without thinking, she picked up her watch from the bedside table. It was then that she noticed the blood on the clay tablet. A tiny smear of red had streaked across the centre of the infant handprint. It must have come from her wrist the night before. It was nothing, but it made Frances shiver. She looked at her wrist. The quick wash seemed to have cleared all signs of injury, for her skin looked smooth and undamaged. Frances wrapped the small handprint back in its scarf and placed it at the bottom of her bag. Determined to be decisive and deal with the day, she put on her sunglasses and went out.

She was struggling with her key when she sensed the presence of a fellow boarder in the corridor. Without even looking up, Frances knew with a shudder that the man, too, was resolutely English. Her shaded eyes hovered over a pair of brown sandals with matching socks. Stooped over her key, she glanced across to see a florid fellow in his fifties dressed in an ill-conceived safari suit. He was minutely examining one of the alumni's works that hung in the hall. He sniffed and took out a white handkerchief to mop his eyes.

'Dreadful. Just dreadful,' he moaned.

Frances pulled out the most useful word of English she had employed since arriving. 'Sorry?' she said.

The man turned to her with a face so pink that he was either a steady drinker or the classic Englishman who went florid at the mere suggestion of sun. He had a pencil-thin moustache and confirmed his utter Englishness by tipping his panama hat to her.

'Cecil Denby, Major, retired, but everyone calls me Buff,' he said nervously. 'I suppose I'm strictly watercolours, although, between you and me, I had been hoping to be bold with other media this year, but I think it is hopeless. They say the new teacher is quite a maverick in his approach, which could be invigorating but I doubt he'll even give me a glance. And yourself?'

'I'm not sure. I haven't really done a lot of art and—'

Cecil smiled a smile as watery as his work. 'I meant your name.'

47

'Oh, of course, yes, Frances, it's Frances.'

'You're English, aren't you? Yet, I suppose you're very good . . . at art,' he added in what seemed like an accusation.

'Yes, no . . . I mean, yes, I am English and, no, I don't think I am very good at art. To be honest my cousin booked me in . . . the house used to belong—'

It was Frances's destiny that morning to be on the receiving end of monologues.

'Three years.' The man turned his attention back to the painting he had been perusing. 'Three years I've been coming here and look at this. It's rubbish. Don't you think? It was the best of last year. In fact, it's the first time one of mine has even been in the corridor, and it is appalling. I know Margaret was just being kind. I thought while I was away that perhaps it would look better when I returned, but it was dreadful then and I fear it is even worse now. It's funny, I was all right about it when I got home. I think I simply forgot what the work actually looked like, but here with it in front of me, it all seems so desperate and overwhelming.'

Frances went over to look at the painting in question. Many colours had been used, many brushstrokes had been engaged, but to no obvious purpose. She pulled her sunglasses down her nose and looked again but couldn't even determine whether the thing had been hung the right way up.

'What is it?' she enquired softly.

'Exactly! Exactly!' declared the middle-aged man, almost beating his breast in the process. 'It is nothing. It's rubbish. It was supposed to be a self-portrait. If Dorian Gray had found this he

48

would have keeled over in the attic. I can't do it. I can see exactly what it is I want to paint but my hand can't bloody well get it down on the canvas.'

There was a danger of tears from the emotional fellow so Frances tried a practical tack. 'I can't seem to get my key to lock the door,' she said. It was a good course of action. Asking an Englishman a practical question, like whether he would mind carving, is always a good way out of any awkwardness.

Buff returned his hanky to his many-pocketed jacket and nodded. 'No, they don't,' he said.

'They don't what?' asked Frances.

'Lock the door,' replied Buff patiently. 'The keys don't lock the door.'

'So what's the point of them?' asked Frances through faintly gritted teeth.

'Ah yes, indeed. I'm not sure and, to be honest, I haven't really liked to ask. Hate to complain. I think it's an Italian thing—having the key is supposed to make you feel better even if it, you know, doesn't work.'

God almighty, thought Frances, plugs that won't go into sockets, keys that go in locks but to no effect—it was a good job she hadn't come to get laid.

'Are you going down . . . Frances?' Buff said her name hesitantly and then blushed as if the very suggestion of them going down together had made them intimate. He indicated the way with a slight wave of his hat and Frances followed him to the main stairs leading to the entrance hall.

A woman about the same age as Frances came towards them in the corridor. She carried a broom and bucket and for a moment Frances thought she

49

seemed familiar but then the bucket clipped Frances on the leg and the woman and the moment passed. Slightly too late, Buff tipped his hat to her.

'*Buongiorno*, Gabriella.'

Gabriella ignored the Major and stomped along the corridor with her head down. Clearly she hated cleaning for foreigners. Rich foreigners who thought they could buy anything with money.

Having been polite to the staff, Buff turned his attention back to Frances and murmured, 'The staff are charming but hopeless, I'm afraid. Leave nothing of great value in your room. I carry it all about my person.' Buff tapped his safari jacket with the quiet confidence of an organised man. Gabriella barged into Frances's unlocked room and sighed the sigh of Sisyphus as she presumably prepared to rummage through her belongings.

Buff marched on unperturbed. 'Isn't Margaret marvellous? So full of vigour. Confidentially, I can tell you that every two or three years she finds a new *passione* with whom she contracts a delightful, if short, lease of life. I have every confidence that it won't be me.' Buff shrugged the shrug of the unloved and eyed Frances anew. 'It's never been a woman but, hey ho, you might give it a try.'

'No, really I . . .' Frances began a sentence which she realised had nowhere to go.

Buff stopped on the stair and, taking her by the arm, said most earnestly, 'Look, I didn't mean to put you off. It's just I find it all so ruddy difficult. I don't know why I keep coming back. I mean, I've no talent for it. No talent at all but, anyway, you know, ever optimistic, still here. Don't you worry about not feeling much cop to begin with. The school is positively plagued with people whose love

50

for art is much greater than their talent.'

Downstairs in the hall the theme from *The Dambusters* was blasting out over the loudspeaker. A rather oily man was rushing from the school office towards the front door. He was gleamingly bald but immaculately buttoned into a white three-piece suit. With his suit and his entirely smooth head, he looked like a well-dressed boiled egg. He nodded to the guests and then, with a look not unlike the White Rabbit's, he scuttled off, late for some very important date.

After a lifetime of touring with shows and staying in hotels, Frances wondered if she should find someone to give her key to, though why would anyone want to take charge of a key that was entirely pointless? Buff had headed for a door to the right of reception when suddenly it was flung open, heralding a crashing and slamming of pans and the appearance of Margaret. Her vast body entirely filled the door and soon her voice filled the hall.

'*Lei è matto!*' she yelled into the kitchen, and then ducked as the sound of a pan came crashing towards her. She escaped into the hall and slammed the door behind her. Frances and Buff thought it impolite to comment so they stood waiting for an explanation.

'Morning!' Margaret beamed as if nothing untoward had occurred. 'Such a lovely day.' She inclined her head towards the kitchen, where the noise had finally abated. 'The penalties of having an Italian chef. The man is a genius but so temperamental. If the aubergines are not quite right there is hell to pay.'

Buff nodded curtly as if he quite understood,

while Margaret continued to smile as if nothing were awry. 'Now what are you all doing in here?' she enquired.

'I thought perhaps . . . breakfast,' murmured Buff.

'Nonsense,' boomed Margaret. 'You must go out and breathe Italian air and life. That is why you are here. Drink coffee in the piazza. Make love to the air.'

Like a mother hen she shooed them towards the door. 'And later,' she continued, 'I thought we'd have a picnic. Major, be a love and get some meat and cheese, Angel, some bread and fruit.'

'I don't want to be any trouble but I was thinking I might try and find a hotel,' began Frances. 'The thing is, my cousin booked me in and I'm really not sure about—'

A sentence she had been prepared to see through to the end got nowhere for, within moments, Frances found herself outside the closed front door in the street. The military wing of the art school stood beside her, looking equally bemused and they both blinked in the sharp morning light. Frances didn't think she could bear a descent into what she knew would be more insights into the Major's artistic soul so she declined his polite offer of coffee and headed down the hill. As the town was small this only left up the hill to Buff who had little choice but to march off awkwardly towards the main square.

CHAPTER FIVE

Chi cerca trova

Seek and ye shall find

Frances didn't mind about the breakfast. It wasn't as though she was hungry. Lately, her bruising from romance had provided her with the best diet known to woman. Biologists have yet to make the connection, but pain from the heart seems to express itself through the stomach and for more than a year she had had no interest in food. Despite the early hour and the fresh air, no appetite was awakened now. Frances needed to take stock and think for a moment. Bread and fruit. Perhaps she should find a phone or a travel agent or a travel agent with a phone . . . She took a deep breath and then paused to think about Alistair. It was still a daily habit. His departure had caused her to feel as if the basic functions like breathing were almost impossible. Each time she filled her lungs deeply it was as though she inhaled thoughts of her old lover. Seeing him again after a year of separation had only made matters worse. It was as though she had an ongoing ailment whose pain she continuously monitored. Even in moments of apparent calm she would stop to feel around in her psyche for the hurt and realise she was no better. On the good days she felt nothing at all. As if she had passed away but no one had yet taken the trouble to organise a funeral. Now, her distress heightened by the recent rehearsals, she found herself in this strange place and was angry.

'Go home,' her family in England had said, but as Frances stood in the narrow street she barely remembered the place. What little she thought she might have recognised had nothing to do with adult existence. She had no idea where one might buy bread and fruit, find a phone, get a drink. These were the streets she had played in, streets she had dreamt of, yet now she was here there seemed to be nothing familiar about any of it. Frances felt intense anger rising up against her cousin Gina and Aunt Emilia. Hadn't she suffered enough without this push to the absolute limit of emotional hurt? She was down but did she need a good kicking in the process?

With no memory map of the place and having arrived in the growing dark the night before, Frances looked about for a moment to get her bearings. A woman stepping out into the streets of Montecastello five hundred years ago would have had much the same experience as Frances did now. A beautifully preserved medieval *borgo*, the narrowness of the lanes and lack of access had left the town untouched by modern life. The route to the hilltop was so constricted that no cars sped through the town and no rush hour would ever mar the rhythm of its day. It was a place built for, and for ever devoted to the pedestrian. But through her dark glasses, Frances saw none of the beauty. Her eyes refused to take in what was all around her. Her ears, however, could not help but be alert.

Gone was the tomb-like stillness of the night before. Now the fifteen hundred souls of the town were up and about their business and no one was being quiet about it. Across the alleyways women

54

were calling to each other as they snapped clean sheets on to washing lines, unmindful of the sacrilege their laundry was committing on architecture that had once inspired the great Renaissance artists with their floppy hats and smiling eyes. Banished beyond the walls, no cars sounded, there was no rush of metal past the pedestrian. That did not mean, however, that silence reigned. Even the remotest of villages is rarely still in these modern times. In Montecastello the deep throat of Vespa scooters could be heard above a cacophony of varied music. Rap music boomed incongruously from a five-hundred-year-old bedroom, while across the way someone was practising the trombone. Just because the place looked like a museum didn't mean that life was not continuing. The noise was magnified by the proximity of the rough stone walls and the strange absence of greenery.

Frances had the oddest sense of standing on a stage on the night before a great theatre opening. Above her head, the balconies along the façades of houses were as convenient as boxes at the opera for the housebound of the town to watch the cavalcade as thousands of characters and hundreds of subplots were played out each day. It was all too loud and too bewildering. She started to turn right but a short fat man dressed in a shabby suit was taking photographs with a long lens. He seemed, in fact, to be photographing her. The suit looked filthy, which considering it was black was quite an achievement. Frances turned and walked the other way. She didn't want to meet anyone. She didn't want her presence recorded. She wanted to be invisible. Unseen.

There appeared to be no obvious shops. No neon signs lured the shopper, no mannequins posed and pointed the way in, yet people were coming and going with bags of freshly purchased provisions. Frances felt bewildered. As if she no longer knew how everyday life worked. She was supposed to buy bread and fruit, but where? Beside what seemed to be a post office, a shuttered building looked as near to tourist information as was on offer. It was, of course, closed, but a framed pencil drawing of the town hung in a low window. It showed that the hilltop settlement with its surrounding fortress wall made a perfect heart shape. The town was balanced with a giant church on one side and a tranquil little park at the other. The buildings were perfectly picked out in the finest of pencil with a chart of numbers for some of the lanes and particular houses. *Passeggiata del Toppo*; *Vicolo della Torre*; *Il Torrione*; *Mura perimetrali*. Frances walked the town with her eye until she reached the diminutive Chapel of St Illuminata. There it was depicted in perfect detail and Frances took such a deep breath that she thought she was going to faint. This time it was not Alistair but her childhood friend Sophia who flooded her mind.

Frances could still hear the calls echoing through the village.

'*La capella va a fuoco.*'

What a phrase to remember. 'The chapel is on fire!'

Frances's family, the Angellis, had lived on the edge of town above the small lane that ran down to the chapel. It was a large place but ramshackle and decaying. Frances's father leapt from his bed and

56

all the men ran half-dressed to help douse the flames. There was no fire department. Nothing organised, just people trying to do the best they could, but it was too late. The fire had taken hold and once the roof caved in nothing but the large wooden Madonna could be dragged free of the inferno. Her face was charred and black but the men stood her on the grass and the women knelt in prayer. It wasn't until morning that they found the bodies of Sophia and her parents. They said her grandmother went quite demented and could not be consoled. With the memory of a five-year-old, Frances felt as though her parents had put her on the train within the hour, but that couldn't have been possible. For years afterwards she dreamt of Sophia in the fire, her friend Sophia, charred black like the Virgin Mary they claimed to have seen.

Frances put her hand out to a rusted drainpipe that ran down the uneven stone wall beside the window and tried to calm herself. The crinkled paper of a yellowing poster crunched under her hand. An official notice had been fixed to the pipe. *'Esche rodenticide collocate in fognatura.'* The local authorities were clearly keen for their message to be widely understood—the notice was concluded with a portrait of a rather friendly looking rat and the English suggestion to 'Avoid any contact with rat carcasses.' Frances lifted her hand in revulsion as if the poster itself were infected. The town was beautiful yet all she seemed to see was horror.

She turned away and could not remember which direction she had come from. She looked left and saw a woman standing in the centre of the street staring at her. She was tiny, dressed all in black and hunched from perhaps seventy-five years of

57

carrying her life. Her hair was set in the immovable bonnet of hairspray common to the generation who visit the hairdresser once a week and never touch it in between. Her eyes bored into Frances, who knew what it was—the evil eye. What the hell was it called? She must protect herself. Nullify the evil glance. Make the sign of what? Double over the middle fingers and make horns by holding out the first and little fingers. *Gettare il malocchio'*. Frances's head was spinning and she turned and ran down the lane away from the woman. These were not the things she wanted to remember.

Faint and foolish, Frances reached the edge of the battlements. She felt claustrophobic in the small town and desperately needed a vista, some air in front of her eyes. She stopped by a rough stone wall. At a gap in the wall a dirt track ran steeply down to a chapel on the hillside. The place whose drawing she had run from stood below her. Even the novice tourist would have recognised it from the pencil sketch as the tiny Chapel of St Illuminata—a small single-storey structure devoted to God. It had been rebuilt and the terracotta of the roof looked surprisingly bright against the green hills beyond. A wooden fence of neat, angled crosses marked the track which passed the chapel and went on into the valley below. There were no signs as to where the road might eventually lead. It was a route for locals who already knew. A small bell tower, unimpressive and only just fit for the purpose of a call to prayer, rose from the roof of the chapel. A young man whizzed up the hill on a battered moped carrying an infant casually on his lap. The road was wide enough, yet he skimmed past Frances and took her remaining courage away with him. She shouldn't have come. She had expected many feelings but not this panic, this overwhelming sense of childish terror. It was ridiculous. She was forty years old, officially a grown-up. No one was after her. Frances turned round and tried to breathe more calmly. Lanes ran off at either side of her and once again she had no sense of which way she ought to go. She felt lost and afraid. She shook herself. This was madness; she was a successful woman, a self-made woman. She could do this. OK, she could do this for a very short time and then go home. She tried to imagine Gina by her side and began giving herself a good talking-to.

'If I follow the town walls round I must eventually come back to the art school. The place is tiny. I will find the art school, I will find Margaret with her big shoes and fat ankles, she will find me a plane . . .'

Frances began to walk clockwise round the perimeter wall. *Mura perimetrali . . . perimetrali . . . perimetrali . . .* it would be like finding the electrical socket in the room.

'Follow the yellow brick road, follow the yellow brick road . . .'

Although Montecastello was small, the town seemed to have concentrated itself in the centre. The outer reaches of the place, in fact the buildings with the best views, were neglected and in some stretches in danger of tumbling back down the hillside. Great chunks of stone wall were missing, perhaps plundered to repair some more central location. The views across the valley showed the abrupt division between town and country. Not for the Umbrians the straggle of

English suburbs crawling reluctantly towards a centre. Here there was a distinct division between nature and settlement. Frances's feet echoed along the stone path as she walked the narrow way. Sometimes walls encased her on both sides and sometimes there was a gap on the left as the view swooped in and tried to take her breath away. She saw no one. Her own feet mesmerised her and she began to be uncertain that she hadn't already passed the school and was going round for a second time. She looked up from her shoes and found herself staring through a metal grille into a courtyard.

The rusted bars supported the brick arch of an old doorway. Through them she could see the rough-hewn walls of a large room or terrace. It was impossible to tell whether the original design was interior or exterior as grass and flowers had overtaken the floor and the roof was open to the sky. Stones of every shape and size had been wedged together in a random yet somehow even pattern to make the structure, which perhaps had stood for half a millennium. Memory flooded through. Wave upon wave of pictures from the past filled her mind. This was her home. This was where her parents . . .

It is always bad if a person is having a personal, dramatic moment and some stranger interrupts it. Part of the problem associated with intimate revelations is that other people carry on with their lives at the same time. In the midst of her most intense feelings about returning to her home town, Frances suddenly realised there was someone standing in the centre of the courtyard. In the centre, in fact, of *her* courtyard. Knee-high in grass

60

and purple flowers, a man was dancing with an old-fashioned Fred Astaire cane. The cane was slim and black with a silver tip and on closer inspection she realised that the man and the cane were dancing independently of each other. It was the most bizarre thing. The fellow held out his hands in front of him and the cane with its silver top seemed to float in the air between them. Sometimes the cane rose up by itself only to sink down again and then float horizontally without being touched at all. The man twirled and moved and the cane bounced and bobbed in response with no human help.

At the man's feet a small scruffy dog was sitting with its head to one side, up until now the only audience for this extraordinary show. After a few moments the man paused, seized the cane in the middle and turned to give a deep bow towards the door where Frances stood. Automatically she began to applaud and then stopped abruptly. She was embarrassed and tired and angry with herself and the world. She had had no idea he had noticed her and now didn't know whether to run or stand still and pretend she had seen nothing.

'Scusi . . . dov'è . . . art school?' she said hopelessly.

The man smiled and shrugged. He was perhaps fifty, dark-haired, olive-skinned and when he spoke it was with a slight Italian accent. He was not handsome, being too thick-set, slightly squat with faint pock-marking on his face, but he smiled again and Frances did not feel afraid. He had the fullest head of hair and the most perfect teeth she had ever seen in a man. This could not be a dangerous person, for his mother had clearly taught him to

61

brush regularly. He walked towards the metal grille that separated them.

'*Ciao, inglese*, did you see the stick dance?' he asked.

'Uh, yes,' Frances replied.

He squinted his eyes and looked at her more closely. 'Are you sure?' When she failed to answer, he shrugged and slipped the stick under his arm. 'You want your room, yes?' he asked.

'My room? Yes, at the art school.'

'*Naturalmente*. Everything has been prepared. You have been expected. Here is your key.'

'Look,' she began, 'I don't think you understand and I am really not in the mood for mucking about. As it happens, I don't think you should even—'

He held his hand out through the grille as if dangling a key and without thinking Frances pretended to take it. Their hands brushed together. The man tucked his cane under his arm and eased open the grille, which gave with a rusty sigh. He bowed slightly to indicate she should come in.

'*Benvenuta, signora*. I trust you had a reasonable journey. So tiring, travelling. Your name?'

'What?'

'I need your name for the registration.'

'Frances. Frances Angel.'

'Be careful who you tell that to. You know what they say in Italy—*angeli non Angli*.'

'What the hell does that mean?'

'We want angels and not Angles. The English come, they take the best things and they go home. Giacomo.'

'Giacomo?'

'My name. The bellboy, he is Auroch.'

'It's a dog.'

Giacomo wagged his finger at her. 'Treat him like that and you will carry your own cases. *Avanti.* Come.'

'I know what bloody *avanti* means.'

Giacomo moved into the courtyard where wild fennel and figs crept in profusion across the disorder.

'This is our beautiful, medieval hall where every piece of art has been inspired by the landscape that surrounds us. Notice the colours—the Prussian blue, the burnt umber, the Indian yellow, colours gathered from round the world just to delight your eye.'

'Nice. Look, you shouldn't be here.'

The man looked concerned. 'Why?' he asked.

'Because, because . . .' Frances wanted to claim ownership, say it was her house and he had to leave but she realised she wasn't sure. Just because the house was abandoned didn't mean it belonged to her. Besides, she didn't want to tell anyone her story. Not yet. Not before she understood it herself. 'You see,' Frances continued.

'Ah, you see,' repeated the man. '*Guardi.*' Once again, he held the cane out in front of him and then let go with both hands. The stick hovered quite still and then slowly began bobbing up and down. The man swayed from side to side and the cane floated in the air in response. After a few seconds he grabbed the cane in the centre and tucked it back under his arm.

'Very clever,' commented Frances sarcastically.

He looked at her and frowned. 'Perhaps you will be less bad-tempered by the pool.'

'I am not bad-tempered. I have not had a good

morning and the only person I have found is you, and you're pissing about when I need to—' Frances suddenly realised how bad-tempered she sounded, and stopped.

The man ignored her and walked away across the overgrown courtyard. His dog stayed close to his heel and, if only to finish her sentence, Frances followed. The dog was tiny but he didn't seem to know that. He moved with the swagger of a Great Dane. His hair was long and slightly curled, a patchwork of white, greys and black, none of which dominated. A bastard of the highest order, he trotted happily through the long grass. A gate in the corner led out on to a wide terrace overlooking the valley. It was a breathtaking view that stopped conversation altogether.

The terrace was as overgrown and wild as the courtyard. Flowers and stones competed for space alongside old bits of rusted metal and corrugated iron. Posts whose purpose was forgotten stood at various intervals; stone urns, perhaps once planted with profusion, stood empty on moss-covered plinths. The place was a junkyard but the landscape beyond was spectacular. Had it been this beautiful all those years ago? wondered Frances. Had she lived and played in the face of such spectacle every day?

The man led the way through long grasses to a low stone bench and moved to take Frances's hand to help her to sit down. She snatched it away from him and nearly toppled on to the bench in the process. He sat and waited. After a moment's silence he stretched out his hand and pointed.

'You see that our swimming pool is shaped with natural rocks and blends perfectly into its setting.

Here you can float as safe as the waters you first swam in inside your mother.'

'My mother . . .' Frances tried again but the man clicked his fingers in the air and the sound echoed against the old stones.

'I will call to the waiter for a glass of *prosecco*. Please notice how beautiful the light is on the red roof of the house.'

The house lay beyond the terrace and slightly above them. Frances looked up towards the dilapidated building. It had little or no roof but for a second she saw it whole. Unlike any other building in the town, this one had a wooden front. Struts of honey-coloured wood gave shape to the structure. The curved arches over the door were echoed in the decorative strips laid in a lattice across the front. Slats of greeny blue had once filled in the walls but now many sagged from their place or were missing. It was an entirely individual building and had been built by her father. Frances could almost smell the food bubbling in the kitchen, hear the laughter in the garden. This had been her home. She felt sick. All the years she had kept away from this place in her mind and now she had stumbled in without thinking.

Auroch barked at the edge of the garden. The grass was too long for his short legs and he demanded attention.

Giacomo shook his head. 'The dog is a fine creature but he has abandonment issues.' He got up and swooped the little animal up to his chest.

Abandonment issues. How could a dog have abandonment issues? Frances had sat on that roof with her father. He had gone up to fix the tiles but instead they sat and looked at the view. She could

65

see her father's face, leathery and tanned from the sun, and when they came down her mama had pushed his kisses away.

'Franco Angelli, don't you try and get round me. You were supposed to be fixing the roof. Look at this place. The rain falls on us whenever the good Lord pleases.'

Papa shrugged. 'If it pleases the good Lord . . .'

'What were you doing up there?' she demanded as she served great bowls of fresh *tagliatelle* made that afternoon. 'And don't tell me you were fixing anything. You didn't even take your hammer with you.'

'The view, Mama, you should have seen the view.'

'I see the view every day when I hang out your laundry,' she snorted.

'But it is not just a view. What is it, Francesca?'

'A history lesson, Papa,' she replied.

He smacked the table with delight. 'Of course, a history lesson. You should read Herodotus, Mama. He said our people, the Umbri, had land so vast it went right up to the very north of Italy, that it stretched from the Adriatic to the Mediterranean. Can you imagine how great we once were? We had our own art and culture. When you look out you can almost see the past in front of you. Imagine the Huns passing over the land like flames eating up the valleys.'

'Papa says when Hannibal fought here the battle was so fierce the army didn't even notice an earthquake,' interjected Francesca.

Mama kissed her on the top of her head and smiled.

'Eat your pasta or I'll show both of you an

earthquake.'

Giacomo, the man with the dancing cane, had returned to the bench and now the dog sat between them. Both seemed unconcerned with Frances's detachment.

'He is blind,' said Giacomo quietly.

Frances closed her eyes. It was terrible but being blind suddenly seemed an attractive option. Not to see where you were. Not to have old images flooding back.

'Who?' she asked at last.

'Auroch. The dog,' explained the man. 'I only ever think of it when I sit here. From here you can look out over Italy. I should like him to see it. It's an extraordinary place. I wonder if he senses all these tiny medieval castellated villages? Places once fought over tooth and nail and now sitting on the sidelines of history. Each one fighting only to be remembered. Who comes here now? Not conquerors but ignorant visitors from all parts of the five known continents to fill every available space, seeking Culture with a capital C. Have you come perhaps for culture?' he asked.

'Culture?' Frances gave a short laugh. 'I shouldn't think so. I work in the theatre. I'm not even sure what that means.'

'Culture is "everything that gives the mind possession of its own powers". Who said that? Some clever *bastardo*. Anyway, it is a wonderful thing. To love and to work is to know something of the wonder and richness of life and through work and love united comes the strength to live.'

Frances stared at the strange man. His eyes were alight with a passion for life she had not seen for years.

'Is that *de rigueur* for an Italian?' she asked.

'What?'

'That you have to have some tin-pot philosophy about everything? Can't you just sit?'

He shrugged again. 'We sit.'

The two sat silent for a moment soaking in the endless vista.

'OK, I cannot just sit.' He grinned at her. 'I have more—what did you say?—philosophy in the pot.'

Frances groaned.

'Why do you suppose that a country which is so beautiful and has no need of adornment is so famous for its art?'

Art.

In this environment, you will paint and sculpt under the same light that spawned the Western world's greatest art. Here is the architecture and countryside that inspired Renaissance artists and later masters like Poussin, Ingres and Corot . . .

What would her parents have said if they knew she had come to Italy for art? Were they artistic? She could not remember. They would have said nothing. They hardly knew her. Frances realised Giacomo had turned towards her and was looking for an answer.

'Mark Twain, you know, the American?' he asked again.

'Yes, yes, of course.'

Giacomo nodded. 'Mark Twain said, "The Creator made Italy from designs by Michelangelo." You agree, eh, *l'ambiziosa*?'

'*L'ambiziosa*?'

'The ambitious one. Am I wrong? Are you not *l'ambiziosa*? You are not a pilgrim, I am sure. You are hardly dressed for art, no. Your pearls, your sunglasses, you look like you've come for a takeover bid, or something else perhaps.'

Unsure what to say, Frances resorted to what every English person abroad does when faced with the linguistic skills of their continental friends. She spoke down to him. 'Your English is very good.'

He nodded his head. 'Yes. It is good. I can even spell patronise.'

Frances stood up so quickly she nearly fell. 'Listen, you know nothing about me. I wish everyone would stop making presumptions about me. Deciding I'm no good at art or not here for art at all. As it happens I—' Frances stopped in mid-sentence and the man shrugged.

'I have to go now.' She faltered. Frances realised that there had been a brief moment when she had almost felt normal but now panic returned and flooded through her. She couldn't stay here any more. She needed to be on the move.

'Don't forget to leave the key to your room at the desk on the way out!' he called after her.

She muttered to herself, 'There is no bloody key and if there was a bloody key it wouldn't bloody work.'

Now she hurried along the lanes. She had to get the hell out of here, back to the place where she belonged. Back to somewhere where at least she knew what everyone was talking about and nothing unexpected lurked around the corner.

CHAPTER SIX

There are three classes of people: those who see. Those who see when they are shown. Those who do not see.

Leonardo da Vinci
Italian draughtsman, painter, sculptor, architect and engineer (1452–1519)

'A plane? To go home? Today? Of course we can do that. We only wish for you to be happy.' Until Frances had returned from her walk Margaret had been rather cheerful, pretending to get on with paperwork while whistling along to hit songs from *My Fair Lady.* Now there was clearly a slight edge to her day. 'Paolo?' she called out to the office at the back. *'L'Inglese*, she wishes to go home. Paolo? Oh, for goodness' sake. Paolo, where are you?'

Margaret sailed off into the office calling for the missing Paolo and quite forgetting *'how loverly'* things might be. Once again Frances was deserted in the hall. It was, however, the hub of the revolving set on which the drama of I Gelosi was played out and it wasn't long before another member of the *dramatis personae* pitched up. A woman wheeled her bag in from the front door. The two steps up into the hall were awkward and there was a great thumping as the woman, perhaps in her sixties, bumped her smart white case up the stone impediment. She was extremely tall and thin and dressed entirely in beige, including a beige smock and a beige beret, presumably from some shop selling artist's clothing. She had clearly gone in for the entire painting experience, costume and all. She also managed to have travelled without attracting any dirt whatsoever. She looked, in fact, like a soap-powder advertisement, as if small cartoon birds ought to be flying round her shoulders, overwhelmed by freshness. The brilliant costume was good, which was just as well, for the woman in beige was not—as the unkind might have put it—an oil painting herself. Her large hook nose more than adequately held up her even larger glasses and several moles had taken up residence on her chin. It was a look that would have sent Hansel and Gretel running. She ignored Frances completely, but then Frances was getting used to that.

Unable to think of anything else to do and still waiting for Margaret's reply about her flight, Frances went to sit on one of the sofas in the hall. Clearly they had been provided for guests exhausted from waiting for an answer, a cup of tea or indeed anything else they might have requested. The giant grandfather clock in the corner ticked sonorously. It was a pleasant sound. Frances had a loathing for digital clocks, which taunted her that time was slipping by and she was doing nothing useful with it. This clock beat slowly and steadily and soothed the Protestant work ethic in her breast long enough to allow her to relax. She was just sensing a loosening of her shoulders when the old timepiece seemed to give a slight snore. Frances listened again and there was the distinct expiration of air through troubled nasal passages. She glanced over the back of the sagging floral sofa. A man, a large man, a large bald man dressed entirely in black leather was lying flat out on the stone floor. Uncertain whether he was asleep or ill, Frances was trying to decide whether to poke him when suddenly his eyes snapped open and he spoke.

'*Ich bin gestorben und jetzt sehe ich einen Engel,*' he exclaimed.

'Are you all right?' asked Frances, thinking how German had the misfortune to always sound like a command.

'I am well. I am Anselm Heimer—performance artist from Germany. I do Berlin-style cabaret in my own way, sometimes with and sometimes without paint. It has no intrinsic meaning so I would appreciate no interpretation,' he said without bothering to get up.

There was no time for interpretation, for Buff had returned with the picnic. Here was a British major who might well have been brilliant in the face of battle but it seemed was hopeless in the midst of anything domestic. He stood helplessly, clutching endless bags of provisions as he tried simultaneously to maintain manners by holding open the door for another guest. The upright gentleman with a shining head of waxed hair, whom Frances had seen the night before, was also returning. He too was a man of civility and was attempting to hold the door open for Buff. In the throes of politeness, the two men spent some moments engaged in a sort of mating dance as each tried to outdo the other in solicitous behaviour. The matter came to a head when Buff dropped all the bags he was carrying and both men went scurrying off after escaped tomatoes. When the food was gathered, they continued, without

72

conferring, to lay it out on a large table that stood near the clock.

Once order had been returned, Buff stood uncertain of how to proceed. The brillianteened gentleman grabbed the social bull by the horns.

'Good morning,' he boomed as if nothing untoward had occurred. 'A glorious day. You must be some fellow artists. I am Carlos, *Capitán de Corbeta* Carlos Simionatto. My friends call me Pito.'

Buff swallowed hard. The two men were roughly of an age and he eyed Capitán Simionatto with suspicion. '*Capitán de Corbeta?* You're Argentinean?'

'*Sí. Fuerza de Infantería de Marina Rio Plato. Retirado* . . . retired.'

Buff nodded. 'Cecil Denby, Major Cecil Denby, Scots Guards, retired. My friends call me Buff.' The final instruction was issued with the clear understanding that Buff's nickname would not be appropriate for the Capitán's use.

Now it was the Capitán's turn to stiffen.

'Scots Guards?' he enquired. 'So you served in Los Malvinas?'

Buff flinched. The near emotional wreck he had been in the upstairs corridor with Frances and his appalling art had entirely disappeared.

'The Falklands. Yes. And you I believe —Argentinean Marines?'

The Capitán gave the briefest of nods and clenched his jaw. Clearly they had gone from seeing each other as fellow students for a summer of profound expression to something else entirely. Frances sensed the encounter was not going well and barring the arrival of Kofi Annan she had better involve herself. With the strongest sensation of having entirely disappeared from view, she stood up between them and stuck out her hand.

'How lovely to meet you, Pito. Frances Angel. My friends call me . . . uh . . . Frances Angel, actually.'

The Argentinean was a gent and he dipped his head to kiss her hand.

'Angel.' He seemed to have calmed down but as soon as the formalities were over his irritation returned.

'Can you believe it?' he exploded.

'What?' asked Frances.

'Yes, what . . . ah, yes, what . . . there was no *colazione* this morning.'

'Breakfast,' translated Buff. 'I know. It was absurd. I have to say this is my third year and I have never gone without a meal before.'

It must be true that an army marches on its stomach for in the absence of breakfast the two men had found common ground.

Pito nodded enthusiastically. 'The brochure plainly states that there are three delightful Umbrian meals per day included, to be shared in company with the faculty.'

'Still,' declared the florid Buff, 'I got rather a splendid picnic lunch if I do say so myself.'

Pito rubbed his hands in anticipation as he eyed Buff's many purchases. 'That is splendid,' he commented. 'As they say in Italian, "*Un uomo deve mangiare!*" '

'A man needs to eat,' explained Buff to Frances. 'Your Italian is impeccable, Capitán,' he added with all the civility an English army officer prides himself upon.

The Capitán nodded and gave a slight click of the heel in thanks at the compliment. Frances felt as though she had stepped into a poorly rehearsed production of *Privates on Parade*.

'Sorry,' interjected Frances. 'I've just remembered that I was supposed to get the bread and . . . uh, well, I didn't. Or fruit. Sorry.'

The men looked at her. At once she knew what it felt like to fail a military mission. They both knew fruit and bread to be essential. There was joint shaking of heads at the inferior quality of today's lower ranks and, without conferring, the two soldiers set off back to the town. Frances sat down on the sofa. This really was the most extraordinary place. Obviously there was no entrance exam for the art school students and all comers were accepted. So far, there were two soldiers from opposing sides in the same war, the German performance artist who still hadn't emerged from his position on the floor and the tall, thin woman in beige who continued to wait with the patience of Job for Margaret to reappear. Unexpectedly, Frances almost felt a slight regret that she was leaving.

Enter the next character actor in this curious drama. In the doorway, the man in the white three-piece suit, who had gone out earlier in such a hurry, had returned. He was accompanied by a woman dressed in an excess of road kill. She was older than she wished and swathed in faux leopard-skin prints overlaid with minks still glassy-eyed from their encounter with death. Her platinum hair had been teased into a style that added some six inches to her head. It was not just her appearance that was loud. She spoke with a Texan drawl at a decibel level that made her, despite her presence in Europe, still audible in parts of the prairie.

'Oh, but this is delightful. So charming, so quaint. Why, Paolo, you old dog, you never said it was pretty as well. Oh, I just love it. I love it. Look at the quaint woman sitting on the sofa. That is so artistic. Someone just waiting to create. I am hoping, Paolo, I might end up with a painting that will go in my home. I brought some fabric samples from my designer so I can match the colours.'

Paolo was bright red either from the strain of her seven matching cases or from the excessive gushing.

'Please, Ms Beauyeur, allow me to give you a tour of the school,' he panted.

Ms Beauyeur raised a cerise gloved hand. 'No, Mr Bertelli, no. I have come a long way on my own and I intend to be independent. Mr Beauyeur always said I could never manage, but I will, you know, I will. That bastard had no idea what I could achieve. I believe, Mr Bertelli, that the good Lord is watching over me, that he has a purpose for my life, and that you and I are marching through his vineyard with work to be done.'

Paolo crossed himself and nodded uncomfortably. He too believed the good Lord watched over him but he was sufficiently European to think that mentioning his private relationship with God was in poor taste. The Italian in him also worried about the idea of being alone in a vineyard with a woman who was not his wife. Ms Beauyeur took out a postage stamp of a lace hanky from her pink clutch purse, dabbed her nose and smiled.

'I am unique. I will explore, I will discover, I will

be triumphant,' she declared.

And with those words from a business-development seminar ringing in everyone's ears, Ms Beauyeur exited. Drawn like an ageing butterfly to the light, she headed down the corridor towards the doors to the garden. Her exit was perfectly timed with the reappearance of Margaret from the office, who watched the fur-drenched woman retreat.

'Paolo, where the hell have . . . who, may I ask, is that?'

Paolo removed his cravat and mopped his brow. 'Ms Beauyeur from Dallas in Texas. I . . . uh . . . collected her from the station.'

Having been quite calm, Margaret suddenly went into orbit. 'Collected her from the station? Collected her from the station?'

'Please, my darling,' pleaded Paolo, half glancing at the woman in beige still standing quietly, waiting to be dealt with, and at Frances sitting on the sofa. Frances realised she was quite enjoying herself. She had rarely seen better theatre and was quite content not to be too involved in the production. So this was the redoubtable Margaret's husband. He was a full head shorter and considerably rounder than his voluminous wife and, not surprisingly, she appeared to dominate in every way. Paolo took Margaret gently by the arm and attempted to steer her towards the backstage area.

'We need to talk, my darling, *amore mia,*' whispered Paolo.

'Talk?' boomed Margaret, who had no volume control. 'Too bloody right we need to talk. What are you thinking, Paolo? We never collect anyone from the station. We have enough problems without you drifting off to the terminus. I suppose it didn't hurt that she was attractive?'

'Attractive? I didn't even notice,' protested her small but feisty husband. 'Besides, no one has ever been attractive to me since I first held you in my arms.'

'Now, Paolo—'

'Come here, you *gatta*.'

Margaret gave a surprisingly girly shriek as Paolo chased her into the office. Noises of frolic followed through the open door as they continued to bait each other.

'Let me sink my head into your field of poppies, *cara mia*.'

Frances smiled at the signs of their continuing passion but the sight and sounds cut into her. She realised with a start how much she longed for that connection with another human being. Perhaps she had clung on to Alistair out of fear that it would never come. Perhaps she was fundamentally unlovable.

'Paolo, you are a disgrace.' Margaret could be heard giggling in the office. 'Would you have collected a man or that ugly woman waiting at reception? I don't think so.'

Paolo lowered his voice. 'What ugly woman?'

'The one at reception,' repeated Margaret still booming in her usual fashion. There was a Pinteresque pause, followed by a marginally more subdued but still entirely audible voice from Margaret.

'Paolo, there's an ugly woman at reception. Go and deal with her.'

There was the slight sound of a scuffle and then

Paolo reappeared at the front desk smiling, patting down his shirt collar and emitting Italian charm as if nothing could have been overheard.

'Signora, welcome, welcome to I Gelosi. And you are?'

'My name is Madeleine Lacroix,' said the patient beige woman. 'I made a booking from Bordeaux. I have here all the relevant communications.'

Madeleine removed a pristine beige leather folder in which no doubt all her paperwork was alphabetised. She was the neatest woman Frances had ever seen and she spoke with a pleasingly caricatured French accent. The place was turning into a United Nations of waifs and strays. Paolo took her passport with a slight kiss of the hand and passed it immediately to Margaret, who had appeared behind him.

'How many is that?' he asked his wife out of the corner of his mouth.

'Six, that's all.'

'Six!' exclaimed Paolo. '*O Dio*, we can retire now.'

'Don't be cheeky, it doesn't suit you. Yes, six. The Major, as usual, Capitán Simionatto, Miss Lacroix, your leopard woman in the garden, the German behind the sofa, that little Yugoslavian who hasn't come yet and Miss Angel on the sofa, who would make seven except she's leaving.'

'Leaving?' Paolo threw his hands up in such a classic Italian display of horror that Frances thought he was rather overplaying his part. He rushed over to her with charm enveloping him like an invisible opera cloak. He smiled and then he twinkled. Frances had heard about Italian men

79

flirting, but this man was actually twinkling at her. It should have been nauseating, but he did it with such sincerity that somehow he got away with it and she found herself as near to blushing as she would ever get in her life.

'Miss Angel, you cannot leave us. Why, we shall not allow it. You have met my wife. *She* will not allow it.' Paolo lowered his voice confidentially. 'I must warn you. Everyone says she is *lei è' la carta di briscola* . . . you know?'

'No,' replied Frances honestly. It was, in fact, the reply which at that moment she would have given to any question.

Paolo beamed. 'The trump card. You will find that Margaret is never wrong about anything. If she says you should stay then she will not be mistaken.' He turned to admire his winning wife. 'Is she not beautiful? She has, how you say, a harmonious behind . . . like a double mandolin.'

'Paolo!' protested Margaret, who clearly had the ears of a bat, from behind the desk.

Paolo threw his arms up in the air and called back to her. 'What? I am a man. I have to speak when I find beauty.'

Frances was still pondering the idea of having a bottom like a double mandolin. It was an image she simply could not formulate in her head—but there was no time to linger. Paolo was single-minded in getting her attention.

'You have been to Italy before?'

'Well, I . . .' faltered Frances.

Paolo shrugged as if her answer was the least of his concerns. 'No matter. You will stay, and within a week you will have *cose all'italiana*—all those strange habits and practices unique to us Italians.

You will be unable to speak without using your hands.'

Before Frances could emphasise her desire to go home the front door once more opened to reveal the triumphant return of the troops. Buff and Pito were laden with bread and fruit. The outing had clearly been a success with regard to provisions (there were many paper bags) but less fortunate on the diplomatic front.

'But you are absurd,' exploded the Argentinean Capitán. 'Our claim to Los Malvinas goes back to the papal bull of 1493—'

'Oh and we should count that instead of the open, continuous and effective possession, occupation and administration of the islands since 18 . . . something or other by the British who—'

'Who live nowhere near the islands—'

Both men dumped their groceries on an empty sofa and, without conferring but with military precision, moved the table into the centre of the hall so that everyone would be able to sit down.

'What about the UN's recognition of the right to self-determination?' continued Buff. 'In 1960 . . . something . . . they decided that—'

'1964,' interrupted Pito.

'Was it?'

'I believe so.'

'I've always been hopeless with dates,' conceded Buff.

'Ah.' The Capitán smiled. 'There is a trick for remembering them which I was taught at school. You need to visualise the date in association with the event and then . . .'

Frances had not given food a thought for some time but suddenly she felt drawn to the picnic laid out before her. There were *panini* so fresh that wisps of flour floated into the air as they were placed on a cutting board, gleaming plum tomatoes still clinging to their vine, plump white balls of mozzarella glistening from the liquid bath they had been resting in, olives as large as small plums, olive oil like a sweet syrupy wine and prosciutto so silky and succulent that even a pig would have thought the sacrifice worthwhile.

'We have not been introduced.' Madeleine, the beige-clad woman, loomed over Frances. 'I am Madeleine Lacroix of France.'

'Frances Angel . . . London.' Frances held out her hand but Madeleine's attention had drifted. Ignoring Frances, she walked towards one of the doors in the far corner. It was the one the old woman had been attempting to open the night before.

'Yes, I thought so,' declared Madeleine quietly but with great confidence. 'It is a *trompe l'oeil*, you know, the door. Technically brilliant. You can see that, no?'

'No. I mean, yes.' Frances got up to have a closer look. The door was brilliant. It had been painted to look like the other entrances and exits in the hall but in truth there was no exit or entrance. Just a painted wall.

Paolo was bringing plates from the kitchen. 'But it is also a real door,' he explained. 'This *trompe l'oeil* is more than the perfect trick of the eye. It pretends to be a door but there is also a real door. You have to look beneath the surface. If you look carefully at the paintwork you can see the shadow of the *porta della morte*—the door of the dead. The paint covers a small, bricked-up opening which is knocked through only when you need to bring a coffin in and out of the house.'

'Why?' asked Frances.

Paolo laughed. 'It is a Montecastello tradition. You wouldn't want that kind of bad luck coming through the door you use every day, now would you?'

Madeleine gave a loud and long sniff. 'I am an engineer, Monsieur Bertelli,' she confided. 'I do not believe in luck. I believe in structure and order, although I confess that I hope this summer might unlock something a little, well . . . wilder in me.'

Frances looked at the tall woman with the challenging face. Under her artist's smock Madeleine wore a beige long-sleeved jersey tucked into beige leggings tucked into beige boots. She was in fact, entirely tucked. It was clear from her astonishing cleanliness that she had not interacted with anyone or anything for some time. An unlikely candidate for a walk on the wild side. As if there was not enough of a cavalcade, the old woman, the *cucciola*, now wandered across the hall and came and stood beside Frances. In contrast to Madeleine's pale ensemble, the old woman wore black, the traditional black of grief from some past sorrow. She took Frances's hand and placed her head on Frances's shoulder. Sandwiched between the two women, Frances felt as though she were being escorted to the door of the dead.

'Your grandmother?' asked Madeleine.

'No,' insisted Frances. 'I don't know her.'

'Strange,' said Madeleine, who clearly liked everything to have its place. 'She seems to know you.'

She came with the house, thought Frances.

83

Didn't Margaret say the old woman came with the house?

CHAPTER SEVEN

Come il cacio sui maccheroni

Like cheese on macaroni (just what the doctor ordered)

Soon the hall was filled with the sound of chatter as everyone dived into the picnic. As well as Capitán Pito and Major Buff, there was methodical Madeleine, leather-clad Anselm, who had roused himself from behind the sofa, Margaret and Paolo, Felicity Beauyeur from Texas, who wished everyone to call her Fliss, the *cucciola* and Frances. Then, at the last moment, a wind blew in the small, round figure of Goran Toranovic, the black-suited photographer from the street. He turned out to be from Montenegro and his suit was as filthy up close as Frances had noticed from afar. He was the last of the art students and one could only hope that he would find expression in his painting for he didn't have much to say. Goran kept his distance from the group—which was probably just as well—via a long lens through which he photographed incessantly.

Although the food looked tempting, Frances had almost got out of the habit of eating so she stood and watched the others. The conversation was about art and the season and what excitements were planned. Frances felt like a spear-carrier on the edge of the scene. When the front door flew open and a dog bounded in across the stone floor, she was the first person the new visitor came to.

The dog greeted her as an old friend the way only children and animals can manage after a single encounter. It was Auroch, from her parents' deserted garden, and he was soon followed by Giacomo, the man with the dancing cane. He carried a pad of paper and a red clay tile.

'Come on, Auroch, this way, boy,' the man called. He caught sight of Frances and smiled. 'Hey, how you doing, Angel?' he asked in an unmistakable American accent.

Stating the obvious Frances blurted out, 'You're American.'

He nodded. 'I know, ain't it a burden? Can I just say that I never voted for that president. May he choke on a pretzel.'

'You made me think you were Italian.'

Giacomo struck a heroic pose. 'I speak Spanish to God, Italian to women, French to men and German to my horse.'

'And you save American for people with special needs?'

Giacomo winced. 'Ouch.'

Frances turned back to the picnic table and, irritated by the man, took a slice of cheese and a tomato to busy herself. He stood sheepishly beside her.

'I don't really speak all those languages. I was quoting Charles the Fifth.'

'Listen, you can quote stock prices for all I care. I'm just not crazy about wasting my time playing pretend.'

'Pretend? Pretend?' Giacomo's voice boomed out in mock disgust. 'I'll have you know I was acting. Don't you know an actor when you see one?'

86

'Probably not,' murmured Frances.

'My dear Angel, Italy is full of actors. Fifty million of them. Check out anyone in the street and they will give you a great show. This is the land of theatre. Do you know that Nicolo Paganini often used to finish playing his most complex sonatas after breaking all the strings on his violin except one? Can you imagine the drama?'

'Frankly, no.' Frances knew she was being rude but she couldn't help herself.

'Oh, come on, be nice. I nearly lost my life coming here, you know.' He held up the jagged remains of the red clay tile he was carrying. 'It's off the roof. Almost took my head off. Must be five, six hundred years old. Imagine that. That tile has been sitting around all that time and it chose me to land on. What are the chances? It was my fate that it picked me.'

'And mine that it missed,' added Frances.

Giacomo ignored her and held the tile up for closer inspection. 'Look, it's hand-made. See.' He pointed to a small indentation at the edge of the tile. 'That's the thumb print of the guy who made it.'

Frances brought the piece of tile closer to her eye. Not only was the thumb print completely clear but the very ridges and swirls of the maker's individual mark could be clearly made out in the sun-baked clay.

'Neat.'

'He might as well have signed his work,' agreed the man. 'Imagine that—a hot Italian day five hundred years ago and the workman places his thumb in the clay as he makes this tile.'

Frances looked at Giacomo. He was not

87

handsome but each part of his face was pleasing. Perhaps, she thought, the face whose attractions defy analysis exudes the most charm. Aware that she was staring at him, she bit into her tomato, only to be surprised at how sweet and juicy it was. Some juice escaped from her lips and ran down her chin. Giacomo reached out and wiped it away with his hand. It was an intensely personal thing to do, yet somehow it didn't feel invasive.

'So, you believe in fate?' he asked.

Frances shook her head but replied, 'Yes, well, no, well . . .'

'Kind of undecided. Me too. I think fate means believing someone is in charge—that there is a plan. I suppose if you were given some kind of sign then having faith would be no problem.'

Frances was lost and didn't feel another tomato would be the solution. 'What are you talking about?'

'Well, I figure if you had some sign from God, like a burning bush or whatever, then you could stop wondering. I mean, it would make it easy to believe.'

'Yes, right.'

Frances could not think how they had started this theological discussion. Perhaps he was mad. She longed for someone else to join the conversation but the others were busy eating and chatting.

'So, would you like me to give you the stigmata?' he persisted.

Frances laughed. 'The what?'

'You know, the marks on your hands or feet that appear by themselves. Like St Francis had, and Jesus.'

'I know what stigmata are.'

'Well, just imagine if you had them. Then you could be really sure not only that there was someone out there, but that you had been specially chosen.'

'What are you, the Angel Gabriel now? You can give me the stigmata just like that?'

'Sure. Imagine what you could do with that in a business situation. Things get tough in negotiations and you hold up your hand and say, "Hey, don't mess with me, I've got the stigmata."'

Frances smiled. He was charming, and it was annoying. The man removed a piece of charcoal from his pocket and drew a small cross on the clay tile. He turned the tile over and showed her that one side was blank while one had the cross mark, then he threw the tile on the stone floor and stepped on it so that it cracked into many pieces.

'Give me your hand,' he commanded. He took her left hand and pulled her down into a crouching position so that her palm hovered on the broken tile. 'Now look.'

Frances turned her hand over and there, in the centre of her palm, was the faint but unmistakable sign of the cross, just as Giacomo had drawn it on the tile.

She looked up. 'It's a trick, right?'

'Do you know it's getting harder and harder to impress a girl.'

'Is that what you're trying to do? Because you're wasting your time.'

'Thanks for the info.' He smiled. 'Of course it's a trick. But tell me, when the priest holds up the solid vial of St Gennaro's blood and makes it liquid again, does the fact that there is red wax in the

89

container and it's the heat of his hand that causes it to liquefy again make it less impressive? Do the people who want a miracle need to know that?'

Frances shook her head. 'Everything about you seems to be a trick. How do I know you're really American?'

'I have great teeth, no sense of irony and I find cutlery a trial.' Giacomo stopped and looked at her. 'Listen, I'm sorry I kidded around with you earlier. I had seen you in the town. You looked so miserable. I thought it would cheer you up.'

'You bastard.'

'Most people call me Jack.'

The meal was coming to a conclusion, with the table picked as clean as if a biblical plague of locusts had descended upon it. Then, like a royal arriving to inspect a cheese factory, Margaret swept into the middle of the group to claim the floor. She clapped her hands and dramatically sniffed the air.

'Ah yes, I sense a hint of the debauched bacchanalian revels to come,' she declared.

'You'd know,' muttered Jack.

Margaret shot him a glance and continued. 'Welcome, welcome to Italy. Ah, Italy. You will fall in love. Especially you British, and possibly the French, but you Germans and Slavs will be hard work.'

'I like love,' declared Anselm, clearly a little offended.

'But only if you bring your own handcuffs,' muttered Jack.

Margaret steamed on as if no one had spoken. 'I know you may think you like to call a spade a spade but once you learn to think of it as a *badile* then you will understand how intoxicating this place can be. So *benvenuti* to Italy but most especially to I Gelosi, our own little piece of paradise. I Gelosi—named and destined for greatness. Let me transport you to a scene of great drama. It is 1575 and the great city of Florence contains a talented but restless group of actors. These kings of the stage are bored. They are tired of repeating the same lines over and over. Of having to speak someone else's lines. You can imagine.'

There was general nodding of heads, so apparently everyone except Jack and Frances could imagine it.

'And so these actors formed their own *teatro dell'arte*. They invented their own business, they improvised and they became a huge success at no less than Catherine de' Medici's wedding.' Margaret winked at Frances, who had the unnerving feeling of falling further and further down a rabbit hole.

'Together, for the next few weeks, we—' Margaret threw her arms out wide as if to take in the entire room '—we shall be the I Gelosi of today. We shall be the *zingari*, the gypsies of the art world. We shall repeat no one's ideas, we shall improvise, we shall dare and we shall have only one watchword—passion. Together we shall be passionate about art, about food, perhaps even about each other.' Over in the corner, the English Major, quite overwhelmed, had to sit down. Margaret ploughed on. 'We shall conclude, as we have every year, with a sensational piece of performance art.'

Anselm nodded enthusiastically. 'This will be

91

magnificent,' declared the resident German expert on performance art.

Margaret agreed. 'In addition to our work on canvas, each year we present a tableau for the people of Montecastello. It is, I have to tell you, hotly anticipated.' Margaret continued. 'I like to think we are helping to build the growing international reputation of this hilltop idyll and we cement that with a very special piece of work prepared jointly by our students from all over the world. This year that piece of work, for the first time, will be presented on stage as a piece of theatre. We have been given special permission to perform at Montecastello's own *teatro dell'arte*—'

'A great honour,' interjected Buff.

'—and our performance will be attended by Cardinal Vacceccio from the Vatican City himself and Signora Biche from the Italian Commission of Culture.' Paolo crossed himself at the very mention of these names. Clearly they were people of some significance. Margaret nodded in agreement. 'This is a great tribute to the growing reputation of our small school and I know you will all treat the occasion with the honour it deserves. Everyone will play a part but the key figure will be our *trovarobe*—the man or woman charged with finding the vital props, the person who will stage-manage, the one responsible for the scenery and illusions. The guiding hand of our final piece of art.' The room was hushed and no one moved as she glanced at each one. 'I shall watch you all and then decide.'

'And brilliantly. You will decide brilliantly. She always does,' beamed Buff, clutching a cushion and looking slightly breathless with it all.

Frances felt like the girl at the side of the netball court destined only to cut up oranges in the break. Margaret clapped loudly. 'This is your chance to be yourselves. To be unique,' she declaimed and spread her arms out in a dramatic gesture of inclusion. 'You must take this chance and cry out, "Liberty, you are mine!"'

'Liberty, you are mine!' cried Buff enthusiastically and alone. 'Sorry,' he mumbled to his shoes. 'I thought you meant all together.'

'Ah, Liberty! What crimes they commit in your name!' countered Jack. 'Madame Roland, on the way to the guillotine,' he added by way of explanation.

Frances laughed, and as the room broke up into conversation she turned to Jack. 'So, Jack, are you going to commit artistic crimes? Are you another one of the people here whose ambition for art far outstrips their talent?'

Jack thought for a moment. 'I do hope not,' he replied finally. 'That would be disastrous.'

Frances smiled. 'Why?'

Jack leant forward and whispered in her ear. 'I'm the art teacher.'

CHAPTER EIGHT

The sun, with all those planets revolving
around it and dependent on it, can still
ripen a bunch of grapes as if it had
nothing else in the universe to do.

Galileo Galilei
Italian astronomer and physicist
(1564–1642)

The picnic moved on into the evening and a
cocktail party of Chianti, Frascati and the
inevitable mistake that is grappa. Somehow the
chance for Frances to speak to Margaret about her
departure never arose and it was with a light head
that Frances excused herself to bed. Although she
could not admit the fact even to herself, she had
enjoyed the gathering. They were an eclectic
bunch unlikely ever to assemble again and it made
the conversation relaxed and unedited. Everyone
had left their homes and habits behind. For a brief
while they could be who they wished to be rather
than who they were. The only strange moment had
been when she thought the Argentinean Capitán
had been trying, rather formally, and certainly
ineptly, to ask her out, but then she also thought
that Buff had tried to kiss her. That had been post-
grappa so it was probably all nonsense. Frances got
into bed and then noticed that someone had been
in her bag. The little clay handprint was
unwrapped and propped up against her broken
watch. She put her hand out to touch the tablet

94

and realised that the faint markings of the stigmata still lingered on her palm. She rubbed the mark with her thumb and it faded into the lines on her hand.

She turned out the light and held the small handprint in her palm. Somewhat befuddled by the day and drink, she tried to think. Today she had been in her parents' garden. Tears of tiredness and emotion slowly fell from her eyes. She clutched the clay tablet tighter. Sophia had been a timid little mite, easily the smallest of the three friends, and the slightest thing could make her jump. She had been afraid of the dark. Sometimes she spent the night at Francesca's and they would lie holding hands till Sophia fell asleep.

'Trade with me, Francesca,' Sophia had said on the way home from school. 'You give me your handprint and I'll give you mine. Then we will always have each other's hand to hold. Then I won't be afraid of the dark.'

Now Frances was lying in Sophia's house trying not to be afraid. Perhaps her old friend had slept in this very room. Frances could not remember. The fire in the chapel was bright and glowing. They said the villagers who tried to put it out had to shield their eyes from the fierceness of the light. How anxious all their parents had been. It was a game that had gone too far. They had always played next to the little chapel; it was close to the house and, of course, they had played games about the Church. The Church was everywhere in their lives. Frances remembered the dusty olive branch from Palm Sunday her father kept tacked to the stable wall, the small amulet that, like so many devout Catholics, her mother wore pinned under the lapel of her Sunday coat. The girls had played saints and visions. Maria was best at the game, and when she fell to the ground claiming to have seen the Black Madonna it was easy to follow along. Then it got out of hand. Someone saw them, heard them and told Father Benito. They had been taken to his house and made to wait in his study. Once they were alone Sophia and Francesca became afraid.

'It was a game, Maria,' pleaded Francesca. 'We have to tell them. It was just a game.'

Earnest little Maria shook her tiny dark head. 'To you, maybe, but not to me.'

Sophia was in tears. 'We didn't see anything. You have to tell them. It was just a game.'

'You don't know what I saw,' snapped Maria. 'You are not in my head.'

Father Benito entered the room where the girls had been told to wait. 'The Bishop wishes to see you now,' he announced.

'I can't,' wept Sophia. 'It isn't the truth. Don't make me, please don't make me. God will know that we made it up.'

Francesca's head was spinning. The game had seemed so real. She tried to think what they had really seen. She shut her eyes and tried with all her might to see with her heart.

*   *   *

The next morning, when Frances awoke, she felt she was in a timeless space. That she could have been any woman, in any age, awakening in this ancient house. She could not shake the thought that perhaps she lay in Sophia's bed. Sophia,

Francesca and Maria. Maria, who was still here. Maria, the last connection to what had happened all those years ago. She was still alive. Still playing the game. Perhaps Gina was right: it was time to face the unfaceable. Today she would find Maria and speak to her. She probably couldn't leave straight away, so at the very least she would see Maria and sort out one or two things that remained muddled in her head.

In her mind Frances played out the scene of their meeting, how Maria would look, what she would say, how they would lay the ghosts of the past to rest. Entirely preoccupied with this pre-planned dialogue, Frances got out of bed and opened the shutters to her room, thinking only of getting dressed in the light. As she pushed them open a flood from the sun burst in. Perhaps it was the sudden influx of brightness that caused Frances to gasp, but more likely it was the astonishing expanse of beauty below.

Frances's room was built into the stone wall of the palazzo, which rose straight up from the steepest side of the mountain village as if it had grown there by itself with no human assistance. Had Frances in that moment jumped from the window, she felt she might have fallen for ever. Below stretched miles and miles of impossibly yellow sunflowers. Miniature suns, their heads turned in uniform obeisance to the great master in the blue sky. Picking out the best of the blue with shades of green, the Tiber river snaked through the valley. Saplings planted in military rows and even ranks of terraced vineyards suggested a passion for geometrical patterns. Seen from above, the landscape had the texture and plan of an elaborate piece of needlework. It was both an unashamed example of horticultural showing-off and a simple attempt to tame the more uncontrollable and unpredictable hazards of life and nature. Frances felt as though she had been asleep not for a single night but for months and years. She had the strangest sensation of seeing colour for the very first time, and it made her head swim.

Girasoli. The Italians called sunflowers *girasoli*—turn to the sun. All day they would follow the arc of the sun, turning their heads to worship. Such magnificent colour.

Frances's father would stop and look across the fields of yellow and sigh. 'If only we could see them properly,' he would say.

Francesca was confused. 'What do you mean? I see them properly. I don't need glasses.'

'Ah, but no one sees them properly, my angel.' He sat down and pulled her on to his knee. 'Where do we get the light to see the sunflowers from?'

'The sun.'

'Yes, the sun, and the sun is more majestic than you and I could ever imagine. It gives out such light that even Michelangelo could not imagine. Did you know that ninety-nine per cent of all the colour in the world goes past our eye without us even realising?'

'Why?' asked Francesca.

Her father put up his hands and shrugged. 'Who knows? Perhaps God thought it would all be too much for us.' He turned his small daughter to look at the fields below. 'You need to concentrate. In one minute something will appear to be one colour and the next it will have changed completely. In a single second something will be startlingly clear to you and in the blink of an eye it will be as if you never saw it at all. Come back and look at the sunflowers in an hour and they will look different to you. Do not trust your eyes to tell you what things really look like.'

'So how will I know which is the real colour—the one now or the one in an hour?'

Papa smiled. 'That, my darling girl, you have to let your heart tell you.'

'Papa! Are you wasting time chatting?' called Mama from the house.

'No, Mama,' he answered, 'I am talking to Francesca, our gift from God, and that can never be time wasted.' He turned to his daughter. 'Twenty years we waited for you to arrive, you slow coach. How could any of this ever be wasted time?'

He had loved her and then he had given her away. Why had they not come with her immediately? Why had they left it till later to come after her? An acute childish pain swept through her. Frances turned away from the window longing for darkness, but the light seeped into every corner. Just like her eyesight, the sundial too had begun to function. Now the sun sent a shimmering shadow across the stone floor. Frances walked around it and then across it, feeling time playing on her face. She put her hand in and out of time as it turned her white skin golden. The dial seemed to say ten to eight but she did not trust herself to have got that right. Sundial reading was not something that had ever come up as a necessary life skill before. Unable to make any decisions, Frances had put on the same clothes from the day before and then, in defiance of Jack, her ambitious pearls and a cashmere sweater. Today she would find Maria and talk to her and after that she would go home. Last night had been fun but she had not come to play at colouring-in with a UN of wannabe Rembrandts. She reminded herself that there was no hotel in Montecastello; that she had had no choice but to stay here; that she had come not for art, but for a reason. It was time to seek out the place of miracles.

Coincidentally, a meeting about the miracle business was taking place downstairs. Paolo emerged from the back-room office in the company of a serious-looking group of men just as Frances descended into the hall. The half-dozen fellows were all dressed pretty much identically in dark, charcoal-grey suits and narrow black ties. There was something so *Mafioso* about it that Frances would have laughed had she not noticed that on their lapels each man wore a gold pin shaped like three children at prayer.

The men solemnly shook hands. Although Paolo spoke in Italian, Frances seemed to gather the gist of it. The mists of time that had obscured her native language were slowly clearing and in the furthest recesses of her mind she found nouns and verbs of her mother tongue. He was concluding a conversation about something to do with the Vatican and the status of their local shrine. There was more but Margaret arrived from town dressed in a vast marquee of a frock and the gathering broke up. Each of the men gave a small bow to their hostess as they left. She dismissed them with a wave of her hand.

'Miss Angel.' She smiled with immense charm at Frances. 'You will want my attention. I shan't be a moment. I just need to deal with a slight infestation.' Margaret marched towards her husband, once more leaving Frances waiting in the wings. She was beginning to think she ought to give up trying to get Margaret to organise anything. Margaret was charming, she was delightful; she promised the world but failed to deliver so much as a small principality. Frances couldn't even be bothered to sit down so she hovered in the middle of the hall.

'Paolo, what is going on?' demanded Margaret. 'I have told you I don't want the committee meeting here. This is an art school, not some council office.'

Paolo held up his hands and pleaded with his wife. '*Bellissima*, this is for the town, for all of us. People will come here from all over the world to pray at the place of miracles.'

'It is heathen, superstitious nonsense and I don't want anything to do with it. For goodness' sake, we are here to glory in the arts not sink down into the mire of hocus pocus and religion. Every tin-pot town in Italy has some stupid cult or other and there is no reason for us to follow suit. We—' Margaret swept her arms out wide and knocked the ledger off the front desk '—we, Paolo, are artistes!'

Paolo crossed himself and said a silent prayer. Today the office seemed to be like one of those old clown cars at the circus from which an impossible number of funny men in large shoes keep emerging. Ms Beauyeur was next to appear. She wore a pink Lycra tracksuit in which no one was ever intended to run. In her carefully manicured hands she clutched a tape measure and a pad of paper with many notations.

'What was she doing in there?' demanded Margaret, her eyes narrow with suspicion.

Paolo held his hands up in innocence. 'She was measuring.'

'Hmm,' snorted Margaret. 'Well, that can't have taken long.'

'I believe there will be plenty of room, Mr Bertelli,' declared Ms-call-me-Fliss-Beauyeur, waving the tape in the air.

'Plenty of room for what?' demanded Margaret.

Ms Beauyeur stopped and smiled beatifically. 'For the Lord's work, Mrs Bertelli, for the Lord's work.' And with that she swept off to measure something else.

Margaret moved threateningly towards her husband.

'Now, darling, *tesorina* . . .' he began.

Margaret's dress was a vibrant green with enormous hand-painted red poppies running wild across her body. It was a garment that required sunglasses for proper viewing. Paolo appeared about to be enveloped in this field of a dress when Margaret was unexpectedly galvanised into action. Capitán Pito was coming in by the front door and Major Buff was descending down the stairs.

'Quick, Paolo, the kitchen.'

She bustled her husband into the kitchen and slammed the door shut. Both men were clearly on a mission for breakfast, which, considering how preoccupied Margaret and Paolo were with other things, Frances held low hopes for. The sound of pots and pans being hurled and intense Italian shouting ensued from behind the closed door and both men sighed as they entered the scene.

'A man could starve to death,' declared the

Capitán.

'It is a disgrace,' agreed Buff.

Frances was pleased to see the Falklands War had been laid aside in favour of the rather more significant topic of sustenance. She had no idea she was about to be propelled centre stage.

'Ah, Miss Angel,' Buff was looking more florid than usual. 'Might I have a word?'

The Capitán looked incensed. 'No, no, it is I who wishes to have a word.'

'Please, Miss Angel, I believe I spoke first,' the British guns responded.

'But you will not speak last,' replied the Argentinean force.

Now the two men were being silly, stepping in front of each other and gradually pushing Frances back against the wall in their desire to get closest to her.

'Stop!' she cried, once her back was against the painted door. 'What is it? Buff, you begin.'

Buff smiled rather triumphantly at the Capitán and removed his panama hat. 'I wondered if we might confirm last night's rather tentative arrangement?'

Frances lost the plot. 'Sorry?'

'Dinner,' explained Buff. 'We discussed the possibility of, uh . . . stepping out together one evening.'

'We did?'

The Capitán threw his hands up in horror. 'No, no, it was I who requested dinner and it was I who—'

Incredibly Frances realised she had become the new territory of dispute and was only saved by a rather loud crash from the kitchen. Noise erupted

103

from behind the closed door. There was shouting and pan throwing followed by what sounded like weeping and the gnashing of teeth. It brought instant silence to the duelling officers.

'Our breakfast,' breathed the Capitán.

'Oh no,' declared the Major.

Margaret dramatically appeared in the doorway, her back to the door, which she slammed behind her. Her hair was wild and unkempt and she looked extremely startled.

'The chef . . . says . . . he needs a moment,' she managed, and disappeared into the office.

Frances had a sudden recollection of *Henry V* with saucepans in the wings in place of actors.

'Gentlemen,' she began, 'I believe action may be required. I have discovered why there is no breakfast.'

Pito nodded. 'The troublesome chef.'

'No,' said Frances. 'There is no chef. We only ever hear noise from the kitchen when Margaret is in there. She has been pulling a fast one with a few pots and pans.'

There was an audible intake of breath from Buff. 'Good Lord!' he exclaimed, as if he were unexpectedly in the presence of Miss Marple.

'Yes! I shall leave the detective work to you military gentlemen but that is my theory.' Having successfully diverted attention from herself, Frances chose that moment to exit stage left and continue her own drama.

The town was waking up to preparations for the day's tourists. It was not a big place—in fact, Frances had been to bigger outlet stores—but it was busy. Montecastello was relatively new to its full title of Montecastello de Sanctis. The Sanctis part, although approved by neither the regional government nor the Vatican, had been added by the locals keen to celebrate and promote the local cult of the Miracle of the Innocents. In the square of V. Emmanuele II, named for the king who had united a fragmented Italy, stalls selling holy water, candles and other religious paraphernalia were being carefully laid out in the shadow of the town's main church, renamed the Church of the Innocents. This was a much bigger building than the chapel on the outskirts. Frances was not at all sure where to find Maria, so it seemed as good a place to start as any.

Rosary beads, ashtrays and amulets were placed in ranks to herald the arrival of the afternoon's pilgrims. The town was not quite Lourdes or even the home of the legendary Padre Pio, but its fame as a holy site was spreading. The miracle itself was less than forty years old and these things took time. There were, as yet, no hotels, but that would come. Already some houses displayed yellow 'to let' signs seeking tenants, and rooms were being rented in the outlying farms. The sale of 'miracle' memorabilia had become an important part of economic life. Many a local woman stood at her tap each morning filling plastic bottles of holy water to be carried far and wide across the world. Tea towels with the Virgin Mary appearing to the three young girls were a big hit and there was talk of a snow globe with the church in it. A committee of locals had taken a trip to Assisi to check out the marketing possibilities and the snow globe had been a big favourite. No one had any worries about this brazen commercialisation of religion. St Francis of Assisi himself had been the son of a successful linen merchant—Pietro di Bernardone—and it was a pleasing thought that had he been alive, Papa Pietro might well have made good use of the tea-towel concession.

It was odd to think that in the same way that Gina's daughters discussed pop stars, Frances and her friends had once discussed saints—who was their favourite and why. Frances had always plumped for St Nicholas, who had stood on his own feet for two hours as soon as he was born. As if that wasn't enough for a baby, he had then practised abstinence from food, receiving milk only during Wednesday and Friday evenings. Sophia thought St Hilarion, who had once been besieged by the whole of Palestine, was 'dreamy', and Maria had had a thing about St Mamas. Now Frances looked at the retail opportunities and thought how ridiculous it all was. Aunt Emilia had brought up Frances and Gina with an ambivalent attitude to religion. 'The Church ruined your life and your parents,' she would say to Frances as they headed to the park on a Sunday morning. Then she would cross herself and say, 'God rest their souls,' just in case the good Lord was still listening. What would she make of all this?

There were some truly awful things for sale. Ashtrays shaped like the church terrace edged with pink glitter, bottles of holy water in the guise of the Madonna with her head as the stopper, a plug-in bust of the present pope, which lit up and played 'Ave Maria', and rosary beads in shades to match every outfit. Perhaps this was what she had come for. To stop this nonsense. To tell the truth and sweep away the absurdity. The idea pleased Frances—a cleansing of the temple. Not some

106

therapy nonsense, but to right an old wrong. She was an adult now and no one could make her afraid.

A few determined tourists were already perusing the goods. These were travellers on a strict schedule who had to fit in the holy site before their half-day in Florence and then the race up to Venice. For them the church itself was a disappointment. The rectangular nineteenth-century building was dull and plain. It had been built with the economic help of first Pope Gregorio XVI and then Pius IX, but neither Holy Father had been generous enough to provide anything too grand. In so far as they had given it any thought at all, both Gregorio and Pius had no doubt been quietly confident that the dull little hilltop town of Montecastello would never produce anything as exciting as a miracle. Consequently they had not provided the wherewithal for a church actually worth visiting. It was an altar for the blindly faithful not the snap-happy tourist.

Inside, the dark and cool neo-classic structure had two aisles, one nave and some indifferently painted pillars by Nicola and Federico Caxi. At one time the *braccio santo* had been the most revered part of the church, containing, as it did, the relics of the saints Filippo and Giacomo. Indeed, the church had once been dedicated to them, but those boys had been rather left by the wayside since the Innocents had pitched up. Gone were the days when some sandal-wearing church scholar with a faded copy of Ruskin would come to admire the fingernail of Filippo or the vestments of Giacomo. Today the church was in the hands of the very young.

A few candles along the length of the aisles provided the only illumination. From the central door a jagged line could just be seen running up the middle of the floor all the way to the altar. It marked a small earthquake some fifty years earlier that had almost split the building in two. The moving of the earth was a capricious event. It could shake down one side of a street causing damage and destruction and leave the other side entirely untouched. Here, in the church, one half had been badly damaged, while the other had not moved an inch.

On the earthquake side, a large painting of Jesus had been only partially restored. He wore a white shift with a red sash across his shoulders, while clouds and crowds gathered around him. His garments had been rent by the quake and large patches remained missing. Whoever was responsible for the restoration had started on his left side and the Lord's bleeding heart seemed fresh from the operating theatre. It pulsated with a scarlet vividness rarely seen outside the butcher's window. Beside the door, a life-size statue of St Giacomo stood with one hand against his chest and the other against his side, clutching a list. He looked thoughtful, as if he knew he had forgotten something.

It was only on this, her second inspection of the town, that Frances began to see the life she had failed to notice before. There were plenty of shops but none that felt the need to advertise their wares and services in the brash and vulgar manner of British towns. Here the potential customer needed sensitivity and knowledge to spy the hairdresser, the butcher, the grocer. There were few outward

108

signs, but once discovered inside dark, stone doorways, there were worlds of delight. Pyramids of oranges, some sliced to show a bloody flesh, fresh spaghetti looped over a suspended broom handle and tied in bundles with white, red and green patriotic ribbon, great yellow wedges of fresh parmesan, jars of olives and barrels of anchovies. Behind the slashed green and white curtain at the butcher's, whole prosciutto hams and *mortadelle* hung from the ceiling. A pale calf's head, its eyes closed and lips curled with some bovine secret had a carnation stuck between his teeth as if he had met his end in cabaret style. It was a *Babette's Feast*, a veritable celebration of food, if you knew where to find it. Frances could still feel the sensation of yesterday's tomato juice slipping down her chin. She had meant to go straight to the heart of her drama, but she found herself seduced and sidelined by the setting. For no reason at all she bought six lemons and watched with pleasure as the seller placed them in a brown paper bag. Each piece of dazzling yellow fruit still bore a remnant of twig and leaf as if the garden they had been plucked from was only moments away. As she carried the bag from the shop Frances imagined herself living here. Strolling about buying fresh bread, meat for the family and lemons for . . . whatever fresh lemons were for.

It is well known that faith and food are loyal bedfellows in human sustenance, and directly opposite the church the café owner was laying out tables for lunch. Here was a man who understood that the grace and ease of living required oiling from olives and freshly poured wine. He had a small pile of white tablecloths and snapped each one into place with a flick and twist of his wrists like an expert bullfighter subduing his prey. It was the overture to a show. The waiter knew he was being watched and he played his part well. The square was designed for an audience. A low wall and some benches lined the square and men of varying ages sat and admired the daily seduction of the tables. A few of the rustic fellows were smoking pipes and, with the undulating scenery behind them, looked as though they had been set there on purpose for a tourist postcard. One man had brought his donkey, and the combination of the old ass, the stern façade of the church and the excellent use of extras made this a stage set any Englishman abroad would seek. To one side a sixteenth-century well had recently been restored. It was a source of great pride to the town and it was here that two uniformed *carabinieri* leant, keeping an eye on everything and everyone through half-closed eyelids.

Behind them a woman from the hairdresser's was sitting in the doorway on a plastic chair. Brown paste covered her scalp. It was impossible to tell which particular treatment she was receiving but to the uninitiated it appeared to involve sticking her head up the business end of a cow. She was clearly waiting for something to take, but that did not mean she hid away in her half-finished state. No, she sat watching, not wishing to miss any nuance of the daily performance in *V. Emmanuele II*.

A handsome woman with a young baby sat behind a stall of candles ready to make a sale. There were no customers yet and after a night of disturbed sleep, she was not quite awake. The baby, clearly having fussed throughout the early hours, now lay back against her breasts at peace. Neither Madonna nor child moved in the rising heat. It was only when a woman with tightly curled red hair approached to examine the wares that the mother began to coo at the baby. She held her child up in the air and tried to make it laugh; she tickled its feet and brushed its nose with hers. She played the part of the devoted and attentive mother with energy. Everyone in the square was aware of their part in the unfolding drama. Frances smiled. Jack was right. The place was full of actors.

The table-laying at the café was done and slowly customers drifted to sit down. The movement was irresistible and, despite her best intentions to get on with her task of seeking out Maria, Frances found she too was heading towards the smallest table near the wall. Like Mafia men of old, she felt safest with her back to the wall and her eyes to the view. She ordered coffee and here too found herself on the receiving end of another polished performance. Despite the absence of customers, the waiter at first declined to catch her eye. He stood against the wall dressed in black trousers and a white shirt, a clean pinny wrapped across his waist. On one hip hung a change purse and on the other a bottle opener. He had all the professional precision of a gunslinger waiting for high noon. His hooded eyes glanced at no one. A picture of bored disdain dressed in a costume of utter professional courtesy. At last he gave a resigned sigh and strolled over to receive Frances's order. His pad at the ready, he was now a study in curiosity as he waited to hear the extent of her Italian. He allowed her to stumble through and then smiled as he smugly repeated her request in accented English

111

learnt at a Wimpy bar in Tottenham. The exchange was followed by a brief flurry of professional activity. Now he showed what he could do. Napkins were brought, steaming coffee was presented with a flourish, sugar bags delivered as a personal favour and a teaspoon as if magicked from the air. Once it was done, the paper bill was ceremoniously placed under an ashtray advertising the benefits of Campari. The waiter, his performance complete, returned to his wall and a face of bored obsequiousness to await his next moment centre stage.

The coffee was hot in a way that the British never manage. Steam rose from the dark liquid. For a brief moment Frances realised she was entirely content but then, as she looked up through the heat of her first sip, she thought she saw Alistair. There was a man with the same insouciant strut, the same swagger of ownership of his world and everything in it. Utterly unable to control herself, Frances felt her heart, or rather her stomach, lurch from its harbour into turbulent waters. She could see him sitting opposite her, casually smoking and smiling with effortless charm. An actor with a lazy talent and a talent for being lazy. A man content to be a footnote in other people's lives as long as they paid for it. The man she thought had loved her for herself and not just for the house or the life that came as part of the successful-woman package. It had been an illusion. Everyone had warned her. They had all said he was a con artist, a parasite, but she had loved beyond all reason. She had loved from the very heart of herself and it seemed the pain of it would never go away. When she had announced that her biological clock was ticking, that she thought perhaps they should settle, start a family, that she might work less and that he might work at all, he had walked. Calmly and steadily he had simply walked away. The grand passion she had had had melted into air.

Frances considered that thought. A sentence with the word 'had' in it three times in a row. How much more past tense could you get? The very core of her emotional life had not been real. It had not been the truth. She had not wanted to know that he loved the set more than the leading lady. Now he was with someone else. Someone who was also rich, also successful, but who would never pull that hideous children card out of the pack. Frances felt foolish. She was a woman who could organise anything, crunch the numbers on any project, who had allowed her hormones to take over her life. Gina had suggested a therapist, the therapist had suggested she might have issues from her own childhood, that perhaps she didn't really want kids, that . . . Frances had not bothered with therapy for long. It had been an untidy business diving backwards into the past and she had not had the time for it.

'Is this seat taken?'

There are said to be certain definite ways to avoid being joined by strangers in public places. One is scratching with vigour, the other is to claim that you and the Lord are sitting together communing, and the third, if you are British, is to smile winningly as they approach. Frances forgot all three and the red-haired woman she'd noticed at the candle stall plumped down on the opposite chair.

'Hello. Lila Peters,' she announced and held out her hand. 'I'm a writer.'

Frances's civility outweighed her irritation. You can take the well-bred Englishwoman out of England but you cannot . . . and so on.

'Frances, Frances Angel,' she managed and provided a limp greeting.

'You London?' Lila asked her in the universal flow of lazy English from the Thames that now characterised any Londoner under thirty.

'Yes, yes, I suppose I am.'

'Thought you were. Fucking great candles.' Lila removed several tins of wax with images painted on the side. They were cheap and poorly produced but showed the Madonna reaching out to anyone who cared for a cuddle.

'See her face is black?' enquired Lila. 'Oi, boy! *Garçon, señor,* you there . . . coffee, I'm gasping,' she shouted with no hint of interruption in the conversation. 'Fucking clever,' she said, turning back to Frances. 'Black Madonna when the candle isn't lit, white Madonna when it is.'

'That's marvellous,' agreed Frances, if only to prevent discussion. She wished she had a newspaper to hide behind.

'Fucking clever,' restated her new companion.

Frances looked at the dual ethnicity candle. Even to an atheist, 'fucking clever' didn't sound entirely appropriate.

'I thought they might help me find what I'm looking for,' persisted Lila.

'What? Candles?'

'No,' said Lila carefully, as if a wax investigation was not entirely out of the question. 'The Black Madonna. You know the legend here, don't you?

114

You know the little girls who saw the Madonna here in town? They saw her and they say she was black.'

Frances had never seen a black woman until she arrived in England. Being black seemed as exotic as it was possible to be. Francesca, Maria and Sophia had only heard about people whose skin was a different colour. In the Umbria of the 1960s everyone had the same olive tint to their Mediterranean skin. The world had not yet begun its restless movements of whole peoples from land to land.

As if her life was becoming a series of flashbacks, Frances could suddenly see her childhood friends. Maria had taken her cardigan and placed it over her head like a prayer shawl. 'Look!' She pointed up the lane. 'There's a beautiful woman. She is smiling at me. Look at her skin. It is black like boot polish. Shiny and beautiful.'

Maria knelt in the road while Sophia and Francesca watched the play.

'Do you see her?' called Maria. The others got to their feet and ran to kneel beside their friend. 'She's blessing us,' cried Maria. The three little girls bowed their heads. Then Maria suddenly fell forward and seemed to have a slight fit. Sophia laughed but the fit went on a little too long and the laughter died as both Francesca and Sophia became anxious. Francesca ran into the chapel where she knew one of the women who was arranging flowers. Her story came out in a jumble.

'We were seeing the Black Madonna and Maria has fallen over in the road and she's shaking and—'

The woman ran up the lane and gathered Maria in her arms. Soon the priest came in a great fluster. He was young, new to the village and rather grumpy, and the children were all frightened of him. He talked very sternly to them. Said he wanted the truth or their parents would hear of it. God would hear of it. The little girls were only five years old and thought they were in trouble. Perhaps they shouldn't have been playing near the chapel or the game was blasphemous—

Lila was still talking. 'I want to find out more about the Black Madonna. That's why I've come. As a black writer, I feel . . .'

Frances let the woman witter on because she didn't know what to say. The woman was many things. She was red-haired, she was thin, she had freckles, she was annoying, but she was most definitely not black. She had curly hair which might be characterised as straying into the afro area but she was most decidedly white. White as in not black.

Lila carried on. 'I mean, I feel a responsibility to the black community to investigate. What if the Virgin Mary was actually black and the Church has tried to keep that a secret? I mean, that would be bigger than *The Da Vinci Code*. Can you imagine what that would do for my people if she was really black?'

Frances could not because Lila's people were so clearly not black. What the hell was going on? Here she was finally trying to have serious thoughts about her life and this lunatic woman comes and sits with her.

'I'm seeking the muse. Have you seen the photograph?' asked Lila.

116

'What photograph?'

'Of the fire in the chapel where one of the little girls died?'

Suddenly Frances felt cold, as if a great wind had swept up from the valley and across the terrace. 'No. I didn't know there was a photograph.'

'Pretty gruesome actually. It's in the little chapel itself. The door's always open. You can see it if you want. So, where are you staying? I can't seem to find so much as a stable to take me in.'

For some reason Frances didn't want to say, so the words 'I'm at the art school' came out with great reluctance.

Lila frowned. 'You an artist? I didn't have you pegged for an artist.'

'No. I mean, it's not that kind of place. You see, I—'

'Do they take anyone?' persisted Lila.

Frances sank back in her chair. 'Yes, I suppose they do.'

In the distance a voice seemed to echo around the square. It was magnified by a poor sound system which cut out every other word and made nonsense of the broadcast even to the Italian speaker.

'It's her!' cried Lila, her preoccupation with her direct link to Kunta Kinte momentarily forgotten.

'Who?' Frances enquired despite herself.

'It's the Parade of the Innocent Girl. She arrives at the church today so that she can stay and pray for the faithful who come on Sunday. Isn't that why you're here?'

'I was just trying to have coffee.'

'It's fab. We've got such great seats,' enthused

Lila. Frances felt as though she ought to be offering programmes, or ice creams at the very least.

The noise from the loudspeaker drew nearer. It had turned to choral singing and there was much murmuring from the stall-holders. The women placed black lace veils over their heads, crossed themselves and stopped the children running around by yanking them to their sides. Even the unoccupied men on the wall shuffled to their feet and removed a charity-shop collection of hats from their heads. From the corner by the hairdresser's the first signs of a small parade appeared. The woman with the brown paste scalp ducked inside and stood half hidden in the doorway as she watched. The parade consisted entirely of men who marched in two ad hoc columns with their hands clasped low in front of them. The small army wore suits from a bygone age, but wore them with pride. Some had hats, some did not, but each held his head with distinction. They were led by Margaret's husband, Paolo. He wore a sash in the tricolour of Italy and carried a large yellow flag fringed in white and gold. He was followed by three cloth banners held aloft by yet more local fellows with the strong, well-worn hands of the artisan. Some paces behind them a man with a splendid Spaghetti Western moustache carried a pole, its end supported by a sash slung over his shoulders. The pole was heavy, for mounted on the top were two grey loudhailers from which the intermittent music was emanating. Behind him marched the priest, attached to the sound system by a microphone on a curly wire. He was elderly and corpulent and was leaning heavily on a stout cane. He wore a white surplice that fell to the ground and swished as he walked.

Here was a whole slice of Italian history in one scene. A complex story of lands acquired piecemeal by many popes over many battles, some small, some violent, some justifiable, some not. Battles which had ended in the central domination of the Vatican and, some would claim, which had helped to crush genius.

Protected by the holy man and his workaday centurions, walked the centre of everyone's attention—a tiny woman dressed entirely in white. Her dress was full and beneath its fringe peeked white slippers and tights. Her age was impossible to determine for her face was invisible. A long white veil covered her head and fell across her shoulders, almost to her waist. She was clearly the focus of the event. She carried nothing but her own purity, and it reminded Frances of advice an old actress had given her when she first entered the theatre: 'My dear, the trick with doing Shakespeare is always to play royalty. That way you never carry props and you always get a seat.'

This was definitely someone who always got a seat. The impressive nature of the small parade was only slightly marred by one or two technical points. The choral music was issuing from a small cassette-player slung beneath the loudspeakers which gave a tinny though adequate sound but had a poor on/off switch. The priest clearly wished to interrupt the music to say sonorous things but the standard-bearer couldn't turn it off. A Laurel and Hardy burlesque ensued as both men grappled with the equipment. They were not helped by the appearance of Jack's dog, Auroch. Despite his blindness the small animal seemed to have no difficulty wandering around on his own. He was a friendly soul, until, it seemed, it came to the priest. Instantly his hairs stood on end and he began a quiet but menacing growl. All around the square men and women were kneeling, bowing their heads and crossing themselves. Lila was beside herself. She jumped to her feet for a better view.

'You can't see her face. No one ever sees her face. Do you think she's black?'

'Well, she could be black like you,' Frances replied evenly.

Lila gasped. 'Wouldn't that be thrilling?'

'Thrilling.'

Clearly this parade was a regular occurrence and there was little deviation from the usual route, but that day something changed. As the veiled woman turned into the square she lifted her head from eyeing her shoes and appeared to look at Frances. It was her old friend Maria. For a second it seemed as though she was going to lift up her veil but the priest shot out his arm and held her wrist. There was a slight juddering in the procession, which gave Auroch just enough time to leap into the midst of the men and grab the priest by his billowing sleeve. Not quite the animal-loving Assisi of his generation, the priest gave a shriek and attempted to hit the dog with his walking stick. Auroch, a dog of some determination, kept his jaws clamped on the surplice and was lifted quite off the ground as the priest swung round trying to hit him. As the priest turned, his face came into full view and Frances saw what she had dreaded—Father Benito was very much alive. Auroch, however, provided little time for

120

reflection. His tail lashed into the back of the slight woman and she stumbled forward into the man with the loudspeakers, which in turn started the music off again. It was a noisy and ill-formed procession that moved on through the square and into the sanctuary of the church. The carriers of the banners and the flag waited to enter last and as they turned to go in, a gust of wind caught the flag. The yellow silk unfurled and for the briefest second the image of the Black Madonna was revealed. The wind faded as quickly as it had come and in seconds the parade was safe inside the church. The oak doors banged shut, only to reopen seconds later with a strong hand depositing Auroch back on the pavement. They were to remain shut until the Sabbath morning.

Lila sat down with a bump. 'That was worth the whole trip.' She glanced at Frances. 'Oh my God, look at you. You're so pale. Have you had like a religious experience? How cool would that be?'

Frances shook her head. 'It's the coffee. It's strong . . . and the sun . . . I have to go. Excuse me.' She threw money on the table and fled, with Lila calling after her, 'See you around!'

Frances half ran, half walked as she left the square. She had some vague idea of the town layout now but because she was not paying attention she soon found herself in an unfamiliar square. One side had the usual small stone houses. Lanes ran off at all angles but the square was unique because of the dominance of a large pale-yellow building. Anywhere else the size of the place would have seemed unremarkable but in this Lilliputian town it appeared gargantuan. Steps ran up on both sides to a big double front door on the first floor. Above the deep blue of the door hung a sign, *Teatro dell'Arte*.

Here she would feel safe. Here was a world she knew. Frances grabbed the black metal handrail and almost ran up the steps. Inside, the foyer was empty but the lights were on as if visitors were expected. Old photographs from bygone productions lined the walls. Straight ahead a red velvet curtain concealed the auditorium from view. Frances pushed it aside and entered. The theatre was perfect. No more than thirty seats filled the stalls and all were neatly draped with dust sheets. Around and above them eleven painted boxes in gold and cream with flourishes of flowers looked down from two levels. There had been no attempt to be subtle about the decoration. Gold cherubs smiled down from the golden ovals in a blue ceiling, while each box was trimmed in red velvet and bore the gilded crest of some local family. Above the tiny stage a painted clock showed time standing still. An old black-and-white photograph from the very first night hung framed on the wall. The theatre, the legend explained, was an exact scale replica of the La Scala opera house in Milan. This tiny arena had been built in the 1900s by the city fathers in an attempt to show the world that Montecastello was a town worth paying attention to. *Il più piccolo teatro del mondo. Un'oasi di tranquillità.* Ninety-six seats each expectantly facing a stage that was no more than a dozen feet wide. It was utterly unique and utterly enchanting. For a while it had worked. People had come great distances to see such a folly, but not many people worship at the footlights any more and the place had faded in significance once the miracles began.

Did she remember this? Had her family ever come here to be entertained? Was this where her lifelong passion had started? The plain pine boards of the stage creaked as Frances climbed the four small steps on to the performing space. Here was theatre in miniature. Here was perfection. Frances breathed in the smell of dust and singed gel from the lights. The afterglow of nerves and excitement, the aura of performance. This was her world. It was here that she could breathe. It was here that she belonged.

'Ah, an actor alone on the stage. Time, I think, for a solo bravura performance. I am guessing it will no longer be in Italian.' A thickly accented Italian voice from one of the central boxes made Frances spin round. It was dark and she couldn't see who was speaking. 'It's Etruscan, you know.'

'What is?' she said, trying to shade her eyes and see where the voice was coming from.

'The word for "actor". It comes from Etruscan. *Hister*. It was adopted into Latin and it is how the English get histrionic. It was the Etruscans who brought theatre to Rome. You are in the cradle of performance.'

Frances felt afraid. 'Who is it?'

The voice retreated from the box and Frances could hear steps echoing in the walls of the building. In days gone by actors had run cannon balls down tubes in the walls to make the sound of thunder reverberate round the house. That was how it sounded now. Each step crashing towards Frances as she stood centre stage unable to move. At last the thunder ceased and there was a moment's calm before the storm. Then the velvet curtain at the back of the stalls swished aside.

Father Benito stood there, still dressed angel-like in his flowing white and leaning on his cane. Only his costume, including the indispensable little linen collar, gave away his profession. Nothing in his face suggested sanctuary or forgiveness.

'It is me, Francesca.'

'Father Benito,' she whispered.

'Of course. I am always here. I am supposed to be here but you should not have come.'

Frances could not move. She stood stock still, like an actor caught in the light without any notion of the next line.

'How did you know?' she forced the words out.

'Maria recognised you.'

'It's been more than thirty years.'

'And it should have been longer.' Slowly Father Benito began to move round the seats at the back of the stalls. 'It is not good for you to be here.'

'I am a grown woman now. You cannot threaten me.'

Father Benito shrugged and spread his arms out as if it were the last thing on his mind.

'I do not threaten you. I am a priest, but perhaps you must make peace with a higher authority.'

Suddenly Frances felt about five. She was panicked and couldn't breathe. The ghosts of the theatre walk only on pay day, but at this moment Frances could feel every spirit in the place alive and pacing. The priest stood now in the centre aisle and there was no way out except past him. She turned to the back of the stage and desperately sought a door. In one corner, past some black drapes and a large wicker basket, a heavy wooden latch was locked with a pin. She ran to it and struggled to lift it, and all the while she could hear

Father Benito's tread and the thud of his staff as he made his way towards the stage. They say when Hannibal fought here it was so fierce the combatants didn't notice an earthquake, an earthquake . . .

Frances looked back to the theatre and for a brief moment thought she saw the *cucciola*, the old woman from the art school, sitting in one of the boxes watching. At last the pin released, the latch lifted and Frances found herself looking out at the street from the raised platform of the stage. The door was part of vast wooden shutters that opened to allow sets in and out of the back of the theatre. On show days a ramp ran up to the twenty-foot-high doors, but not today. It was a good drop to the ground and she didn't think for a second she could make it. A hand reached for her shoulder and Frances, strong and determined Frances, felt herself faint. She thought she cried out 'Mama' as she began to fall, followed by the strangest sensation that a pair of hands reached out to catch her. Then she drifted down, down into a field of poppies.

CHAPTER NINE

Everything we hear is an opinion, not a fact. Everything we see is a perspective, not the truth.

Marcus Aurelius
Roman emperor and Stoic philosopher
(AD 121–80)

Frances came round in her bed. Someone was holding her left hand and massaging the palm. Considering her fall she felt surprisingly well. She slowly opened one eye to find that Jack was sitting beside her. His attention was entirely devoted to studying her hand, which he rubbed in gentle circles with his thumbs. Auroch lay at his feet, and as Frances stirred he sat up and barked.

'I know, Auroch, I know,' said Jack soothingly. 'I told you, abandonment issues. Welcome back, Angel, welcome back.'

'I need to see Maria. Maria,' she whispered, trying to sit up.

'Sssh.' Jack eased her down on the bed. Out of the corner of her eye Frances once more thought she saw the old woman, the puppy, watching her through a crack in the door, but when she looked again the door was closed.

'I fell,' she said.

'Indeed,' agreed Jack, 'and had the good fortune to land on the harmonious behind of our patron.'

'I fell on Margaret? Is she OK?'

'My dear, even now she is dining out on her tale

of angels falling at her feet from the sky. Paolo carried you home.'

'That Humpty Dumpty?'

'Built like a bull, or so Margaret tells me after a glass too many. You have a bruise on your knee which even now competes with the sunset for its rich palette. A slight cut on your hand. Otherwise, I believe you'll survive.'

Jack continued to stroke her hand and Frances, for reasons she could not fathom, continued to allow him. His thumb played across her lifeline and Auroch once more settled on the floor.

'More room is taken up in the brain for the different activities of our hands than any other part of the body,' he began, for all the world as if she were a child and needed a story. 'Aristotle wrote the first book on palmistry. You'd think he had better things to do but he wrote it for Alexander the Great more than two and a half thousand years ago. I guess even someone with "Great" for a surname wanted a little peek into the future. A little reassurance that he was truly born for greatness. Funny to think of a man like that as unconfident.' Jack pressed his thumb against her lifeline.

'It was a German,' he continued, 'Dr Carl Gustav Carus, personal physician to the King of Saxony, who related the fingers of the hand to a person's conscious mind and their palm to the subconscious: *Die Symbolik der Menschlichen Gestalt und über Grund und Bedeutung der Verschiedenen Formen der Hand.*'

'I thought you only spoke German to your horse?' Frances said drowsily.

Jack chuckled. 'It always sounds so very

127

scientific in German. Basically this'—Jack pressed her left hand—'this for you is your major hand, the one you use most naturally. It's the largest. Same with lobsters, actually. They have one claw bigger than the other, one dominant over the other.'

'Lobsters are right- and left-clawed?' asked Frances. 'And what do you see, Madame Arcati?'

'You have small hands but they like to do things on a big scale, undertake big projects. You are brave but at present your lifeline hugs your thumb so you are listless, lacking in energy and enthusiasm. Half alive, you might say. It doesn't have to be that way—the lines on your hand change as you do. "He sealeth up the hand of every man; that all men may know his work"—Job chapter thirty-seven, verse seven.'

'Don't do that.' Frances snatched her hand away and sat up.

'Don't do what?'

'Quote like that. I hate it.'

Jack put up both hands in surrender. 'Sorry, I'm sorry. I had no idea you were biblically sensitive.'

'I'm not. I just—'

'OK, OK. I forgot the most important thing I also know . . .' Jack took her hand and brought it almost level with his eyes. 'You are a theatre producer.'

'Where the hell do you see that?'

Jack laughed. 'I don't. An email came for you from Angel Theatre Productions in London. Someone called Gina wanted to know if you had arrived safely and Margaret put two and two together. I fear,' continued Jack, 'whether you like it or not, you are set to become her next *trovarobe*.'

Frances moved to stand but she still felt giddy

and weak. 'I can't. I really can't. Margaret is hopeless, you know. At least once an hour she promises to sort something out and then nothing happens. I've been here two days and have barely had a proper meal.'

'And how do you feel when she promises?' asked Jack.

'What?'

'In the moment that she promises, how do you feel?'

Frances paused. 'Well, optimistic, I suppose. As if something might actually be happening.'

'That's the idea. An Italian shopkeeper will never tell you he has no idea when he can get the order you want or repair the shoes you need. He will tell you the day after tomorrow and you will be pleased. And then on Thursday he will shrug and say Monday. That way you have been optimistic till Thursday and then you can be optimistic till Monday. I think it's rather a fine system. These are little transparent deceptions which give you the most pleasant of all Italian sensations—that you are unique, you alone are worthy of service, of extra effort.'

'I don't like deceptions of any kind,' snapped Frances. She shook her head, trying to clear it either from the fall or from some thought which haunted her. Jack gently pushed her back down on to the pillows and then continued to hold her by both arms.

'Frances, why do you fight being here? You've tried to leave since you arrived. I'm sure there is some Chinese saying about that and it isn't good.'

'I can't explain. It's too complicated.'

There was a moment of stillness interrupted by

Margaret bringing a tray.

'Tea! Tea, the great British cure-all,' she sang out. Jack dropped his grip on Frances and turned to pick up the clay handprint from her bedside table as if it fascinated him as art.

'My dear, quite a turn. How very fortuitous that I was passing.'

'Are you all right?' asked Frances, although in the face of Margaret's vigour the question seemed absurd.

'Energised, my dear, quite energised. I don't believe I've been responsible for saving a life for some time. I have to say you're quite the talk of the school. We haven't had anything this exciting here since a local cat ate a tube of red oil paint and did inadvertent modern art all over the cobbles. Now then, good and bad news, I'm afraid. Good news—I was able to get you a flight this afternoon—but bad news, I spoke with the *dottore*, just as a precaution, and he says you really mustn't go anywhere without a jolly good night's rest. I must say your cousin Gina is most concerned about you. She seems to think you might decide to come home early and suggested in no uncertain terms that that would be a mistake. I read the email, I'm sure you won't mind. What shall I reply?'

'I'll go home tomorrow,' said Frances, more tired than she could imagine and with the dull beginnings of a headache.

Margaret patted her arm. 'Capital idea. Heavens, we shall be busy what with your departing and the first day of class. Yes, indeed, tomorrow the creativity begins.'

*   *   *

The next day Frances awoke feeling surprisingly refreshed. She dressed and then opened the shutters to check the time on the shadow-covered floor. Downstairs the hall was deserted. Frances tried the office but it too was like the *Marie Celeste* during pudding. Margaret had promised a flight for today but France had no idea what time. She wandered along the corridor past the garden doors. The art studio lay at the far end of the building. It was a vast white room with ceilings as high as the room was wide. Each year Margaret had the studio repainted white—a clean canvas for fresh endeavours. Despite the brilliance of the paint, the window shutters remained closed and there were no lights on, giving the room a twilight feel. Easels, fresh boxes of paint and jars of sable brushes stood to attention, ready for genius. The class, which was small, had gathered in the studio with a large palette of available emotions. There was a good deal of nervous anticipation, some first-day-at-school giggling, and one or two were obviously steeling themselves for the moment when their own greatness would at last be untapped and allowed to flood forth. Buff, who thought everyone would be the same bag of nerves as himself, was doing his best to prepare his soul for inevitable disappointment.

'I mean, I think about Prince Charles,' he said to his Argentinean colleague, Pito, who was busy lining up paintbrushes in height order and wasn't listening. 'You know he is not an artist per se, I mean he's a prince, and yet he has managed some really rather fine watercolours. I met him once, you know. A formal occasion but he handled it so easily. I wish I could be as adept with my landscapes. He executes them so adroitly. I marvelled at the series he did at Highgrove. Amusingly we turned out to have rather similar cufflinks.'

German performance artist Anselm, who appeared to have been poured into a pair of leather trousers, was holding forth to Goran, the photographer in the filthy suit. 'My work has no distinct or intelligible meaning, that's the point,' he declared, while Goran viewed him only through his lens. Meanwhile Texan Fliss was holding up fabric samples and declaring, 'You see the den looks out over the golf course so I am thinking some kind of painting with green in it would be good.'

Madeleine sat neatly on a bar stool, her feet tucked beneath her and her body rigid, presumably with the desire to go wild. When Buff realised Frances was in the room he cried out, 'There she is!' as though someone significant had turned up. Buff led a smattering of applause for this star entrance on to the scene. Frances was mortified, but the entire class was agog at her fall from the theatre and she found everyone wanted many more details than she was prepared to give.

'I was hot and dizzy, that's all,' she kept saying until she had fairly convinced them that she was a delicate soul who would need to be watched in the midday sun. Anyone who has ever been a star attraction will know that the moment can be short-lived. Lila Peters chose that moment to arrive and quickly stole the thunder. She was breathless and carried many bags.

'Sorry I'm late. God, nightmare. Hello, everyone. Lila Peters from London,' she announced and dropped her bags too near Pito's feet for him to feel comfortable for the rest of the day. Margaret swept out of nowhere and on to centre stage. She clapped her hands.

'Yes, indeed, a last-minute student. Isn't it delightful?'

Frances wondered if she should tell everyone that Lila, pale-faced Lila, was actually black, or whether they would be able to see that for themselves. Was it too late to escape back to her room? She had no intention of joining in.

'Margaret?' Frances began.

'Ladies and gentlemen, *ora*, *al fine*, *il circo comincia!* At last it is time for the circus to begin,' boomed Margaret with the air of a ringmaster about to set the tumblers off for a bit of a tumble. Buff gave a sigh of excitement and led another smattering of applause. Margaret held up her hand in acknowledgement. 'So we begin,' she said. 'Giacomo.'

'OK,' Jack bounced on his feet. 'We're going to start with the basics. This is an international school of art. We have come from all over the world but actually I don't give a damn what language you speak. We're here to make art. Anyone want to define that for me?'

'It is creativity,' declared Lila, who, despite being the newcomer, was clearly not planning to be shy. Fliss, who loathed competition, shot her a look, which Goran managed to capture with his ever-present camera.

'Yes but everyone thinks art is only on paper with paint,' exploded Anselm, sensitive about his performance catalogue. 'There are those who think only of Monet and Renoir but I believe art is expressed best through the body and that we should not limit ourselves.'

'Art is also an acronym for assisted reproductive technology,' contributed Madeleine, stung by the reference to French artists and still not quite managing to let her hair down.

'It's a trick question.' Frances surprised herself by interrupting quietly. 'No one can define art.'

Jack smiled and nodded. 'Absolutely. There is no right or wrong way to do this stuff. Art is the foremost expression of human creativity. Every artist chooses the rules and parameters of his or her work. You choose the medium, you choose the rules for its use and you determine what deserves to be expressed in it—an idea, a belief, a sensation, a feeling, a view, whatever you think will communicate itself.'

'Green, definitely green,' mused Fliss, still looking at her swatches.

Jack smiled. 'Now, some of you may have no idea how to begin and some of you may be utterly confident. Frankly, I don't know which is worse, but today we will all go back to the beginning, which is this—' Jack picked up his small dog and put him on a stool where he sat obediently waiting for his part in the double act '—and this.' Jack held his hand aloft with the palm facing the waiting class. He spoke quietly but with a natural command which left no doubt that here was a man sailing in home waters.

'This is my dog, Auroch, and he and my hand represent the very beginnings of art.'

Fliss, whom Frances suspected of possessing minimal social skills, interrupted the genesis of art.

'D'y'all mind if we open the shutters? Get some

more light in here?'

'I can't bear the dark myself,' agreed Lila. Both forceful women, it was clear that Lila and Fliss were either quite quickly going to loathe each other or end up sharing lip balm.

Jack shook his head. 'No, we begin in this cave. You are not ready for the light yet. In the evolution of man . . . and woman—' Jack gave a slight bow, which unexpectedly made Madeleine even more unexpectedly giggle '—when hands stopped being used for front feet, at last they were free to be used for something else. About two million years ago human beings first picked up stones and began using them as tools. Life was tough then, every day a struggle to survive, keep warm and safe. Yet what do we find if we search deep in the caves they made home? Art. In the midst of the basic battle to stay alive, human beings have from time immemorial needed to express higher feelings.

'Deep in the Altamira caves in northern Spain there are the most magnificent paintings—most of them fifty feet wide and thirty feet high—in the most thrilling and vivid polychrome of red, black and violet. There are bison, boars, horses, even people—and they weren't just chucked on. In many cases the creator of the designs exploited the natural contours of the rock surface to bring the image into focus. Some even include shading to give a kind of three-dimensional effect. Imagine those Michelangelos of their day painting the ceilings of their homes. Imagine lying by a campfire and looking up at that. You will not find better, more immediate art than this, the expression of human creativity and, moreover, you will find it all over the world. And all this work has one thing in common—none is signed by the artist, for they had no written language, but throughout the entire gallery of work the creators left their handprint. This—' Jack held his hand aloft once again '—this is not only what you will use to create your art, it is the first piece of art you will create. For centuries human beings stencilled images of their hands on cave walls. In some places thousands of handprints blanket the red sandstone, some with flat palms and splayed fingers, others painted solid in black, yellow, brown or white. Each one saying that for one glorious moment in time I, an entirely unique individual, was here—for every hand of every human that has ever lived is an original. Each one of us, even if you are a twin, has an entirely personal handprint and that has been the case since man began. Today we shall make our first mark and declare this place our own. Now you can pick any method you want—put paint on the palm of your hand and press it against the wall, blow paint from a tube around the hand, or straight from your mouth for all I care.'

'Sorry, but wait a second,' interrupted Fliss. 'What's the dog got to do with anything?'

Auroch sat patiently on his stool waiting for his big moment. Jack put his hand on the dog's head. 'Auroch is blind.'

There was a general tutting and sympathetic clucking round the room. Jack chuckled. 'Please don't feel sorry for him. Auroch never bumps into anything. That is because he feels things, he senses things and we must learn to do the same.'

'Feel the force, Luke,' muttered Frances.

Jack looked at her. 'The fact is, he has an advantage over you. Throughout your time here your eyes will fool you, they will lie to you.'

A sentence echoed through Frances's head: sunflowers look different depending on the time of day.

'Bear it in mind. Let's begin.'

Now the room broke into an excited bustle of paint selection and wall gazing. For a task so simple there was a surprisingly wide range of techniques. Anselm immediately ingested half a tube of cadmium blue into his mouth and, using a straw, sprayed it over part of a wall, part of the door and fairly liberally on Fliss. Fliss was untroubled with this, preoccupied as she was by picking up and putting down tubes of paint as she tried to recall the exact shade of the eighteenth hole. Madeleine took charcoal and began painstakingly to draw most precisely round her left hand, while Buff spent some moments with a ruler measuring a place which would put his hand in the exact centre of his selected canvas. Lila had managed to fill half a wall before Pito had even finished placing a small blockade of easels around his chosen spot. Goran stood helplessly until Jack gently removed the camera from his hand and placed it on a table. Without his massive photographic phallus, the poor little man looked quite naked. Frances too felt lost. She stood in the centre of the room and didn't move. She had tried once more to focus Margaret on her flight home but she was too busy trying to place handprints on her own harmonious behind. Jack came up behind Frances.

'You are sinister,' he declared.

Frances felt a shiver of the terror which echoed through her life. 'Thanks,' she managed. 'Most

137

people just find me slightly bossy.'

'*Sinistra*. Latin for left-handed. You're left-handed.'

'What? Yes. So?'

'Did you know that the percentage of left-handed people today is about the same as it was during the Ice Age? Isn't that odd? I mean handedness is genetic. Why do you suppose the proportion of left-handers should have remained so constant over thousands of years? Perhaps you have some evolutionary advantage over the rest of us.'

'Good grief. More Palaeolithic trivia. Why, you're a positive Stone Age minefield. How the hell do you know that?'

'About you or about them?'

Frances shrugged and Jack continued. 'Even Auroch knows you're left-handed from the way you stroke him, and as for the Palaeolithic people—that's easy. Everyone paints the opposite hand to their dominant one.'

Jack picked up a tube of paint from the table and reached for Frances's left hand. Without asking permission he squeezed the tube and spread bright red paint all over her hand.

'Press that against the wall and no one will know the sinister truth.'

'Look, I—'

'Just try.'

Jack turned Frances towards a virgin wall and propelled her forward. She put her hand out to stop herself and the paint squeezed from her palm on to the plaster. It felt wonderful. She stood, unable to move, as if she, Samson-like, held the wall upright. Slowly she removed her hand but the

138

print remained behind. A perfect impression of who she was, just as she had sealed a moment of her life into soft clay when she was a child. Now, all these years later, each line and fingertip of Frances's hand was replicated in red, declaring 'I was here'. Jack leant forward and examined her first piece of 'art'.

'Look, in the centre—the faintest mark of the stigmata.'

'Like the roof tile,' she said.

'Unique and not at all sinister,' commented Jack.

'You've got red paint on my sweater,' she replied.

'It doesn't matter.'

'It's cashmere.'

He looked at her arm and then gently pushed her damaged sleeve up to her elbow. 'You will only wear the sweater when you are cold and when human beings are cold they cannot see the colour red very well at all. So, it doesn't matter.'

Unexpectedly, Goran was laughing. Smearing his hands in paint and making great swirls across the wall. A small dust cloud erupted from his suit but no one could help but smile at his unexpected vigour. The room was cheery until suddenly a heart-rending cry went up from Buff.

'Oh no, no.'

Jack wheeled round. 'What's the problem?'

'I've smudged it,' cried Buff. 'It's just a handprint and I've smudged it. I can't even do a handprint.' The large, anxious man began to weep.

'Good heavens, Major Denby, it's only a handprint,' declared Margaret. 'I mean all this fuss just because—'

Anyone might have predicted that a former Capitán of the Argentine military would have disapproved of such a display, but Pito surprised everyone. He stepped between Buff and Margaret and prepared to defend his old enemy.

'Pardon me, madam, but it is not just the handprint. The poor man is starving. He is weak and cannot think and it is your fault. You have provided no food.'

The room was now very still.

'Food was supposed to be included.' Now that everyone was beginning to look at detail, Madeleine was ready to chime in. 'I have my paperwork, which clearly states—'

Anselm rubbed his stomach. 'An artist must eat.'

'There's no grub?' enquired Lila. 'What's the point of that?'

Margaret stood her ground. 'This is hardly my fault. The chef is very—'

Pito held up his hand. 'Please, madam, I have it on very good authority that there is no chef.'

Margaret blushed the colour of Frances's handprint. 'Who told you that?'

'Miss Angel,' declared Pito triumphantly.

The entire room turned to stare at Frances.

CHAPTER TEN

Chi fa falla, e chi non fa sfarfalla

Those who act make mistakes; and those
who do nothing really blunder

'Look, I . . . it's just that . . .' Frances faced the
room and was at a loss as to what to say. 'It's just
that you only ever hear noise from the kitchen
when Margaret is in there and we've never seen
the chef and—'

Now Margaret began to weep. She was not quiet
about it for she was a large woman and tears fell in
great waves on to her chest. Instantly everyone felt
terrible and there was much tutting and
international noises of soothing. No one moved as
they all had hands covered in acrylic paint, which
limits even slight sympathetic gestures, but there
was a definite air of kindness.

'It's true,' bawled Margaret. 'The chef never
came because we never booked him.'

Quietly everyone began to clean up and once
that was done they exited in a silent crocodile to
the hall and the kitchen door. Pito had put himself
in charge of the expedition as Buff was still
something of a hopeless mess over his failed
handprint. The Capitán waited for everyone to
assemble and then slowly pushed open the door to
the food provision area. The kitchen was
charming. It was painted the yellow of sunflowers.
Bright copper pans hung on the walls around a
central cooking unit made of solid wood.

Buff gasped. 'Golly, it's stunning.'

'But useless.' Paolo stood in the doorway. 'So you have the truth at last. We have no chef. There is no one to cook. I told you, Margaret.'

'I know, I know,' his wife sniffed.

Paolo placed his hands on his hips. It was an heroic Italian pose, which to the English in the room looked slightly camp at the same time.

'I am afraid you are all here under false pretences. I tried to tell my wife that we simply could not open this season but she would not hear of it.'

'This place is my life,' whispered Margaret.

'I know, my darling, I know, but I'm afraid your life is bankrupt. Ladies and gentlemen, artists, we must throw ourselves at your mercy. The fact is that this school used to run because the Americans came. They had big money to explore their creative side but since 9/11 and the war in Iraq they do not come any more. The bank has given us, how long, *cara mia*?'

'Three weeks,' Margaret sobbed.

Paolo nodded. 'Three weeks to come up with a rescue plan. I am doing what I can but meanwhile we have no chef and no prospect of hiring one.'

Margaret continued to weep quietly as Paolo moved to comfort her. 'This place, this wonderful place,' she cried, 'we are reduced to living from hand to mouth. Oh, the Americans used to come—it used to be the *American* art school—but now they are all too busy buying duct tape and waiting for terrorists to fall out of the sky. They don't come here and paint. I had one fool write and ask me how close to Iraq we were. I ask you, do these people not have maps?'

'But it is a wonderful place.' Goran spoke for the group. Having been parted from his camera, Goran was unsure what to do with his hands, so he too placed them on his hips. He was a little fellow and round, so the pose made him look like a sugar basin. If there was a lesson to be learnt from this, Frances thought, it was that few men can get away with standing with their hands on their hips.

'*Belle parole non pasoano i gatti,*' sighed Paolo.

'Fine words don't feed cats,' explained Pito.

Buff took a moment to be impressed. 'Really, your Italian is superb, Pito.' It was the first time Buff had called the Capitán by his nickname and there was a brief moment of mutual embarrassment.

'I'm afraid I must suggest that you all go home,' said Paolo.

Madeleine, perhaps thinking that here was an opportunity to be bold, shook her head. 'No. There are still three weeks,' she declared. 'Surely you must have a plan?'

'Yeah, what's your plan?' echoed Lila, who, though not given to much planning herself, thought the idea of it splendid.

Paolo gave a slight cough and Margaret shook her head. 'No, Paolo, please.'

Ignoring his wife's plea, Paolo began to explain how he saw the future. 'As you know, Montecastello is a place of great miracles,' he began. 'A place blessed by the very hand of God.' Margaret gave a loud and dramatic sigh, which her husband ignored. 'I sit on a town committee,' he continued. 'We are working very hard to get the Vatican to agree to a speedy canonisation of our own saintly Innocent Woman—the girl who saw the Black Madonna. The Cardinal is due to come. If he can push the process forward then I believe we can start a pilgrimage centre here, which Ms Beauyeur has very kindly agreed to fund.'

Now everyone turned to the Texan.

'You're buying this place?' asked Jack.

Fliss shrugged as if she were also thinking of getting a new handbag. 'Only if the Church gives the OK,' she said. 'I believe the Lord wants me to do good work here but I need a sign from the Church that my path is the right one.'

'And it wouldn't hurt your financial game plan either,' added Frances.

'I could give you the stigmata,' volunteered Jack, but he was ignored.

'If the Vatican makes this an official miracle site,' continued Fliss, 'then the possibilities for opening a Bible study centre are huge. Without it, well, it's just another pretty little town.'

'You snake in the grass,' hissed Margaret. 'No wonder he collected you from the station.'

'I do not *do* public transportation,' sniffed Fliss.

'So there would be no more art?' whispered Goran, who had just begun to enjoy himself.

Paolo shook his head. 'It was a nice dream but it is not practical. It is not what people want these days.'

'I can cook,' offered Buff unexpectedly.

'You can?' asked Pito.

Buff blushed. 'Well, not brilliantly, but I mean I like to cook. I don't mind cooking. I mean, if no one else wanted to cook well . . . I could . . . do the cooking. I quite often whipped up a bit of a curry in the mess,' he explained.

'I can organise a rota for the shopping,' offered

Madeleine.

'I don't mind washing up,' declared Goran, which from a man with his own personal dust cloud seemed the most unlikely offer of all.

'I can organise a show to raise money,' suggested Anselm. 'The pageant you talked about. We can do it to save the art school.'

Frances shook her head. This was turning into a Judy Garland meets Mickey Rooney movie—hey, kids, let's do the show right here. Maybe she should offer her bag of lemons.

'You don't understand,' insisted Paolo. 'If the Cardinal gives us the go-ahead there will be no art school.'

Margaret pulled herself up to her full height and dried her eyes. 'We have three weeks, Paolo, and I don't care what you say, I . . . we . . . my gypsies . . . are going to save this place for its true purpose—the creation of beauty. We shall produce a show such as no one has ever seen. Money will flood in and art shall be saved. The show is our salvation.'

Paolo shook his head. 'This is absurd. It will never work.'

'Paolo, if you think religious hocus pocus is the answer then go to the church and pray. I don't pray,' explained Margaret to the room. 'God already knows my opinion on most subjects and it's not always favourable. We shall gather in the hall this very evening to begin rehearsals. Bless you all, bless you,' she said softly before turning and snapping, 'Miss Beauyeur, I believe you have become surplus to requirements, and you, Paolo, had better keep out of my way as well.'

Paolo shook his head and departed, leaving the

rest of the room with the traitor Fliss among them. Lines had been drawn in the sand and everyone turned to stare at her. Her face twitched. She was a lonely woman who had begun to enjoy her unexpected foray into the world of art. Now she was clearly the girl who had not been picked for the team. She was the one who had played the religious card only to find herself cast as Judas. Anyone else might have turned and tapped her kitten heels out of the room. Ms Beauyeur, however, did nothing according to other people's social mores. Despite her long-term intentions, Fliss was determined to get her short-term money's worth.

'I am still a member of the art school,' she declared. 'I have paid for three weeks and therefore I believe I will stay.'

There was silence as everyone considered this new development.

'I'm guessing you might not get a very good part in the pageant,' suggested Frances.

The room was silent and stayed silent until Fliss finally took the hint and she too walked out.

Margaret turned immediately to Frances. 'Oh, Miss Angel, Miss Angel, it is fate that you have come. Ladies and gentlemen, friends, Miss Angel is a professional theatre producer and she shall be our *trovarobe*.'

'I'm sorry?' stuttered Frances.

'Yes, my dear fallen Angel, you shall be my new *trovarobe* . . .'

Frances struggled to think of an excuse and rather lamely said, 'Oh no, I can't.'

Buff was genuinely shocked. 'It's a huge honour.'

'We must do this for art,' declared Anselm.

'Really, Miss Angel, you cannot refuse,' insisted Madeleine.

'Frances, you must,' insisted Margaret. 'It is destiny. You do believe in fate, don't you? We need this year's show to be the best ever and by chance, here you are, a real theatre producer. My dear, you must help us. You cannot go against fate.' Margaret took both Frances's hands in her own and looked down into her face. 'Do this and we can all live . . .'

'*La vita di Michelaccio*,' added Pito.

Margaret nodded. 'Yes.'

'The life of . . .' Pito began. 'The life of? *Questo?*'

'Riley. The life of Riley,' explained Buff and the two men nodded with shared satisfaction.

Margaret looked intently into Frances's eyes and spoke with passion.

'It was fate that caused me to save you yesterday and now it is your fate to save us.' It was a sentence spoken with such force that Frances simply could not think of a rejoinder.

Anselm rubbed his hands together. The class had entered his territory and he was determined to lead the way. 'We must think of a subject,' he began, 'for the play.'

Jack shook his head. 'This is ridiculous. Forget it, people. Have a nice three weeks and get out of here. You don't need to get involved.' He looked at his silent assembled students. 'OK, *I* don't need to get involved.' And Jack became the next person to leave the scene.

'Anyone else?' asked Anselm, who was counting cast members in his head. Frances longed to leave

147

but now she felt torn in two. The thought of a Bible study centre in the place of art made her blood boil. The thought of a Bible study centre based on a lie was impossible.

'It should be about the town, about Montecastello or Umbria somehow,' suggested Buff.

Anselm nodded. 'Montecastello de Sanctis is a very special place,' he began slowly, clearly prepared to discuss the subject for days. 'A place of magic and, maybe, even of miracles. A place where the spirit moves the hand of art and of wonder.'

Frances felt as though she had accidentally joined a platform discussion with a mime troupe. If Anselm made them all join hands she really was leaving.

'Who has a suggestion?' he asked.

Apart from *Songs from the Shows* in Italian, nothing came into Frances's head. Goran offered an exhibition of photographs but this was not deemed sufficiently exciting even though he said he could do it on slides. Madeleine suggested an obscure piece by Molière, Lila thought maybe some Pinter but using only the pauses, and Buff said he could do a bit of juggling but only if his arthritis didn't play up on the night.

Pito cleared his throat. 'May I suggest that we break into task forces and reconvene at supper with our suggestions?'

Instantly Madeleine began making lists, Buff began checking the kitchen equipment, Lila and Anselm volunteered for food shopping, while Goran and Pito went to check the supply store. Having only just recovered from her fall, Frances was clearly deemed too fragile to undertake a commission and she was left behind. She sighed. She realised that she alone had the power to stop Fliss's plan and there were no excuses left. She went upstairs, retrieved the small clay handprint from her room and set off in search of the Innocent Woman.

CHAPTER ELEVEN

Nocciolo della questione

Crux of the matter

It was siesta time and the town had fallen into a reverie. The small shops were closed and the religious market had packed up. Frances headed straight for the church but as she reached the square, her nerve and determination began to fail. They say Catholics can leave the Church but somehow the Church never leaves them. Frances did not know exactly what she was afraid of but she trembled as if about to face God almighty himself. She had not been inside a Catholic church since her childhood. She did not in any real sense consider herself a Catholic, yet when she slipped inside the deserted building she had to resist the impulse to reach for the holy water and genuflect to the altar. A shiver ran down her spine.

She half hoped that Maria was no longer at the church, that she had gone home for lunch. Then Frances would have the excuse of not being able to find her and could go home saying that at least she had tried. Frances's good intentions of cleansing the town of its false gods were slipping away and all she was left with was fear. The air in the church was thick with the smell of incense and it made her want to cough. As she put her hand in front of her mouth, she turned and realised she was being followed. It was the old woman from the school, the puppy. The woman smiled and settled herself in a pew at the back, where she began to pray. The place was eerily still, so when the cleaning woman from the school stepped out of the shadows it made Frances jump.

'*Esca!*' commanded the woman.

Frances looked at her and another cloud moved away from her memory. 'Gabriella, of course. You were at school with us. You lived by the town hall. I should have remembered.'

'*Esca!*' repeated Gabriella with less confidence.

Frances put her hands up in a silent gesture of incomprehension. '*Inglese, Gabriella, per favore,*' she said.

Gabriella looked at her and spoke in slow and halting English. 'You should not be here. I knew you were not for the art school. *Bugiarda*. Liar.'

'Where is she?' asked Frances.

Gabriella shook her head. 'You cannot see her. Maria sees no one. No one comes in—no one sees her except me and Father Benito. She can't talk to you. You might interrupt a vision.'

'Maria!' called Frances, and her voice echoed in the cavernous space.

A soft voice carried from within the church. '*Va bene, Gabriella.*'

Gabriella sighed. She stared at Frances and then abruptly turned on her heel and marched up the aisle. Frances followed slowly through the shadows. She still felt afraid but was not really sure what of. Above the white-linen-covered altar Jesus hung on his wooden cross. It was a particularly life-like carving with blood seeping down his side and his face contorted in pain; clearly the thorns on his head were not comfortable. To the right of the altar, seated on a pew, was the Innocent Woman from the parade. She was tiny and thin with a white veil covering her head. As Frances approached, the woman looked up. She was not as girlish as she had first appeared; the first signs of grey were sneaking round her temples. She had few lines but her eyes looked weary with the years. She smiled and held out her hand.

'Francesca!'

In that moment Frances was glad she had come. She took her friend's hand and held it as she sat down beside her.

'Oh, Maria.'

The two old comrades hugged and then sat in silence for a moment. They were unexpectedly calm, which nearly drove Gabriella into a frenzy of fidgeting. Maria squeezed Frances's hand.

'They say you speak only English now,' she said. 'I have been learning. Everyone said you went to England so I thought if you ever came back . . .' Her voice drifted away. She had been waiting a long time. She grinned, and Frances could see at once the child she had been. 'Sometimes Gabriella and I watch English television even though it is forbidden.' She looked gleeful. 'We would like to listen to, what do you say . . . ?'

Gabriella shook her head. 'Pop music. It is forbidden.'

Maria nodded. 'Yes. We don't dare.'

'You shouldn't be here, Francesca,' insisted Gabriella. 'Father Benito will be furious. I am supposed to watch. I am supposed to watch alone. I am in charge.'

Maria made a slight shushing sound. 'Just for a moment, Gabriella, please, just for a moment.'

'Who says it is forbidden?' asked Frances gently.

'I remember your mama. She wouldn't have a TV. What was it His Holiness called it?'

Maria smiled. 'Too "feministic". Mama never got over the death of *il papa buono*—Pope John XXIII.'

'It was a long time ago, Maria. Things have changed. The TV—who says it is forbidden now?'

Maria continued to reminisce. '*Il papa buono*,' she said. 'He came from people like us, Lombards but still ordinary people. How Mama loved him.'

Frances felt as though she was drawing information out of a reluctant child. 'What else, Maria? Pop music, what else would you like?'

Maria smiled and the shadow of the person Frances had known passed across her face. 'Yes. Just once, I would like to have some fun.'

Frances grinned. 'What kind of fun?'

'I don't know. Just something different, something naughty. Gabriella and I are awfully good.'

'Maria!' Gabriella was shocked.

Maria shrugged. 'Well, we are.'

There was a moment's silence, then Frances asked, 'What happened to your parents, Maria. Where are they?'

'They gave me to the Church,' she said matter of factly. 'They left.'

'They died,' snapped Gabriella. 'Father Benito told you.'

Maria nodded. 'I don't know. I have been with Father Benito a long time.' She looked around her and lowered her voice. 'I am supposed to pray and not eat. We are waiting for the visions to come back. Sometimes I think I see them but then I am mistaken. Maybe now . . .' Her voice trailed off.

Frances reached for her hand. It was so thin as to be almost transparent. As if it were not hers at all but a poor copy on wax paper. 'There's nothing to you, Maria,' she whispered.

'If the visions are to come then I must deny my body and every evil thing that comes from it. When St Mamas was imprisoned, an angel provided him with food for forty days.' Maria looked up at her old friend. 'I missed you when you had gone.'

'Maria, I have so many questions.'

'No, you must go,' hissed Gabriella.

Frances shook her off. 'What happened to Sophia? Why did they send me away?'

Maria looked down. 'The Madonna didn't come after you left. I never saw her again. Father Benito won't let me talk to anyone. He says I have to concentrate . . . be ready . . .'

Frances shook her head. 'Maria, I need you to remember what happened. What really happened.'

'Father Benito says if I have another vision then one day they might make me a saint. Santa Maria.'

Gabriella shifted restlessly from foot to foot. 'Francesca. Please! I am supposed to guard her. We must wait for the visions.'

'There are no bloody visions, Gabriella,' exploded Frances. 'Don't you understand? We were children. It was a game. We made it up. We never saw anything.'

'That's not true,' Gabriella almost shouted. 'Maria did. Maria, tell her.'

Maria sat with her head bowed. 'This is my whole life, Francesca. It is nothing to you.'

'I need to settle this, Maria,' insisted Frances.

'It's enough, Francesca,' said Gabriella anxiously. 'The Father will return at any moment.

Don't come here causing trouble. You made enough trouble when we were children.'

'Look at this, Maria.' Frances removed the clay handprint from its wrapping and placed it on Maria's lap. Maria ran her fingers slowly over the surface of the childish hand.

'Signora Alienti!' she exclaimed remembering the teacher who had taught them all. '"Your map of potentials . . ."'

'". . . which is always changing."' Frances finished the sentence and the two women smiled. Gabriella sniffed. Here she was a grown woman and yet once again she felt outside the charmed circle of friendship these two enjoyed.

'You still have yours,' Maria whispered in wonder.

'No. It's Sophia's,' replied Frances. Maria placed her hand on it.

'Sophia.' She breathed out and held her old friend's hand. 'It has blood on it.'

'It's mine . . .' said Frances. 'I—'

'There was never meant to be any blood, Francesca,' whispered Maria.

Frances nodded. 'I need to know what happened to her and I need to know why they sent me away. I need to know the truth.'

Gabriella was beside herself with irritation and nerves. 'Francesca, please!' she said urgently. 'Why must you come now and spoil everything?'

'Because what is happening is not honest and it cost Sophia and probably my parents their lives,' answered Frances. 'I don't want the same to happen to Maria.'

Maria sat with tears falling slowly down her face. 'It's been too long. You waited too long. I don't

155

know any more. It is too many years. Maybe the Virgin came to me and no one else.'

'She could be a saint,' pleaded Gabriella. 'She will be blessed.'

'Don't be ridiculous. No one is going to make anyone a saint just because they don't eat and spend their life in the dark,' snapped Frances. 'Maria, it was a game that got out of hand. We were children. It ruined my life and now it is ruining yours. It has to end.'

Gabriella was beginning to pace up and down. 'Please stop this nonsense. Father Benito will—'

'Father Benito will what?' a voice boomed out from a low door by the altar. It was as if the priest had appeared from the cross itself.

All the women fell silent. Like children caught with their hands in the biscuit tin, they hardly moved. The priest approached slowly. Francesca turned and in the dark recesses of the church she saw the old woman kneeling in prayer. Father Benito's smile belied the atmosphere, which had grown cold and uncertain.

'Father Benito will what?' he repeated.

Both Maria and Gabriella had leapt to their feet, but Frances stayed put. She would not be frightened. Despite his age, the stout priest still managed to walk with purpose and, it seemed, menace. His cane beat out time on the stone floor as he made his way towards the women.

'I tell you what Father Benito will do, Francesca, he will make Maria a saint and the Vatican will pour tributes upon us, upon Maria, the town—'

'And on you,' retorted Frances.

The priest shrugged. 'Perhaps a monsignor. It has been talked about.' There was an ornate chair for the priest near the font. He sat down heavily and clicked his fat fingers. 'Gabriella, wine.'

Gabriella leapt to her duties. She got wine from the sacristy and a single glass, which she placed on a small table in front of Benito. As Gabriella leant across to pour the wine he slapped her bottom.

'Pretty, no? Francesca, you are shocked. How amusing. Don't you know what they say—why would God give a man a pencil if he did not intend for him to draw?'

Frances could hardly speak. 'You're disgusting.'

'Am I? I have saved this wretched little town. This place was nothing before the Miracle of the Innocents. It sounds good, doesn't it? No one came here. The place was dying. A youthful indiscretion and the Church thought they could bury me here away from Rome but they did not realise that I would find a miracle. Maria, my little miracle girl.'

'And Sophia?' asked Frances.

The priest sipped at his wine. 'Sophia was foolish,' he said.

'She was five.'

Benito shrugged. 'There was a fire. It was very sad and then your parents sent you away. They can't have loved you very much, Francesca.'

'The truth needs to be told,' she insisted.

'And what is that?' asked Benito. 'The truth? Who are you to decide the truth? Whose truth? Yours, mine, God's? This town will die without me and Maria. There is nothing else here. We have devoted our lives to these people. They don't need your truth. They will die without the miracle. The Cardinal himself comes next week. He has heard of Maria's visions. He will begin the process to

157

canonise her. Montecastello will be famous and I will be the people's shepherd. *Monsignor* Benito. Forget the past. No one is interested. You are nothing here. No one will believe you. You don't even speak the language any more.'

Frances turned to her childhood friend. 'Come with me, Maria. Come out of here and talk to me.'

Maria did not speak. Instead she shook her head and looked down at the floor.

'Maria, please. Maybe I'm wrong. Maybe you did see something. I need to know,' Frances pleaded but it was no use.

Father Benito shrugged as if the matter was simple. 'It seems Maria doesn't want to come with you.' He turned to Gabriella. 'Not much use as a guard, are you? Perhaps we shall find someone else.'

'Father, please,' whispered Gabriella.

Father Benito dismissed her with a wave of his hand. 'Show Francesca out. And the foolish old woman at the back,' he commanded and gulped his wine.

Frances knew fighting was pointless, that neither Maria nor Gabriella would come with her. There seemed to be no choice. Frances rose to her feet and walked slowly up the aisle. As she did so the puppy also rose and silently followed behind. She seemed docile but as they reached the centre of the aisle she turned, walked slowly back and spat at Father Benito's feet.

The spittle landed on his highly polished black shoe and slowly slid to the ground. He looked down and then quietly declared, 'Don't ever come here again.'

Frances and the old woman slipped from the

church and back out into the square. It was late afternoon and a small crowd had gathered outside the café. Released from the studio, Anselm was doing some kind of outdoor performance art. Her head full of what had just happened, Frances found she had no more impetus to move on, so she stood and watched. The act seemed to involve Anselm lying on the ground wearing the briefest of loincloths. He lay in the position of Jesus on the cross and appeared to have persuaded Lila to shake flour all over him. While Anselm intoned something impenetrable in German, Lila shook a cloud of white powder over his prostrate body. This was sufficiently exciting for the gathered men to shout remarks. No one needed to speak Italian in order to guess the lewd nature of the cat calls. As Frances watched, Lila deposited the final dusting of flour and Anselm carefully got to his feet. Behind him on the stone pavement was the perfect outline of a man, his arms stretched out in agony, a halo of white flour shimmering around the entire form. It was strangely beautiful and the crowd momentarily ceased baying. Everyone gathered around the shape and made quiet noises of interest.

Anselm grabbed a chair and stood on it. 'It is struggle and tyranny that produce art. Order only produces lists and—' he struggled to think of something else ordered '—filing cabinets.'

'Death to the filing cabinet,' echoed Lila.

'This is a land of passion but it reeks of blood from the past,' bellowed Anselm. 'Be warned, even here before the church murder has been done! Even on the high altar! Beware the blood! Beware the passion!' And with that Lila reached into a carrier bag and removed a plastic ketchup bottle shaped like a tomato. She handed it to him and he proceeded to squirt red sauce from on high at the outlined figure on the floor. A large dollop of tomato fell and splattered across the torso and had the desired effect of utterly silencing everyone. Some were impressed by the performance and some, like the café owner, wondered who would be responsible for cleaning up the mess.

It was only when the show was over that Frances realised the old puppy had disappeared back into the shadows. Soon a light mist of rain began to descend and the ghostly image of Jesus on the ground washed away into the cobblestones, as the café customers retreated inside to the warmth of a drink. Frances stayed and watched the flour figure melt away as if it had never existed. She had played the meeting with Maria over and over in her mind for years but, now it had happened, it had not gone according to the script in her head. She stood like a child waiting for her mother to tell her she must come in from the rain.

CHAPTER TWELVE

Mettere paglia al fuoco

Add straw to the fire (tempt fate)

Wet, weary and overwhelmed with emotion, Frances returned to the school. She was desperate to go up to her room and crawl under the covers. Perhaps, she thought, I might never come out again. She was heading for the stairs when Anselm, Madeleine and Goran barrelled in, carrying great bundles of black and white cloth. They were soon followed by Margaret and Pito, lugging all manner of head gear and Lila with assorted props.

'Ah, Angel,' cried Anselm.

'Excellent,' agreed Goran and dumped his armload of fabric on a chair.

'Why, Miss Angel, you are all wet,' declared Margaret. 'Never mind. We shall have you out of those clothes and into your costume in a jiffy.'

'You are a Sister of Charity, are you not?' enquired Madeleine, and without waiting for an answer she shook out the great folds of a frock and handed it to Frances, who looked utterly bemused.

'For the pageant,' explained Goran helpfully.

'Sorry? What?'

Pito beamed. 'I read a local story which we might translate into something.'

'It's really most engaging,' enthused Madeleine.

There were general murmurs of encouragement for Pito to continue. Like a small boy ready to do 'show and tell' to the teacher, he turned an anxious

161

face to Frances. She stood there, damp round the edges, hating her English manners and listened.

'Miss Angel, it is the story of *Il Povero Davide*. Poor David. A local chap, a *barrocciaio*, a carrier, a humble man blessed with great visions of the saints as a small boy.'

'Isn't that marvellous?' declared Madeleine, suddenly struck by how thrilling it would be to have something as bold as a vision. She had once had a dream with Gérard Depardieu in it but it probably wasn't the same thing at all. She had never told anyone about it because in the dream Gérard had been cleaning out her garage and she had never understood what that meant.

Pito smiled and attempted to pick up the thread. 'The visions left him as he grew and then when he was thirty-three—'

'Exactly how old Jesus was when he died,' contributed Anselm, which was ignored.

Pito ploughed on. 'When he was thirty-three, he had a mysterious vision. He retired to a hermitage in the Sabine mountains and returned some months later with a curious sign on his forehead. David told the world that he had been marked out by St Peter himself, who had appeared in a vision with the Virgin Mary and St Michael.'

More people and visions, thought Frances. The country was obsessed. Didn't anybody just get up and see the view?

'Ah, St Michael,' interjected Margaret, who was getting over-excited. 'Like my pants,' which was an impossible thought for anyone.

Pito sailed on ahead. 'Goran, perhaps you might stand here as David?'

Flushed with the excitement of unexpectedly

being thrust into the limelight, Goran stepped forward.

'Now David had—'

'I'm sorry,' interrupted Anselm, displaying his own attachment to things of this world, 'but does this mean that it has already been decided that Goran will play the part of David? I mean, that's not fair. It is clearly the best part. David is the best part and there has not even been any talk about it.'

'But there are lots of other parts,' exploded the exasperated Capitán. 'In any enterprise a leader must have men.'

'Just men?' asked Lila, apparently feeling sidelined as well. 'Is this some kind of misogynistic piece? I mean, we were supposed to be doing this together and as a feminist and a black woman, I—'

The Capitán took a deep breath and tried to be calm. 'David had a team. Men and women, some children too, I think. There were Christian Matrons, Sisters of Charity, Daughters of Song—'

'I was thinking blue and red for the women,' contributed Margaret.

'Blue and red? Together?' pondered Madeleine. 'I don't think that will work at all.'

'Those are the women and we have David and Michael—what about the men?' persisted Anselm.

Pito was beginning to get irritated.

'There are plenty of men—he had a whole army of men. They should wear brown,' he added as an aside to Madeleine.

'Brown?' repeated Margaret as if it were the last colour on earth.

Goran was feeling uncomfortable. 'I don't have to be David. If people think I cannot be David then I can just not be in it at all,' he announced with a slight choking sound.

Now everyone felt embarrassed. It was clear the little fellow had enjoyed his moment in the limelight and there was a strong possibility that he was going to cry.

'I think Goran would be great,' murmured Madeleine.

'I was thinking Goran was perfect for the part,' declared Frances, who so far had been unable to come up with a single contribution. Her remark, given as it was by a professional theatre producer, was immediately followed by other slightly lacklustre endorsements of Goran's exceptional suitability to play the hero.

'Thank you,' Goran gulped through held-back tears.

'I think we should just have black and white,' declared Madeleine who for some reason had taken charge of colour.

'That is very dramatic,' agreed Anselm.

'And slimming,' added Margaret. 'Miss Angel?'

All eyes turned to their new leader.

'Well,' she managed, 'it certainly worked for *My Fair Lady*.'

Pito swept on. 'Anyway, not everyone liked David having all these followers—he had thousands—'

'Thousands?' asked Goran nervously.

'Trust me. You can make that work,' reassured Frances.

'The Church denounced him and eventually he was shot by the local police.' Pito pretended to hold up a gun and said, 'Bang.'

Goran, who was clearly going to be good at taking direction, promptly keeled over. A small

164

barrage balloon shot down in its prime.

'David had three bullets in his brain. Everyone scattered except his loyal hermits who took him home to die.'

There was a long pause and then Frances, who instinctively knew when a performance was over, began a round of applause, which delighted everyone.

'It's brilliant,' sniffed Margaret. 'Quite brilliant,' and went on to declare she could be a Daughter of Song but it would depend on the song as she really couldn't do anything too modern and pretty much only knew show tunes. Meanwhile Anselm's principal interest was in finding out whether David's army had had different ranks and if so could he possibly be a general?

'What do you think, Miss Angel?' Pito asked. The others turned to get her professional opinion.

'It could . . . work,' she said hesitantly.

Anselm rubbed his hands with the thrill of cracking on. 'So we need to decide,' he said. 'Lila, are you a Matron of Many?'

Goran shook his head, 'No, Anselm, I don't think so. Not Matron of Many, Matron of Mary.'

'Oh pardon. So many titles.'

Now Lila put her oar in. Why was Margaret allowed to be a Daughter of Song and why was everything in black and white; had that really been agreed? What happened to the blue and red she was sure someone had talked about?

'But Miss Angel, she said black and white,' declared Anselm stiffly 'Everything will be black and white; like *My Fair Lady*, except *Povero Davide* who will be red . . . and small . . . like a little ball in the middle. A little bouncing ball right in the

165

middle . . .' Anselm was clearly still having a problem with the casting of Goran in the principal role.

They were all most excited and the discussion continued apace. Soon everyone was dressed like a small gathering of Sing-a-long-a-*Sound of Music*. As evening fell, Pito brought out several bottles of wine. Just as Frances was thinking she might slip away, the kitchen door banged open and Buff, who had been absent for some time, appeared carrying a large silver platter. Perhaps it was hunger or perhaps it was the wine but no one said anything as Buff stood holding the dish. Everyone gathered around silently. There was nothing complicated about what Buff had made. Here was not a carved ice swan with caviar nestling between the wings. It was a peasant dish of fresh penne pasta bathed in a sauce made from the sweetest fresh plum tomatoes with pinches of brilliant green basil dotted among the crimson. It looked like a painting.

'It's beautiful,' sighed Pito.

'Amazing.' Goran swallowed.

'A work of art,' breathed Margaret. 'I've never seen such a use of cadmium red with . . . are we to say viridian green?'

'I think we are nearer emerald,' suggested Pito.

'And the *bianco titanio* of the pasta . . .' added Margaret in awe. 'You are an artist, Mr Denby. An artist of the kitchen.'

Clearly unused to compliments of any kind, Buff began to weep. Tears streamed down his florid face and landed in great splashes on his khaki shirt.

'It's just a little pasta,' he sobbed.

'No, no,' cried Pito, taking the platter from the newfound chef and bearing it with great ceremony to the dining table. 'It is genius, it is fantastic.'

The meal progressed with much fuss over Buff's unexpected talent, the appearance of actual cooked food and excitement about the forthcoming production. Even the arrival of Fliss and later Paolo failed to dampen the enthusiasm of the evening. Yet again, Frances realised she had been swept along into activities she had had no intention of taking part in. She was surprised to realise that the only person missing was Jack and surprised that she had noticed.

*   *   *

The next morning, Frances found herself once again in the art studio. She wondered if she was gradually giving up any attempt to determine the course of her life. The truth was that nothing seemed clear any more and she had no idea what to do next. Her conversation with Maria had answered none of her questions. Moreover, it had left her fearful for her old friend in the grip of the priest. She realised her focus had changed from some kind of resolution to a desperate desire to rescue Maria. That Maria needed rescuing was in no doubt, but how to go about it was utterly unclear. She had awoken with no plan and when Madeleine had said it was time for class, Frances had shrugged her shoulders and gone to class. In that sense, she supposed, she had adopted, as Paolo said she would, the *cose all'italiana*.

That morning the art room was freezing cold. An air-conditioning unit had been blasting away and the shutters held out the warming sun. The cold led to a lack of good humour and there was a degree of grumbling from the assembled artists, silenced only by Fliss's arrival in a particularly outrageous tiger-stripe catsuit.

'What?' she demanded of the silence. 'I will have you know that I am still an art student here and I intend to take every damned class I want. Goodness, it's cold in here. What is wrong with this place? Are you worried that your precious Angel might faint again?'

Jack began the class with his usual energy as cool as the room. He looked tired. 'It is cold in here on purpose,' he said. 'Now I know you're all so busy with your damned religious play—'

'Not all of us,' sniffed Fliss, who was still smarting from being left out. 'Even though religion is my life.'

Jack ignored her. '—so let's start with Jesus, who said, "I am the light of the world." Imagine that? To be the light of the world is, of course, to be the origin of everything. Of trees and food and us and art, and it is central to what we want to do. The great German artist Goethe said, "On the twenty-eighth of August in 1749, at midday just as the clock struck twelve, I came into the world. I came into the world as dead and only after various efforts was I able to see the light." That is our job to try and see the light.'

'I love Goethe,' agreed Anselm, rather pleased that a German was being singled out.

'And so you should,' agreed Jack. 'A great traveller and lover of Italy, but he struggled all his life to see what was in front of him. Anselm, do you know what his last words were?'

'"*Mehr Licht*,"' declared Anselm, suddenly rather shy at all the attention.

168

'Indeed, more light,' agreed Jack. 'What do you think he meant by that?'

'Maybe it was just dark in his room and he couldn't find his slippers,' drawled Fliss, and everyone laughed.

'Listen, if you boys are going to prove your virility with a Goethe quote fest, I think I might get a cup of coffee.' Lila headed for a table in the corner set with a kettle and tea- and coffee-making paraphernalia.

'I'm with you. I never even heard of the guy,' agreed Fliss, following.

Madeleine joined the breakaway refreshment party. 'I went to Germany once,' she said. 'Very difficult for the vegetarian.'

'Ladies, ladies, come back,' soothed Jack. 'All I am trying to tell you is that Goethe, the great Goethe, spent a lifetime trying to see what was in front of him. You need to understand that being cold affects how you, how we all see colour.'

'Is this going to be science?' Fliss's voice rose in panic. 'Only I can't do science. Really, I can't. I don't know what happens but my mind just freezes over. My husband used to say I had no brain for anything but decor and he might well have been right. He was always saying how stupid I am.'

Jack held his hand up to calm her. 'Fliss, you are not stupid and your husband is an arsehole.'

There was a sharp intake of breath from the Texan housewife who, nevertheless, did not disagree.

'Look, let's break it down,' continued Jack. 'There are two sets of substances in the world: those you see in your mind and those that actually physically exist—mind and matter. They are quite

169

distinct but, if we do our job well, then we can try to make them relate to each other. We should be able to do this because the sensory system we've been blessed with is so damned clever. Every day, whether we are artists or not, all of us who are blessed with sight use it to seek information about the world. The truth is that light is so amazing that we pathetic humans can hardly take any of it in, but the bit we can see is incredible. Whether by luck or design, our eyes are created to accept those changes in light that are the most informative about the chemical or molecular structure of surfaces and objects.'

'No, I don't get it. I said I wouldn't and I don't,' declared Fliss on the edge of tears.

Jack smiled and walked towards her.

'All it means, Fliss,' he said soothingly as he put his arm gently round her, 'is that our vision is automatically tuned to the bit of light that tells us the most about the world. Isn't that neat?'

'Well, yes, I suppose so,' admitted Fliss.

Having calmed her down, Jack went back to his thesis. 'But that doesn't mean our eyes won't lie to us.'

'Oh shit,' said Fliss. 'Just when I thought I had it.'

'The truth is that all colour is in the mind. It is not an intrinsic part of the physical world, because the colour of something changes depending on the context you see it in. The same red in different circumstances might be red or it might be scarlet, crimson, pink, maroon, brown, grey or even black. And here is a curious thing about colour: if you are cold then you can't see red so well.'

Frances thought about the paint on her

170

cashmere sweater. Jack had said it didn't matter. She watched him teach. He was good, even inspirational. She had come to Montecastello to learn something but this was not what she had imagined. He walked comfortably around the room. Like a good director he knew just what each member of the troupe required in order to bring out their best. Frances realised she was staring at him, when he looked over and smiled. Jack reached for some paintbrushes and quickly juggled them in the air before continuing. He was a show-off. Just another show-off, Frances reminded herself.

'So today I want you to choose just two colours—red, any red, and one other—and paint when you are cold. Tomorrow we will arrive dressed very warmly and see if the work looks different to us. Now, in order to get the point of all this I need you to be cold, really cold. So let's get naked. Well, maybe not naked, I know some of you are English, but I want you to take off as many clothes as you feel comfortable with.'

'Comfortable?' asked Buff. 'It's like Scott of the Antarctic in here.'

'Come on, come on,' said Jack. 'I don't have all day.'

It turned out that Anselm was comfortable in surprisingly little, while Madeleine required a polo neck and Buff could not be parted from his socks. Goran was unexpectedly comfortable with his flesh and padded about like a small fat boy at the lido whose mother had over-indulged him with ice cream. Pito wore a smart white vest and pressed boxers, while Fliss had on a bra and pants that matched her outfit. Frances was wearing a pair of pressed jeans and a light-blue singlet. It was about as casual as she had ever been and she didn't feel there was any more stripping back to be done.

Jack grinned at her and she found herself grinning back.

'No shorts, Frances?' he asked.

She shook her head.

He reached into a stone jar and pulled out a pair of scissors. 'Make some.' He turned away as if cutting up designer clothes was an everyday activity and there was nothing more to say. Frances wondered for the hundredth time why she didn't just stay in her room. Her mind still on the scene in the church she pierced the very expensive cloth of her couture trousers near her upper thigh and began to cut.

'I don't really like red,' murmured Madeleine.

'Can't we have more than just two colours?' demanded Fliss. 'I really don't know if I could choose just two colours.'

'I am not good with colour,' muttered Goran, white for the first time in his birthday suit.

Jack shook his head. 'Today is a learning exercise. Two colours. Plenty of time for that great landscape you want to take home to Texas, Fliss. Try and find the two colours which you feel balance each other, and you follow in the footsteps of Aristotle, Goethe, Mondrian. Aristotle's theory was that all colour is just different mixes of light and dark, while Goethe believed that all colour either came from the dark group represented by blue or from the light group represented by yellow. The duality in all nature. Repulsion and attraction, action and reaction, activity and passivity, male and female.'

'Yin and yang,' agreed Anselm.

'Absolutely. Everything has an opposite and that is why nature is full of conflict. Life is a relentless battle to find balance and it is a fascination you will find throughout art. Reduce your work to the basics. Try and see the light. Find harmony, balance. Now pick your red and then find what you regard as its opposing colour and get painting.'

Buff looked entirely perplexed. He was a watercolour man. His colours ran pell-mell into each other whatever he did. 'What should we paint? I mean, what is the subject, as it were?'

Jack smiled. 'Paint the truth, Buff. That's why we're here.'

Frances felt exposed in her new short trousers, like a small British boy heading for his first day of school, yet mixed with this sense of nakedness there was also liberation. A curious sense of freedom that she could not recall from the past. The work progressed and Frances found herself unexpectedly lost in the task. She had much on her mind, yet the minutes and hours seemed to drift away as she dabbed paint on canvas and did what she had come for—to try and see what she really saw.

CHAPTER THIRTEEN

Time is the father of truth, its mother is our mind.

Giordano Bruno
Italian philosopher (1548–1600)

The days passed quietly with sessions in the art room, work on the pageant and wonderful meals from Buff. Frances knew the time from the sun in her room in the morning and then by its progression around the building during the day. Her broken watch lay unattended on her bedside table. Apart from the classes, Jack kept to himself and she rarely saw him outside the studio. She made several attempts to see Maria, but Father Benito had hidden her away and no one was talking about where. Frances tried to have a conversation with Gabriella when she came to clean the room but she refused to speak English and simply went about banging her bucket. Frances knew that Maria would have to reappear the following week to go into the church. Perhaps she would find a way to see her then.

At night Frances slept well, but each morning she knew the same dreams had plagued her. Sophia's face, her mother's tears and the thud of Father Benito's cane across the stage. One night she awoke sweating and crying. She had no idea what time it was and in an instant felt annoyed at the way in which she had allowed herself to be absorbed into life at the school. The fact that she was enjoying the art and, heaven forfend, even the pageant seemed absurd. 'What am I doing? I'm drifting about not getting anything done. This is ridiculous. It is not what I came for.'

She tried to think where Benito would hide Maria. Not in the church. It was too public. Perhaps in his house? The chapel. Of course. Maria would feel afraid in the chapel. The place had already seen one death, why not another? Convincing herself that Maria might be hidden at the Chapel of St Illuminata, Frances got up and got dressed. Without thinking about brushing her hair or dressing warmly, she threw on her newly made shorts and a sweatshirt and, out of habit, her pearls, and hurried out. The streets were dark and deserted and she could hear her footsteps echoing as she made her way. As she came through the castellated gate at the edge of the town she saw that a low light burned in the chapel. No longer prepared to be afraid she walked down the hill and shoved open the small, wooden door.

'Maria!'

The light came from an old oil lamp that hung on a metal chain. A wooden ladder was propped against a plastered wall and Frances could just see sandalled feet resting on the top rung. Wonderful music was playing and it stopped Frances from blurting out her first thoughts.

Jack's voice called out from above.

'It's Palestrina. Isn't it gorgeous? The Mass of Pope Marcellus. Interesting story. The Pope thought church music was getting altogether too popular so he told Palestrina to compose something pure and sober or music would be banned for ever from the church. Imagine that. On that one man rested the fate of all Italian music.'

'Sorry, Jack, I didn't know you were here. I was looking for—'

'Shit!' The expletive thundered through the small religious haven. 'Sorry. I cut my hand.'

Jack descended from his perch, his left hand streaming with blood and his right awkwardly clutching the offending tool with which he had been scraping the wall. 'Damn.'

'Oh, for Christ's sake, come here.' Frances removed a fresh linen handkerchief from her pocket and looked at his hand. The cut ran across the base of his thumb.

'You've given yourself a new lifeline,' she remarked.

'Marvellous. Now I can have a new life.'

'Excellent.' She smiled. 'No bitterness there then.' She carefully tied her makeshift bandage around the injury.

Jack looked at the piece of Nightingale handiwork. 'I didn't know anyone still carried those things. Haven't you people heard of Kleenex?'

'Six years in a British boarding school. All I learnt was that no one should ever be made to eat kidney, that it is possible to sleep in sub-zero temperatures and the astonishing value of the pocket handkerchief. I bet you never use a napkin either.'

'I use the table napkin made by Mother—the back of my hand.'

'Not for a bit you won't.' Frances pulled the bandage tight. 'There.'

Frances still held Jack's hand in hers and at the same moment they both looked up from the injury

176

and realised how close they were standing. Frances felt . . . what was it? A slight tingle. Something. A frisson. Jack carefully put out his uninjured hand to push a piece of unkempt hair back from her forehead. For one insane moment she thought he would reach for her but instead he turned to his injured hand and admired her bandaging.

'What was it about?' he asked.

'Sorry?'

'Your bad dream. What was it about?'

Frances moved away to sit on a pew. 'How did you know I had a bad dream?'

Jack smiled. 'I don't know. I don't get that many midnight visitors so I figured . . .' There was a pause before he continued. 'Boarding school, huh? What else did you learn?'

'Not much. I know about the hanky, the kidney thing, oh, and that girls should wear two pairs of underpants every day,' she said, moving away to sit on a pew.

'At the same time?'

Frances nodded.

'Why?' asked Jack.

'To protect our virtue.'

'No wonder the British have trouble understanding Italy.'

They fell silent again as Jack opened and closed his injured hand against the fresh binding. Frances looked up at the wall where Jack had been working. A fresco was taking shape on the ceiling. Charcoal outlines spread across a large section and here and there, where paint had been applied, lambs and birds began to play across the roof.

'Is this how you spend your time?' asked Frances. 'We never see you out of class.'

'I follow St Francis. One day he was in this dilapidated church in San Damiano, south of Assisi. He was there by himself and suddenly he heard a voice calling out from the crucifix, "Francis, repair my house. You see it is falling." Well, he stopped for a second, I mean you would, and then he heard it again. "Francis, repair my house. You see it is falling." And again. Three times the voice called out. Well, that shifted him, so he rushed around ordering materials and doing the church up. It was only after he got the first coat of paint on that he realised the voice meant he was supposed to reform the institutions of the Church, not take up DIY. I figure the Church wouldn't want my help, so I'll stick to the painting.'

A stack of drawings lay scattered on a pew. Frances stood and leafed through them. 'What are these?'

Jack shrugged. 'Just a few ideas for the rest of the decoration in here. There was some kind of fire and the people had the money for a new roof but nothing to bring the art back to life.'

'God almighty, Jack, why the hell are you wasting your talent on Texan housewives and mad men from Germany? Look at these. These are brilliant.' She turned to face him. 'It really pisses me off when people waste their—'

Jack held his hands up in self-defence. 'I have offended God and mankind,' he interrupted, 'because my work didn't reach the quality it should have.'

Frances sniffed. 'Oh for God's sake, don't be so dramatic.'

Jack shook his head. 'That wasn't me. It was Leonardo da Vinci. If he felt like that, what possible chance is there for the rest of us? The trouble is, Frances, that I have seen brilliance, I know how to recognise it and it isn't in my hands.' He stretched his hands out before him and looked at them.

'I'm sorry, but I've heard that before and it's tosh,' said Frances firmly.

Jack looked at her. 'Tosh? Is that some English way of saying "balls"?'

'It's an excuse not to be your best, that's all. So it's hard work to be good, to produce your best. Just get on with it and stop moaning.'

'I don't know.' He sighed. 'Perhaps I sit in the chapel waiting for a revelation. There was an artist called James Tissot who became famous painting shop girls and the demi-monde. Then he had a religious vision which changed his life and his work.' Jack paused and then grinned. 'Also his girlfriend died of consumption and I think that can do it to you.'

'Jesus, you can't move two feet around here without tripping over someone having a vision.'

'I'm guessing you're not religious,' commented Jack. 'Me neither, but I've tried. I think it must be very comforting to believe in something greater than yourself, outside yourself, guiding you along.'

'You don't need that. You have a God-given talent—'

Jack raised an eyebrow at the expression.

'OK, whatever,' Frances conceded. 'You have a talent and I can't bear to see it wasted. It happens all the time: the musical people who are careless about playing, the actors who would rather stay home, the writers who think a short story will do.'

Jack sat studying his own work. 'Look, the

179

Virgin is appearing.' He pointed to the top of the ladder where he had been busy creating a portrait of Mary. Her face was gentle and beautiful. 'I want to do the women from the Bible. That wall will have Eve, and over there Martha and Mary.'

'It's wonderful.'

Jack shook his head. 'No. I am the Jack of all trades—a patina on someone else's surface. Perhaps I shall change my name to something Italian. Giacomo Dilettanti.'

'Does it worry you that hardly anyone will see it in here?'

Jack shrugged. 'That's not the point, is it? There is a place near here called Montefalco. It is a nothing place. In the middle of the fifteenth century the citizens of that unremarkable town had the will and found the money to hire and detain the great Benozzo Gozzoli. He spent several years in that Godforsaken place decorating the churches and convents with genius. I suspect it was wasted on those fucking monks and nuns but he thought it was worth it.'

'But you don't need to hide away. Your work is great,' persisted Frances. 'You don't need to be in some obscure town unless you are running away from something.'

Jack stroked the linen that was bound round his injury. 'Well, I suspect we all have wounds to lick here. Just some are more obvious than others.'

Suddenly uncomfortable, Frances got up and wandered towards the altar. The church was tiny. Perhaps thirty feet long and half as wide. Against one wall a large stone bowl served as the font. Above it, hanging in a chipped and mould-ravaged golden frame was the photograph Lila had mentioned. It was a black-and-white, twelve-by-eight image of the chapel taken from above, on the town wall, the day after the devastating fire. The building entirely filled the photograph so that details of the damage it had sustained were very clear. The roof of the chapel had entirely collapsed and you could see through to the murals on the back of the altar wall. A few struts remained of the original roof beams, but the charred walls gave testament to a violent and raging fire having passed through. There were no people in the shot, but Frances didn't need to see them to know what had happened. She felt sick. She could almost hear the screams. Frances took the picture down from the wall and sat in the front pew looking at it. For the first time in years she began to cry, and once she began she could not stop. All the pain from long ago flooded into her and she shook as she held the image from her past. She cried for her friend who had died and for the one who was trapped by a childish game played all those years before. She cried for her parents and for the loss of her home. She didn't hear Jack move but she felt his arms reach round from behind her. Gently he took the photo from her hand and placed it on the nearest pew. Then he turned her head to his shoulder and she released her grief in great sobbing waves.

How long they stood like that, Frances did not know. After some time she began to quieten. Jack was stroking her hair and making soothing noises. When she at last looked up at him, he very slowly leant forward and without another word kissed her gently on the mouth. Then he took her hand and they left the church. Silently they walked up the lane to the school. Inside, Sally Bowles from the musical *Cabaret* was enquiring what the point was of sitting alone in your room. Jack led her to the art room and then through a door into his unlocked and untidy living space. In the room above they could hear Margaret and Paolo having noisy and unbridled sex. Clearly their differences over the school had not tempered the physical passion between them.

'*Sgualdrina!*' Paolo called out breathlessly.

'*Sgualdrina?*' Frances asked.

'Trollop.'

On that word, Jack took her in his arms, and as they made love she could feel his fingerprints on her body leaving their tender stigmata.

CHAPTER FOURTEEN

The pious say that faith can do great things, and, as the gospel tells us, even move mountains. The reason is that faith breeds obstinacy. To have faith means simply to believe firmly—to deem almost a certainty—things that are not reasonable; or, if they are reasonable, to believe them more firmly than reason warrants. A man of faith is stubborn in his beliefs; he goes his way, undaunted and resolute, disdaining hardship and danger, ready to suffer any extremity. Now, since the affairs of the world are subject to chance and to a thousand and one different accidents, there are many ways in which the passage of time may bring unexpected help to those who persevere in their obstinacy. And since this obstinacy is the product of faith, it is then said that faith can do great things.

Francesco Guicciardini
Italian statesman and historian
(1483–1540)

Frances awoke in the most dishevelled bed she had ever been in. Her arms and legs were tangled in a pattern of confusion with Jack's. She knew she had pins and needles somewhere but couldn't connect the sensation to any particular limb. She tried to move and Jack's eyes flickered open.

Frances smiled. 'Was there an earthquake?'

'Wow,' gasped her American lover. 'Cool. Are you telling me the earth moved for you?'

Frances laughed and tried to sit up. Jack pulled her back.

'It may just be, Frances Angel, that you are saving my life.'

He spoke with such intensity that Frances could think of nothing to say. Sometimes new lovers are not prepared for the emotions unleashed and Jack sensed he had been hasty. He smiled as if he had been kidding and swept an imaginary paintbrush through the air.

'I would paint you now. There is nothing more beautiful than a drowsy woman.'

'I bet you say that to all the girls. I'm surprised you didn't ask me up to see your etchings.'

'As I recall, I didn't need to say anything at all.'

'Smug.'

'Absolutely,' he agreed.

'I expect you bed some poor talentless middle-aged woman each year. A regular Casanova.'

Jack looked horrified. 'Don't say that. Do you know how Casanova died?'

Frances hit him with her pillow. 'Oh, wonderful. You don't deny the description. You just don't want to die like him.'

Jack placed the pillow under his own head and pulled Frances to him. 'Giacomo Casanova—'

'Giacomo! Aha, another Jack in the box.'

Jack ignored her and continued his tale. 'After a life of relentless lovemaking, Casanova ended his days as a destitute old man. Someone took pity on him and he was given a job as a librarian in a castle in Bohemia. There he became embittered by humiliating squabbles with the castle servants who played backstairs tricks and practical jokes on the defenceless fellow. A sad end to a gloriously decadent life.'

Frances looked at this man she hardly knew. His appetite for life and its minutiae was greater than any she had ever come across. Slowly she began to wonder if it was possible to feel again after Alistair. The thought was frightening and she pushed it away.

'Anyway, I don't want you to paint me,' she said lightly, 'because then you would have to get up and I'm too comfortable. What would you paint if you could do whatever you like?'

Jack shrugged. 'I do what I like.'

'Lucky you.'

'OK, I would like . . . to paint . . . Signora Fratelli.'

Frances felt the light-heartedness of the moment slip from her grasp. 'Signora Fratelli? She's dead.'

Jack looked at her quizzically. 'Dead? She's old, all right she's very old, but I do see her every day, unless I am operating on some other plane to everyone else. Signora Fratelli . . . Margaret's old puppy. Apparently she came with the house. I don't think it was part of the actual deal or anything, but when Margaret and Paolo moved in, the old bird just refused to move out.'

Frances sat up in the bed. 'Sophia's grandmother. It must be her grandmother. This was the Fratellis' house. *E per me.* She said she'd been waiting for me and maybe she has.'

'Hmm. Post-coital babbling,' mused Jack, 'and a most unusual example of it. Any chance of letting me know what you're talking about? Why would Signora Fratelli be waiting for you?'

'She was my friend Sophia's grandmother. Sophia Fratelli—she died in the fire.'

'At the chapel?'

'Yes.'

'Boy, talk about me being a dark horse. You used to live here? Does that mean I get to meet the cousins? Please don't tell me Margaret is your mother.'

Frances smiled. 'My parents are long gone.'

Jack settled back on the pillows. 'I feel a story coming on. Shoot.'

And for once Frances was ready to tell.

'I was born here. My parents were already in their late forties when my mother became pregnant,' she explained. 'They couldn't believe it. They went to church and wept, saying I was a gift from God. My aunt Emilia says they doted on me. As I grew up I had two friends I played with every day. Sophia Fratelli and Maria Rocco. We played by the chapel—it was halfway between our houses and our mothers could all call us home from there. We used to watch the women come and arrange flowers for our blessed Mary or come to clean the chapel. Being Catholic permeated every corner of our lives.

'One day—I don't know who suggested it—we played a game where we had a vision. We knew all about the saints. We had been told the stories since birth. And so we pretended to have a vision like a saint. I don't think we can have explained it properly because the next thing I knew the bell in the chapel was being rung and the whole village called to prayer. The Father stood up and told

186

everyone we had been blessed. That we, "the innocent ones", had been visited by the Black Madonna and what a wondrous thing this was for us all. I knew then I should have said something, but I didn't. All the women were crossing themselves and many of the men, including my father, were kneeling and bowing their heads while we stood in front of the altar. That night I couldn't sleep. I knew it was a lie. I knew we had made it up and I wanted to tell, but the next day everything had changed. People treated us differently, and when I went to see Maria she wouldn't hear of us telling the truth. She started saying that she had always seen the Virgin and maybe I just wasn't as holy as her. Sophia was frightened and for days we didn't say anything. Priests came from Rome and wanted to talk to us and the Father showed us off to visitors in smart suits. It seemed too late to put the story right but I knew I had to. I knew I would be damned if I didn't, so I told my mother. I told my mother the truth.'

'What did she say?' asked Jack.

'She kissed me and said I was a good girl.' Frances could feel a sob rising in her throat. That moment, thirty-five years ago, was still as clear as if she stood now encircled by her mother's arms. 'We went to the Fratellis, Sophia's parents, and they agreed that the truth must be told but Mr and Mrs Rocco wouldn't hear of it. They were so passionate about Maria's vision that Mr Rocco closed the door in my father's face.'

'So what happened?'

'I'm not sure. That night there was a fire in the little chapel. The roof caved in and the place was almost destroyed. Sophia and her parents were killed.'

Jack looked at Frances, who was shaking with the telling of her story. 'And your parents?'

'I never saw them again. My parents were afraid. Father Benito—'

'Benito? What, the old guy at the church?' Jack asked incredulously.

Frances nodded. 'Father Benito knew I wanted to tell the truth and I think they were terrified something might happen to me the way it had happened to Sophia. They took me to Rome and put me on a plane to London to be with my aunt. They thought I would be safe while they packed up the house and then came to England themselves. It was terrible. My father was a farmer, he loved the land. It broke his heart to leave. They were driving to Rome, when there was an accident. The brakes failed. I never really found out what happened, but they were killed and—'

'You suspect Benito?'

Frances shrugged. 'I don't know. I came back to try and answer some questions, but Maria is still here and I am afraid for her.'

Jack nodded. 'Benito keeps her in his house. It's weird. He won't let anyone speak to her. I've often wondered about him.' Jack saw how pale the story had made his new lover. He seemed to know that enough had been said.

'Come here.' He took her in his arms and for a while they lay in silence. Then slowly he began to kiss her shoulders.

'Jack, I—'

The door flew open and Margaret appeared in the doorway.

'*Allora*, air, we need air.' She marched to the

188

shutters and flung them open. Outside, the morning sky was a still blue cloth of anticipation.

'Margaret, it's still early,' protested Jack. 'What the hell are you doing?'

'It is not early. It is nine thirty and there are matters to attend to.' Margaret stood at the bottom of the bed and smiled. 'We are late for rehearsals, Major Buff commands us to the kitchen and . . . my Giacomo has been waiting for ever *a farsi una ragazza.*'

Frances raised an eyebrow to her new lover, who blushed.

'I scored,' he explained.

'And you, Angel,' continued Margaret, as relaxed as if they were all sitting down to tea, 'you look so *sfatta*—worn out with debauchery. It is a good look. You should paint her now, Giacomo.'

Jack looked quizzically at Frances, who laughed.

'It's a conspiracy,' she giggled.

Margaret shrugged. 'It is Italy. Conspiracy is in the blood. Life here could not function without intrigue and some has just turned up at the front door. You must dress, and quickly.' She handed Frances Jack's denim shirt from the floor.

'Why?' Frances asked, still sleepy. She could hardly believe herself. Here she was naked in a virtual stranger's bed chatting with some fully clothed woman and she didn't mind in the least. What had happened to her?

'There is a beautiful young man downstairs,' continued Margaret. 'Well, perhaps not so young, but very beautiful, who commands your attention. Hair like an angel. Alistair, his name is Alistair, which I have to say is one of my least favourites. I knew an Alistair once who was a perfect prig

189

and—'

Frances had no time for Margaret's reminiscences of men called Alistair. A cannon could not have fired her out of the bed more quickly.

'Alistair? Oh my God, Alistair. What the hell is he doing here?' She threw the shirt on and, like a naughty schoolgirl caught after lights out, she ran for the door.

'He says he has come for you,' revealed Margaret.

'Who the hell is Alistair?' asked Jack.

'He claims to be a knight in shining armour,' yelled Margaret.

'Frances!' called Jack. But she was gone, flying down the corridor, wearing nothing more than a faded man's shirt and a faint odour of love.

CHAPTER FIFTEEN

Chi non risica, non rosica

Nothing ventured, nothing gained

Alistair was standing at the desk with Lila and Pito, clearly charming the pants off them. He appeared to be quoting poetry to Lila, who looked paler than ever. Alistair was famous for his poetry renditions and he knew it. He let the words drip to his audience like honey to a hungry bear. Although he clearly saw Frances coming, he continued his recital to the end.

> '... *crimson the creeper's leaf across*
> *Like a splash of blood, intense, abrupt,*
> *O'er a shield else gold from rim to boss* ...'

Alistair gave a slight nod of his head in acknowledgment of his own genius. 'It's Robert Browning on the colours of Tuscany,' he explained. 'I couldn't help but think of it as I journeyed here. We travel ever in the giant footsteps of others.'

Frances stopped on the bottom stair and looked at the great love of her life. For the first time since she'd met him her heart did not skip a beat, but she was tired and she felt somehow guilty. Even though they were not together any more, she retained some strange sexual loyalty to Alistair. Jack was her first lover since she and Alistair had

191

split up.

'Hello, chicken,' he smiled. 'Here I am. Should have been here last night, but I confess to over-indulging on the plane. I have to say the stewardess was more than generous with the contents of her trolley and I had to lie low in Rome for a few hours. How's the colouring-in going?'

He acted as if they had never parted as he confidently pulled her into his arms. It was very familiar. Perhaps he had come to whisk her away. He was, after all, here. In all the years of their relationship, Alistair had never done any of the running. This was what she had dreamt of. Perhaps she didn't need to deal with any of this nonsense after all. He would laugh and say what a ridiculous story. They would rush back to London and amuse their friends until late into the night.

Alistair pushed her back and held her at arm's length.

'Chicken, what are you wearing? Is this some kind of Rembrandt look? I'm not sure about it, not sure at all. You look so, well . . . untidy.'

Frances pulled the large shirt tightly about her. Margaret had reappeared at the foot of the stairs and was watching with a great grin.

'I wasn't expecting you,' Frances said. 'I wasn't expecting him,' she explained to the others.

Alistair smiled all round. 'I know, surprise! I spoke to Gina and she said you had done some bizarre thing and gone off to Italy and I thought, that can't be right . . . Sir Alistair to the rescue. "Cometh the hour, cometh the man."'

'Pretty late hour.' Frances tried to smile.

'Certainly for the man-cometh part,' muttered Margaret.

'I know,' agreed her shining knight. 'Some misunderstanding with the grumpiest taxi driver ever known to man. I did not tip,' he added, confident that his action had finally taught the ungrateful fellow the lesson he needed. Pito and Lila had been watching the entire exchange in silence but now Lila gave the Capitán a slight shove. He coughed and introduced himself into the scene.

'Miss Angel, we have had the most marvellous idea for our pageant. Mr Alistair is such a wonderful actor . . . he has been telling us all about his work . . . a great professional . . . and we thought, what luck, now we have two professionals. We have already hinted that we might prevail upon him to take part in our little show.'

Alistair held his hands up in mock horror. 'Oh, I couldn't possibly. I've only just arrived. I mean, I haven't rehearsed, I don't know the lines . . .'

'We need someone very special to take the part of St Michael.'

'St Michael?' queried Alistair, his ears pricking up at what sounded like a principal role.

'The angel of the vision . . .' explained Pito. 'We have selected an excellent story and we thought . . .'

'. . . with his hair,' sighed Lila.

Alistair ran a quick hand across his locks. 'St Michael, eh? Don't think I've ever given a saint. Not that I couldn't, but I mean a part like that would require the right costume, lighting—'

'Yes, well, before you call your agent,' interrupted Frances, 'let me take you upstairs and we can . . . chat.'

With promises to return the budding saint to his

flock as soon as possible, Frances finally managed to lead Alistair away and upstairs to her room. Always a man to make himself at home, Alistair dumped his bag on the floor and threw himself on to the bed.

'So what are you going to be in this little play of theirs?'

Uncertain of what to do with herself, Frances pretended to fiddle with the shutters. 'Nothing. Maybe a nun.'

'I've always fancied doing it with a nun.'

'You have?'

'Actually, I did once. Tour of *Sister Bernadette.*'

'But we were together then.'

Alistair laughed. 'Don't fret. God, she was awful.'

Frances stood by the window with her hands grasping the sill. She turned back to the room to find him lazing with his hands behind his head. He was grinning and relaxed. A saint ready for action. 'Alistair, what are you doing here?'

He grinned. 'I told you. Gina said you were here, I'd finished the play, God, I was good, and I thought it sounded like you needed saving.'

'I can't believe Gina told you where I was.'

'Ah, well, I might have read one of her emails in an idle moment in your office.'

'Well, where the hell is Pandora? Remember her? Agent with nice Jag? Woman who was going to keep you in the style to which I had got you accustomed?' Alistair had the decency to wince through his smile. 'Doesn't she mind you chasing across Italy after your ex?'

'Oh, don't call yourself that, chicken. We had a little interruption, that's all. You know we're meant

194

to be together.'

'You moved out, Alistair. You moved out of our house and in with Pandora. I seem to recall I said I wanted to live in the country and stop working, and you suddenly found yourself another woman in show business, who lived in London, had a big house and didn't want to stop working. Pandora bloody Box.'

'Baxter actually.'

'Box, Bax, whatever. She's not even good-looking. That woman has a chin big enough to land her helicopter on. Wasn't the name enough to stop you, even if the jaw wasn't?'

Alistair slowly got up from the bed. 'My darling, I had to choose an unattractive woman to stop me thinking about you. Anyway, none of this matters. Pandora is, as it were, back in her box.'

'What happened? Did she have enough of you lying about the house smoking your Gitanes?' Frances could feel the old bickering rhythms which had marked their years together returning.

'As it happens she is rather dull, and Mr Baxter, who is a complete arse, decided he rather preferred it at home.'

'Oh, so chucked out, eh? Basically, Alistair, you had nowhere else to go.'

'Ssshh,' soothed Alistair in his deep, melodious voice. 'Let's not go over it all. I was coming back to you anyway. It was just a matter of timing. I'm here now, aren't I? We can start again. You must know how much I love you. I can't bear foreign food and yet here I am. Think of the fun we'll have. They say Italy is such a romantic country.' He came up behind her and put his arms round her waist. 'Remember this?' He nuzzled her neck.

195

'Remember how good this is?'

The tension in Frances's shoulders eased and she sank back against his chest. He smelt so familiar, felt so safe. She had loved him more than anyone in her life, but now things were changing. Just one day sooner and she would have melted, packed her bags and gone away with him, but not now. She wasn't sure. Frances stroked his arm absentmindedly.

'I'm sorry I didn't get here last night,' he said. 'We missed a whole night in each other's arms. It was never the same with Pandora. You and I belong together. It was as though a piece of me was missing.'

Frances gently pulled away. She couldn't think. It was all too sudden and confusing. She realised if Alistair had arrived as planned she would never have spent the night with Jack. It was all a matter of timing. Perhaps being here had just been a mistake? She should pack her bags and go back with Alistair to the world she knew, but Jack and Maria . . .

'I need some time. Please, Alistair, you must be tired. Sleep.'

'Actually, I am a little weary,' he conceded, moving back to the bed and plumping up the best part of the pillows behind his head. 'This shining knight business is the devil's own work, you know.' And, with that, the golden boy fell fast asleep, confident of Frances's and the world's love.

Frances slowly removed Jack's shirt. For a moment she held it in her arms. It smelt of paint. It was a nice smell. She laid it on the chair and stood naked for a while at the window, letting the air play across her skin. Then she got dressed and sat on

196

the bed beside her lover from the past.

She felt her eyes close as the events of the last few hours crept up on her, and she fell asleep. She slept fitfully for about an hour. Dreams of coloured handprints chasing her across cobbled streets disturbed her. As soon as she awoke, she stood to ease the cramp that ran across her entire body. She felt as though there had been an earthquake and a line now ran down her body where it had split in two. She looked at the sleeping Alistair. She had to speak to Jack before Alistair awoke. She had to explain. She crept from the room heading for Jack's room. The door was ajar and she pushed it open.

'Jack? I need you to—' She paused in mid-sentence. Lounging across Jack's bed lay Lila, completely naked.

'Hey, Frances,' she called but Frances did not stay. She stumbled to her room. Alistair was waking and he reached for her.

'Hello, chicken, want to play with the fox?' he oozed. Alistair began to make love. His hands played across her body and for the first time she noticed how white they were. Alistair was a skilful lover but throughout his efforts Frances watched the shadow of time passing across the bed.

CHAPTER SIXTEEN

Chi più sa, meno crede

The more one knows, the less one believes

Alistair and Frances reappeared downstairs just as Buff was serving morning coffee and biscuits. Everyone had gathered for rehearsal and Madeleine and Margaret were already dressed like overgrown members of the von Trapp family. Anselm looked Alistair up and down. 'I don't think we were properly introduced?' he demanded.

Alistair, who could be charming to either sex, smiled an entirely captivating smile and leant forward.

'Alistair Barton. I believe it has been indicated that I might give my St Michael.'

Pito clapped his hands like a boy scout in the face of a particularly useful knot. 'Isn't it absolutely splendid, Anselm? A genuine St Michael. I'm sure this year is going to be the triumph Margaret yearns for.'

Madeleine continued her wardrobe organisation. 'Now then, saint costume . . . saint . . .'

More rummaging occurred until a shift of pure white was produced and pulled over Alistair's head. It fell in fine folds to just above his feet. A slight hush descended on the small troupe. With his wispy blond hair and fine features he did look very saintly indeed. Frances, however, looked

198

absurd. The black dress with black-and-white veil was not a fashion look anyone but the Singing Nun could get away with.

Frances looked along the corridor to the art room and saw Jack standing in the doorway. He stood completely silent and they looked at each other. Embarrassed, she turned to enthusiasm as her cover.

'I think everyone looks splendid,' she declared, starting a chorus of oohing and aahing and congratulations all round. When Frances looked again, Jack was gone.

The day was spent rehearsing for the pageant. Alistair was marvellous and everyone was delighted he had joined the company. He and Anselm bonded as fellow professionals, and by late afternoon Frances was able to leave them comparing great performances. She slipped out to get some air on her own and wandered on to the terrace that spread out behind the school. It was warm from a day baking in the sun and she let the shafts of light relax her stiff shoulders. The light and the view were stunning, and from below a grove of olive trees gave off a heady scent. That evening the ancient town of Montecastello was so steeped in romance that a critic might have accused it of overplaying the part. The view almost hurt her eyes. For a brief moment she felt as though she had come home. It was as if there was something in her DNA that told her—this was where she had come from and she was where she belonged. Frances gave herself a mental shake. She needed to stop having romantic ideas and decide what to do.

Tomorrow she would see Maria and then the

next day she and Alistair would go home. She had what she wanted. Alistair had seen sense and returned. It was what she had wished for. It was all going to be . . . thoughts crowded into Frances's mind. So much had changed in a short space of time. She remembered her first days in Montecastello. The man in the street who had called her *donnaccia*—slut—and how, perhaps, that was now true. She had slept with two men within a few hours. Jack. Yet he had turned out to be just like any other man. He had filled his bed within a minute. Smiling Jack who had opened her eyes; who had made her sees things differently. She thought of Goran, naked with his art. How Pito and Buff had both tried to prove their virility with unexpected dinner invitations. The pageant? What about the pageant? Frances had never deserted a production in her life, but this was nothing. A tiny performance in a ridiculously small space. She would tell Jack. What would she tell Jack?

Frances turned to go back into the house and, as she did so, her eye glanced through the kitchen window. Shadows were beginning to fall across the half-closed shutters and it was impossible to see clearly into the room but she thought she saw Pito take Buff in his arms.

Buff and Pito? The two military men? Surely . . . Frances was beginning to feel that she knew nothing; that all the set parameters of her life were blurring and fading away. How on earth had she got so involved with these people whose existence she had been happily ignorant of for most of her life? She had come to clear her head, her conscience and then go home. The calm she had experienced when she was painting had left her and she felt foolish. This was ridiculous. She had no real link to this place. Her parents had packed her away. Why should she stay? They could stuff their stupid school. Frances banged into the house and straight into the kitchen. Buff was standing alone at the central cooking island examining a large fish as if he had never seen one before.

'Look at this, Miss Angel, isn't it extraordinary? The silver flecks against the grey and then inside this impossibly beautiful pinky orange. I mean, who would have thought of it as a combination? That's the sort of thing might make you think there is a God.'

Finding God in a fish had never occurred to Frances. 'Yes, I suppose so.'

Buff looked up and smiled. 'Isn't it silly? Margaret is having a most beastly time and I don't think I've ever been happier.'

'No.' Buff was so content that Frances's steam of intention completely evaporated. She also felt slightly bewildered by the absence of Pito. Perhaps he hadn't been in here after all. Perhaps she hadn't seen him at all. Instead of announcing her imminent departure, she found herself saying, 'I've got some lemons if you want them.'

'That would be marvellous.' An entirely contented and secure major from the Scots Guards smiled.

Frances went to get the bag of fruit and shook her head. Pito was nowhere to be seen. Perhaps she was starting to imagine things. Frances delivered the citrus offering and learnt that Alistair was looking for her in the garden. She was not ready to talk to him and there was a moment of genuine fear as she suddenly realised she might bump into Signora Fratelli when she wasn't ready. Frances almost ran from the house to find herself a drink.

It was twilight. The time when witches haunt the crossroads and pedestrians must fling them a coin in order to keep safe. She pushed the childish thought away. Who had told her that? Her mother. Her mother whom she missed. It was not a thought Frances ever allowed herself. She did not live here, had no intention of living here and whatever any of the wretched peasants chose to believe made no difference to her. Having spent all day trying to see, Frances now wanted to be blind. Blind drunk.

The mind may be slow with its colour palette but it is quick to map the unfamiliar, and the small lanes to the central square had fallen into place. Frances knew which shadows hid the doorways of shops, which was the *macelleria* and which lanes led away to the homes and offices of the locals. She had committed the landscape to her mental map and walked with a newfound confidence. She passed under window boxes, past doors closed against the coming night and ignored the doors of the dead whose outlines could just be seen in the stone walls. As she rounded the corner into the last lane off the square she thought she heard footsteps behind her. She stopped and looked back but could see no one. A few childish fears niggled once more. She walked on a few paces and heard footsteps again. This time the shuffling feet seemed closer. Ahead was a dim streetlight, high on a stone wall. A narrow lane peeled off to the right and Frances quickly ducked down it. She leant against the wall and held her breath. The feet came closer and closer until Frances could stand it no longer and leapt out to face her pursuer.

'Signora Fratelli!' she exclaimed. It was the puppy, the old woman from the school. It was Sophia's grandmother. The old woman grabbed Frances's hand and began to kiss it with great passion.

'*Finalmente*,' she repeated over and over again. Frances could not get her to let go and as she began pulling and shuffling down a side lane Frances had no choice but to follow. She had too little Italian to help the old lady and too much English to push her away.

The puppy was tiny but surprisingly strong. A head shorter than Frances and bowed with age, nonetheless she moved them both along the lanes at quite a pace. They were heading downhill from the top of the town. The lanes got narrower, steep stone walls of three-storey houses loomed above them. Even in the gloom Frances was aware of the honey and red of the masonry, occasionally broken by a suspended box of brilliant geraniums or the orange and yellow of marigolds. Frances found herself wishing she had worn a sweater. Not because she wanted to be warm but knowing that then perhaps she would have been able to see the colours more clearly.

Signora Fratelli reached a metal gate at the foot of one of the lanes and pushed it open. The two women had arrived in a high-walled enclosure. Neat gravel paths led between miniature buildings of varying styles. Each was no larger than a fancy garden shed but some were made of concrete slabs, some of the local stone and still others in formal red brick. Some were highly decorated with carved angels bearing bouquets of flowers, while others were austere in their simplicity. Each had a central arched doorway protected by a metal grille and through them you could see the names and resting places of the dead of Montecastello. The old woman had brought her to the churchyard. She continued to lead Frances past these Lilliputian estates until, in the far corner of the plot, they came to banks of plaques set into high walls. Each space was perhaps two foot square and carried the name and an enamelled photograph of the deceased. On a thin ledge before each of the remembered stood small silver pots of flowers, some fresh, some fake. These were the memorials of the working people. These were the Montecastellians who had tilled the land, cleaned the lanes. They had not had the money to lie in a private house and wait to be carried in comfort to the next world. They lay in serried ranks, six high and many deep. Frances looked at the faces immortalised in black and white on the enamelled pictures. Hardly anyone smiled. These were records for posterity, taken in formal clothes and waiting to look out from the grave.

Still the old woman walked on until at last she came to a spot near the end of the wall. She pointed to one of the portraits and Frances stopped to look. It was a little girl, perhaps five years old: Sophia Fratelli.

The old woman tapped on the picture. 'Sophia,' she said. Then she reached into the folds of her black dress and pulled out a small brown parcel neatly tied with string. She pressed it into Frances's care. '*Finalmente*, Francesca Angelli.'

It had been years since anyone had called her

that. Frances looked down at the parcel and knew what it was. Slowly she opened it and inside was a matching handprint to her own. The old woman pointed to it and then to Sophia's picture. Here was her own hand pressed into clay. The hand Sophia had held so as not to be afraid in the dark. The old woman pointed to it and then to Sophia's picture. Beside Sophia a handsome couple stood frozen in time on an enamel plate. 'Fratelli, Alfredo, Luisa' read the inscription. The old woman pointed to herself. 'Fratelli,' she said.

'I know. Fratelli,' repeated Frances. 'You're Sophia's grandmother. Nonna Sophia?'

Signora Fratelli nodded and smiled and once more pulled Frances away. This time to another wall with more photos and more memorials. There in the middle of a rank of many were Franco and Adriana Angelli, Frances's parents. Signora Fratelli looked straight at Frances and said again, 'Francesca Angelli, *finalmente.*'

The portraits of her parents were formal. Her father in a suit and her mother in a black dress that Frances could almost feel against her face. It was her mother's best for high days and holidays. She was well turned out to meet the Lord. Her parents stared out in black and white at their long-lost daughter. Signora Fratelli took Frances's hand and placed it on her mother's portrait. Unable to communicate, she pointed to the necklace her mother wore round her neck. Frances nodded. It was a small cross her mother had been given for her first communion. She had worn it always. The old woman reached into her pocket and removed a small piece of tissue, which she carefully unwrapped. Inside lay the same small silver cross on a thin matching chain. Signora Fratelli handed it to Frances.

'*Finalmente,*' she repeated and began to cry. So too did Frances. This tangible, recognisable piece of her mother's past was too much. The two women turned and held each other like grandmother and grandchild united in their grief.

Sometimes we think others are foolish because we cannot see the whole picture. The old woman had been right from the moment Frances arrived—she had indeed been waiting for her. The question was, what was Frances supposed to do about it? After some time Frances returned Signora Fratelli to her room. She sat with her while the old lady drifted off to sleep. There was so much they wanted to say to each other but could not. The only word the signora kept repeating was the name of the priest. 'Benito. Benito.' It was said with frail determination and Frances wanted to reply, but all she could manage was to stroke the hand of her friend's grandmother. She knew the old woman had waited for her to return. She had waited for her to sort things out, but Frances had no idea what she was supposed to do. She had no idea how to put things right.

CHAPTER SEVENTEEN

We must not always try to plumb the
depths of the human heart; the truths it
contains are among those that are best
seen in half-light or in perspective.

François-René de Chateaubriand
French author, diplomat and traveller in
Italy (1768–1848)

Next Sunday, Frances slipped from her room and
went out to clear her head. Alistair had already
gone for a walk with Fliss who inexplicably had
offered to help him with his lines. Frances was
glad. She needed a moment to herself. Where she
had once lain in Alistair's arms for hours amazed
that a man so beautiful might choose her, now the
oddest thing had happened. She didn't like the
smell of him. While she completely understood
that her visual sense was receiving an education,
something had happened to her nose as well.
Frances went down into the hall to sit but the
school had begun to feel like a spider's web.
Whichever way she tried to escape, she kept
finding herself further and further enmeshed.

She knew Maria would be at the church and she
half wondered if there might be a moment to speak
to her. It was a beautiful day of crisp blue sky and
the people had dressed for High Mass. Mothers in
smart coats fussed over their small boys' hair,
chastised girls for climbing walls and admonished
fathers for putting their hands in their suit pockets.

Up in the square outside the church, the stalls of religious iconography were doing a roaring trade. Frances sat for a breakfast coffee and watched candles, tea towels and plastic rosary beads exchanging hands.

A group of lads, maybe sixteen or seventeen years old, appeared from the narrow Via Catalano degli Atti that ran off to the north of the square. They moved in a pack, and anywhere else they would have looked like trouble. Their hair slicked back with either gel or Sunday morning ablutions, they wore leather jackets with sharp collared shirts and smart pressed jeans. It was Sunday and no one was excused. A middle-aged couple, he in a dark suit and somehow getting away with tan shoes, she unashamedly wearing fur, entered the square. Without speaking, they headed for the low brick wall that separated the terrace from the drop into the valley below. The husband carefully removed a newspaper from his pocket and with great precision tore the personal ad section from the back. He laid it neatly on the wall and waited for his wife to sit. His wife made herself comfortable, the man bowed slightly and moved to talk to the large group of his compatriots now gathered at the café. There was something of the Jewish wedding about the gathering. Each new arrival seemed automatically to know the group to which they belonged. The café was, apart from Frances, exclusively male and exclusively older male: grey-haired fellows with V-neck sweaters under their ancient suits and a fair smattering of flat caps or fedoras. Men with young children were confined to the wall near the well. There they sat staring at babies with a slightly mystified expression. The older women in the smartest coats occupied the commanding position at the heart of the square in front of the shopping stalls. The divisions of the sexes made the pecking order in the town very clear. The men ran the country but the women ran the men.

Frances ordered a shot of espresso and it came with a small glass of water and a packet of sugar. Beside her, two men were engaged in an argument that they played out loudly for the benefit of the crowd. Jack was right—in Italy you didn't need to be in the theatre to see a performance.

Frances's musing was interrupted. Lila thumped down in the next chair.

'Thought I was going to be fucking late. Fuck, Frances, the whole town is here. God, can you imagine what this place would be like without their miracle? I mean, it's their life, isn't it?' sighed Lila. 'This place would be fucking nothing without it. I mean, I can't imagine anyone would ever come here.'

Lila required no response. She spoke rapidly and seemed to have made no connection between the piece of theatre she had been rehearsing at the school and the pageant she was watching being played out in the square. Lila sank two coffees and went into 'the fucking church'. Singing could be heard starting up. It was in a challenging key and signified a general shuffling from the terrace towards the main doors. Frances did not want to enter. She was afraid of confronting Benito, but soon the square emptied and she felt like the latecomer at the theatre. Taking a deep breath, she entered the church.

The back of the church was filling up first, with

209

the gang of lads all sitting in a long row together. As Frances headed for a pew she noticed that some bore the names of local families: Fratelli, Ippoliti . . . Angelli. Here were the places where her parents had sat. Frances could not bring herself to sit in their seats but instead moved further along the pew. An extremely fat altar boy moved up the aisle without ever lifting a foot fully from the ground. He wore a small white cape over his shoulders and looked like a mobile iced bun. He reached up behind the lectern and pressed the button on a ghettoblaster which at last silenced the dreadful music. Then he rang a small bell and everyone stood. No books or leaflets were handed out. This was religion by rote and there was not one person who needed to be told what to do. They had all learnt their parts and were ready to perform.

Frances sat and looked at the cast of characters. There was a statue of the Virgin Mary wearing what looked like a golden bag on her head. It was not unlike something her aunt had filled with ice when she had migraines. Another was of a saint holding up two fingers of one hand in a blessing, while clutching a pig in the other. There was one which she thought to be St Luke. He had an uncanny resemblance to her old chemistry teacher, a man who had taught her what things were made of and what could be done to change them. There was her mother's favourite, St Filippo Neri, a man who once he felt he had learnt enough, sold his books and gave the money to the poor. Frances wondered what Jack would have made of him. Jack, who never seemed to think he knew enough. Jack. Frances felt her stomach take a turn at the very thought of him. What the hell was happening to her? She and Jack had not spoken for two days now and she realised she had to try and see him.

Frances was deep in thought when Father Benito appeared from the sacristy. Behind him walked Maria, her face covered in a white veil. Everyone bowed their heads as she took a seat in a carved throne to one side of the altar. The star had arrived. The show could begin. Maria looked at no one. Indeed she appeared almost to be in a trance. Father Benito took his place centre stage and paused. He turned to look straight at Frances and she felt a shiver of fear. The service began.

'*Mea culpa, mea culpa,*' the congregation repeated. In front of Frances an elderly white-haired woman in black beat time, hitting her right hand against her left breast. It was hard to imagine what the old woman had to take blame for. A young man with an eleven o'clock shadow read from the lectern. He spoke poorly and hesitated over the occasional interruptions of 'Hallelujah' said in quiet repetition. Not for this audience the excesses of the Baptists or the cries of the Born-again. It was familiar and comfortable to them. Like breathing. A grandfather walked the aisle with an irritable and vocal baby with no thought from him or anyone else that the child might be taken outside.

'*Altare privilegiato perpetuo,*' began Father Benito. Perpetual life, thought Frances. How exhausting—but it was what the crowd had come for. It was the truth that they sought. The bored altar boy leant back in his chair, no doubt thinking about lunch. Frances watched the town press forward to hear Father Benito. Even the lads at the

211

back were silent and attentive. Here was the father of their flock; the town's mediator between the human and the divine. The man who could provide them on this day with the sacraments and so bring the gift of God's grace. Without it they would be damned. She imagined what it would have taken for her parents to go against him. No one in Montecastello could survive if the priest turned against them. What if he didn't bless the house, the fields, the tools they used? What if he damned the flour for the bread?

Jack was right. Here was the core of the town. Whatever happened, Montecastello was Catholic to its heart and it was Maria who gave it a sense of self-importance. She looked around the congregation. Where was the harm in having something to distinguish it from every other tiny hilltop town? She could not take everything away, yet she felt a great sense of responsibility to Signora Fratelli. Sophia's grandmother had waited a long time for the death of her family to be avenged. Frances looked at her old friend Maria. Who knew what she had or had not seen? She needed to find a way out for everyone.

After Mass, Frances waited to see Maria but she was marched out in a parade of local dignitaries and there was no speaking to her. Frances left the church and walked to her parents' deserted garden. She thought of what they had been through. Her mother nearly mad with grief, yet consumed with fear. Father Benito. It all came down to him. As she made her way across the terrace she realised with a start that Jack was sitting on the stone bench with Auroch, looking at the view. The involuntary pounding of her heart

212

meant she didn't trust herself to speak. Thinking that perhaps he hadn't seen her, she turned to go, but without looking round Jack called out, 'I'm worried about you.'

Frances stopped and took a breath.

'I'm fine.'

'Good.'

'And you?'

Jack looked up at her. 'Sure. Come, sit.'

Frances sat down and Auroch, who knew nothing of the subtleties of their relationship, welcomed her with kisses.

After a few moments, Jack said, 'I thought you might come here.'

'Jack, I'm sorry. I didn't know that—'

Jack held up his hand. 'Please, don't be. I need to learn to be less foolish.'

'No, you weren't foolish. It's just—'

They turned to look at each other and Frances longed for him to kiss her but he moved away.

'Look, Angel, I wanted to warn you. I know you're angry. I know you feel the town is based on some kind of lie, but there's nothing you can do about it. I know you have things, personal things, you need to sort out, but don't come here and destroy the balance. The town, in its own way, works well. You don't have the right to change things.'

Frances exploded. 'Works well? Maria is terrified for her life. Benito is an evil man. What's the matter with you? I thought you were on my side.'

'This is not some game. It's not about sides. I'm trying to get you to be cautious.'

'Cautious? You don't understand, do you?

213

Father Benito laid the fire in the chapel. My father was sure of it. That's why he sent me away. Benito killed Sophia and her family.' Frances looked at Jack. 'That doesn't shock you?'

He shrugged. 'Priestly intrigue is part of the lifeblood of Italy.'

'That's it? I think he may have killed my parents as well and all you can say is "That's life"? Don't you think someone ought to find out the truth, or are lies another part of Italian life that I have forgotten?'

'Italians know the truth when they see it but maybe they don't attach so much importance to it. They know their prime minister is a crook but it doesn't worry them unduly.' Jack turned, put his hands on Frances's arms and looked into her face. 'What the hell have I been trying to show you? There is no such thing as perfect truth, Frances. I have been living in Italy most of my adult life and what I have learnt is that this may be the land of culture, art and ideas but that doesn't mean they'll thank you for it. Look at how they treat their own. Machiavelli died penniless and never managed to get his work published; Vico, the father of modern thought, lived in a garret; the great Galileo was persecuted for his ideas; Dante had to go into exile. There are two Italys. On the surface everything is brilliant and bright, yet behind that is unbelievably feeble behaviour. The art is magnificent, breathtaking, the architecture is sublime, but try and get anything done here. The place is badly organised, badly governed, corruption is admired. These are not particularly honest, reliable or law-abiding people. They have the most vivacious surface and if you stay for a short while you will see the most spectacular performance of life, but stay longer and you will find melancholy. You have to understand that no one here may be interested in your truth.'

Frances, stung by his words, lashed out. 'What are you doing here, Jack? This is not your home. Why don't you go back? Can't face the truth of your life?'

'Maybe. I meant to go back years ago but now I suspect that I'll end up buried in the corner of an Italian cemetery reserved for heathens and heretics, or perhaps shipped home to distant relatives who don't recall me. Perhaps I like being the perpetual outsider. The observer. It's what the artist is supposed to do.'

'I would have thought the artist was supposed to save the art school. Why are you just letting it go?'

Jack shrugged. 'The town will die without the church. You cannot take that away even if it is an illusion.'

'I'm only trying to take away a lie. Anyway, what the hell are you doing defending the church?'

'I don't know. What are you doing wearing a cross?'

Frances's hand went to her throat, where her mother's necklace now hung. 'It was my mother's.'

Jack's voice was so gentle when he spoke that she could hardly hear him. 'Frances, I know you want to *do* something. That you have some notion of putting things right, but this is Italy. I wish you would just leave it alone. You have this bizarre notion that there is some fundamental core of belief that everyone will recognise. You have to understand how much of life here is just surface. Remember the stigmata I gave you?'

215

'Yes.'

'OK, it's a trick. I drew the cross on the tile with charcoal. When I held the tile over your hand I put my thumb on the cross and the charcoal transferred to my skin. Then I held your hand over the broken pieces and put the cross on your palm with my thumb. That's it. A trick. The dancing cane—it's a trick. There is no fundamental truth about anything. There are just things we do and things we don't understand. Frances, I—'

He seemed about to kiss her, but she could no longer think. She broke from his grasp and stood up.

'Oh, for Christ's sake, Jack, who are you to lecture on truth and acceptability? I thought we had something and two seconds later you had Lila in your bloody bed.'

'No, I didn't,' protested Jack.

'I saw her!' yelled Frances, building into complete fury.

'Well, then I didn't teach you to look properly,' snapped Jack and walked away.

'Jack, come back here! Jack!'

The man was impossible. What had she been thinking? Frances marched from the garden but as she turned into the lane arms reached out to catch her.

'Frances!'

'Gina!'

CHAPTER EIGHTEEN

Chi ben comincia è a metà dell'opera

A good start is half the battle

Gina had not caught Frances at the optimum time for a big welcome.

'What are you doing here?' Frances demanded.

Gina smiled. ' "My dear cousin, how lovely to see you" would have been nice.'

'Sorry.'

'I came to save you, Frances.'

'Join the queue.'

'I heard Alistair came after you, so I came after him,' explained Gina. 'I felt terrible once you'd gone and when you didn't reply to my email . . .'

'Oh God, I forgot. I'm so sorry.'

'Yes, well, as you're not the forgetting kind, I thought I would find an excuse for a short break.'

Frances was bewildered. 'How did you know I was here?'

'I didn't,' replied Gina. 'You weren't at the school, so I went for a walk. It's not that big a place.'

Frances realised how distant her everyday life suddenly seemed. She tried to get back on track. 'Right,' she said. 'Did you bring the kids?'

'Of course. I thought it would be educational for them to watch you ruin your life.' Gina looked at Frances. 'Don't be ridiculous. I came on my own to sweep you out of here and take you to the biggest spa Italy has to offer. You look like you could do

217

with a bit of a deep clean.'

Frances shook her head. 'I'm going back with Alistair.'

'I knew there was something grubby about you. No, Frances.'

'It's fine, Gina. He realises he's made a mistake. The only thing is, I don't think he'll leave until the play is done.'

Gina was entirely confused. 'Play? What play?'

*　　　*　　　*

By the time Gina and Frances reached the school, Frances had managed to update her cousin on Father Benito, Maria and what was happening in the town. All she left out was any mention of Jack. Gina was horrified by what she heard and determined that Frances must leave as soon as possible.

'Benito sounds deranged. This is not your battle, Frances,' she was saying at the very moment the other students were applauding another astonishing revelation of the talent Buff was proving in the kitchen. Gina and Frances entered the hall as he was producing the lightest veal scaloppini with prosciutto and sage accompanied by floating butterflies made from carved crisp vegetables. With each meal his ambitions grew and each time he surpassed his previous effort: the beef served with small tomato baskets filled with herb butter; the fish baked en croute in piscatorial shapes—each meal was an artistic revelation of balance and harmony.

'Ah, your cousin is discovered.' Margaret sailed towards them like a galleon entering home port.

'How delightful. Isn't family the greatest blessing? *Alzate il gomito*, everyone.'

'Yes, indeed,' agreed Pito, who was laying the table, 'Let us raise an elbow—have a drink.'

Everyone except Jack and Paolo was waiting to eat and such a fuss was made of Gina that any suggestion that she had come to help Frances pack and leave was shouted down.

'So, Miss Angel, what do you do?' enquired Margaret after her third or fourth glass of Chianti.

'I work with Frances. We run a theatre company in London.'

Gina might as well have brought manna directly to the table with her announcement.

'This is heaven sent,' declared Margaret.

'Two angels to help us.' Anselm shook his head in amazement, and even Goran tapped the table in a slow beat of appreciation.

'No, I mean, Frances and I—'

'Is she going to be in it?' asked Lila, anxious not to be overshadowed by a professional.

'I don't act,' said Gina, 'I'm a producer, but anyway . . .'

Affected by both wine and good fortune, Margaret began to weep quietly. 'The tale of *Povero Davide* is going to be unparalleled,' she declared to a light ripple of applause round the table.

Gina, who did not know how difficult it was to do anything other than what Margaret wanted, looked to her cousin for help, but Frances merely shook her head. As Buff served the pudding Frances knew that whatever else happened no one would be departing until the pageant had been performed. Everyone wanted to bring Gina up to speed on rehearsals. *Il Povero Davide* was going well, but they all agreed there was only enough material in it for the first half. Discussions about what to do after the interval were intense and Gina, much to her own amazement, soon found she had an opinion about what they should do. By nightfall, she not only realised she was staying but she was put in charge.

With Gina taking over the producing side of the piece, Frances had time to continue with the art classes. She told herself it had nothing to do with Jack but each morning she was first into the studio. Jack, on the other hand, had taken to arriving late and beginning work without any preamble. The class had settled down into a comfortable routine. With the discovery of his culinary talent, Buff had become much more relaxed. He no longer seemed on the verge of tears with each brushstroke. It was as though he had found his calling and the rest was simply fun. Something had been released in the repressed Englishman and it was spreading its effect through the class. Pito, now that his hunger was sated, also seemed less stiff, and the others too, having passed through nakedness or near nakedness, appeared to adopt a more casual approach. Lila and Anselm had clearly formed some kind of entirely cerebral performance partnership and spent many hours rolling on the art-studio floor covered in paint. Goran even looked happy to be divorced from his camera, and Madeleine emerged in a shirt without a high neck and with a dashing splash of red paint on one sleeve. Meanwhile, Alistair's part as St Michael was growing by the minute and his acting was widely admired.

'It is possible,' confessed Madeleine to Frances over a particularly splendid plate of langoustine one evening, 'that I am falling in love . . . into great affection . . . with Goran . . . from Montenegro,' she added, as if the place were awash with Gorans. 'It is most unexpected. A little wild, even. What do you think I should do?'

Frances looked across the table at the little round man who seemed to carry a personal dust storm with him. 'I'd give him a bath,' she suggested.

Fliss, too, was not impervious to the charm of the artistic gathering. She appeared to have bonded with Alistair and could be heard moaning to him that she was beginning to feel bad about her plan to close the school. 'If God had not called me here to start the Bible centre, why then I would love it to stay as an art school. You don't suppose, Alistair, that the good Lord might have sent me the wrong message, do you?'

The only person who seemed resistant to the charm of evenings gathered around food and wine was Jack. He set off each night for the chapel to do his painting and Frances suspected he did not return until morning. He didn't seem to be speaking to anyone personally but each day as he continued his lectures on art he could not hide the enduring passion he had for his subject.

The classes continued. They looked at colour in the cold, colour in heat. They examined spectrums and prisms and wondered at how little they had seen in the past. Jack was wonderful, but he looked pale and tired and avoided being alone with anyone. One morning, Jack moved to the central table and held up a drawing. It was in black and white and looked like a piece of 1960s op art. A spiral disappearing into a central vortex.

'Anybody?'

'Bad art?' ventured Fliss.

'Cool,' declared Anselm.

'It is a spiral,' announced Pito, slightly sniffily. He liked art but not games. His sniff suggested that this was going nowhere but he was too polite to say so outright.

'Is it, Pito?' asked Jack. 'Are you sure?'

Now everyone crowded around the drawing and examined it closely. There was much muttering.

'It is a trick,' declared Goran quietly. The remark was much admired, partly because it was right and partly because Goran rarely said anything at all.

'Indeed it is,' agreed Jack. 'It is an illusion called Fraser's spiral. If you trace the lines with your finger you find concentric circles composed of segments angled towards the centre. The fact is that your eye is lying to you. It has made up a connection that does not exist. There are similar effects. Look at this.'

He took a marker pen and drew on the white wall between the handprints Madeleine and Frances had created in the first class. As he drew, Frances looked at the red imprint her hand had made on the plaster. The paint had failed to seep into the deeper lines and she could clearly see her life played out in the impression. It was quite different to Madeleine's. It was unique.

Jack drew two parallel lines and then marked each one with angled lines veering away from each throughout their length. Immediately the original parallel markings appeared to angle away from each other.

'That's called Zöllner's illusion and there are lots of others in which a sequence of tilted elements causes the eye to perceive phantom twists and deviations. The truth is, we see things in our mind all the time that differ substantially from the facts. Our eye and our thoughts are not always to be trusted. It was only when these things came to be understood that art began to include perspective. Before that art was full of strange bug-eyed people and horses no one could possibly ride. Illusions in art are commonplace. You need to be wary of assuming you know what you are looking at. Take your time to decide what you really know about something. Now grab a cup and spoon!' said Jack enthusiastically.

'Coffee, thank God,' declared Lila.

'No,' said Jack. He held up a cup and saucer in one hand and a teaspoon in the other. He placed the spoon horizontally on the saucer.

'How long is the spoon?' he asked. 'Is it the same as the height of the cup? Is it shorter? Or maybe longer? If I stood the spoon up in the cup to stir something, how much of the spoon would you see? All of the bowl? Some of the bowl? None of it?'

'Why don't you measure it?' demanded the ever practical Madeleine. 'Then you would know for sure.'

Jack smiled. 'It's not engineering, Madeleine, it's art. You're supposed to use your eye, not a tape measure. What is the relationship between the spoon and the cup? Decide together.' Jack placed the cup and saucer on a table and clapped his hands. 'Grab a piece of paper and try and draw what you think the spoon would look like standing up in the cup. Be careful—between illusion and reality lies anxiety and no one wants to go there.'

A flurry of activity erupted with Madeleine holding a pencil in the air and squinting, Goran taking a digital photograph which he could pixilate for a closer view, Anselm staring at his shoes for inspiration, Pito taking an old pair of pince-nez on and off and Fliss declaring that she didn't feel that sort of teaspoon went with that style of cup, which made it very difficult to concentrate. Frances stood and stared at the cup. She felt as though she had never seen a cup before. Her pencil hovered uncertainly over the pure white paper.

'Commit yourselves,' Jack called from across the room. 'Remember, people, you draw the cup as you see it and the spoon as you imagine it.'

Slowly she began to draw and when she looked up again an hour and a half of her life had passed in peace and quiet.

'Not bad.'

Jack appeared at her shoulder and almost made her jump.

'Now why don't you try . . .' He reached from behind and placed his hand over hers to move the pencil. His hands were larger and rougher, and hers quite disappeared. She let him move the pencil across the page, shading and highlighting.

Frances turned and looked at him. She was aware how happy her time in the class felt and could not work out if her feelings for the art and for Jack had become confused.

'Jack, I need to talk to you,' she said.

'We're not here to talk. We're here to paint,' he said and moved away.

By late afternoon everyone was tired of wrestling with illusion and reality and most people went to lie down. Alistair had taken to rehearsing his lines with Fliss. He claimed Frances was too pernickety as a producer to help him with his 'initial exploration'. Gina was at the theatre, discussing lighting, so Frances went to her room alone.

Her door was open and Gabriella stood in the middle of the room. She was clearly distraught and pale from crying. In her hand was the small clay tablet with a child's handprint.

'It is Sophia's, yes?' enquired Gabriella.

'Yes,' replied Frances.

Gabriella nodded. 'Mine got broken. I remember.' She looked at the small imprint, at the lines for ever caught in the dry clay of Umbria. 'You were so close the three of you. Always together.'

It felt like an accusation.

'I'm sorry,' said Frances, like a reflex.

'I have watched Maria all my life. I have sat with her as we waited for the visions. She is like a saint. She sees no one, she hardly eats, she could be a saint and I would be the one who was there with her.'

'Gabriella.' Frances moved to comfort her but she moved sharply away.

'She is not well, Francesca. The Father does not let her leave the house. She has fits. I don't know what it is. There used to be a few but now it is often. I want her to see a doctor but she won't go. I thought maybe you . . .'

Aware that she had allowed things to drift indecisively, Frances knew she had to do

225

something. 'Where is she now?'

'At Benito's, but he will never let you in.'

'Does he go out? Is there a time when he is not there?'

'Wednesday. He has lunch with the men of the council but if you come and he finds out, I don't know, I think he will kill you.'

'I'll be there,' Frances promised. Gabriella placed the clay tablet on the bed and nodded. She left the room and took all of Frances's energy with her. She felt exhausted. She went to retrieve the handprint and sat on the bed. She was still holding Sophia's hand when Alistair returned from a successful afternoon being brilliant. He smiled and pushed her down on to the bed ready to be sexually satisfying.

'No,' she said firmly.

'What's the matter, chicken? Do you know, this could be rather fun,' he continued, ever oblivious to Frances's thoughts. He lit a cigarette and lay back, pulling hard on the rank-smelling weed. 'A little holiday in Italy, jolly people, good food, bit of a play.' Recalling how fine he was going to look as St Michael, he sighed with satisfaction. 'Ah, yes, the play's the thing.'

It was as if the sky had fallen on Chicken Little. Frances felt hit by lightning.

'What did you say?'

'I said, my little chicken,' oozed her lover, 'that we could have fun.'

'No. No. You said—the play's the thing,' repeated Frances getting up from the bed. ' "The play's the thing wherein I'll catch the conscience of the king." There is no fundamental truth, only illusion. Oh my God, that's it.'

'Ah, Henry the Fifth,' nodded Alistair sagely. At one time Frances had found Alistair's ignorance charming, now she was incensed.

'Hamlet, you twat,' she corrected.

There was little time for the twat to reply for Frances was already heading for the door. Of course, how stupid of her. She was a theatre producer and she hadn't even thought of it.

'Where are you going?' called Alistair, unused to such a short scene.

'To catch the king,' replied Frances.

'Did you call me a twat?' whined Alistair, only just getting up to speed with the conversation. But Frances was gone, calling out Gina's name as she ran.

CHAPTER NINETEEN

Quando la pera è matura, casca da se

When the pear matures, it falls on its own
(all things happen in their own good time)

Frances found Gina returning from the theatre
and spilt out her plan in the five minutes it took to
walk back to the school. She and Gina were on
fire; this was what they were good at. This was
going to be stunning. Gina jumped into action
making notes and doing quick sketches for what
they would need. Frances found Margaret, and
within half an hour the esteemed mistress of I
Gelosi had managed to gather everyone at the
teatro dell'arte. Margaret might not be able to
organise a plane ticket but she was a regular
Thomas Cook when it came to marshalling the
troops to save her beloved school. Lila, Madeleine,
Buff, Goran, Pito, Anselm, Margaret and a slightly
delayed and bewildered Alistair sat on the red
velvet seats in the auditorium.

Goran had clearly taken his role as Poor David
to heart and had spent a considerable amount of
time with Madeleine working on the costume he
now wore. Tiny and round, he was clad in a long
flowing robe in red with a blue sash and blue
mantle lined with matching red. On his head was a
cap of woollen stuff with a point falling behind and
decorated with three feathers, a dove and an olive
branch. It was not quite heroic and he had rather
the look of Dopey wondering where the rest of the

dwarves had got to. The red robe bore a sign of the cross framed by mirror images of the letter C. All this would have been quite startling enough had one's eye not been drawn to Goran's forehead, where the same symbol appeared to have been etched with an eyebrow pencil. It was a look that could not be ignored. Madeleine sat beside him and squeezed his hand. Gone was the stiff beige woman who had first appeared in the hall. Indeed, she looked slightly grey round the gills. Frances suspected that far from taking her advice about bathing Goran, Madeleine had instead decided to follow her beloved's path of indifference to dirt. Buff and Pito sat with their legs crossed towards each other, while Lila and Anselm sat with Margaret between them in a curious threesome. There was no question that, as Margaret had promised, everyone had begun to understand how intoxicating this place could be. Frances and Gina took to the small stage and for a brief moment they grinned at each other. This tiny arena of the arts reminded them why they had fallen in love with theatre in the first place. Here they were entirely at home, doing what they did best—fearless theatre producers who could bring audiences roaring to their feet.

'Right,' began Frances. 'Gina and I have been thinking, and we believe that what is needed is a spectacle such as has never been seen before.'

Gina picked up the thread seamlessly. 'If this pageant is a success, not only will it raise much-needed funding for the school but I think the town will realise that they need art. That they need this place and that they need I Gelosi.' There was much murmuring from the gathering as they made the sort of noises that extras listening to Julius Caesar might come up with.

'We have discussed a great deal of art while we have been here,' continued Frances in full and fine voice. 'Now it is time to turn to the theatre and there is no better place to do it. It was here in the Renaissance in Italy that the very invention of perspective painting in the fourteenth and fifteenth centuries, which Jack has talked about, led to the painted scenery that for the first time in history began to create the illusion of reality on a stage. The two are utterly connected and we shall pay tribute to those great Italians whose art transformed theatre. Sebastiano Serlio, the man who invented angled side-wings, which masked the space on either side of the stage and stopped the audience from seeing anything but the pretence before them. The legendary Giacomo Torelli, known to all Italian theatre fans as the Great Wizard, who in 1645 invented movable scenery and allowed chariots, angels and clouds to pass before the mesmerised audience.'

It was a talk Frances and Gina had given before but never with such passion. 'In the early days of theatre,' Gina continued, 'actors and producers knew how to create great effects. In surprisingly small spaces they restaged Roman chariot races, made men disappear and ghosts rise from nowhere. The Baroque Italians created an age of display with stage sets of miraculous splendour where storms at sea, floods of real water, flying birds or angels appeared before fantastic panoramas stretching apparently into infinity. The audience felt transported to somewhere real, yet they knew it was all a show. We shall have all this and more.'

Goran raised his hand timidly. 'We are still doing *Povero Davide*, yes?' he asked, anxious about losing his principal role before it had even been aired.

'Indeed. We shall still do the story of Poor David,' agreed Frances, 'but the story needs balancing. Let us seek the balance—the harmony which we have tried to find in the art room we will create right here. The story of Poor David is about a good man, perhaps a little off the wall but a man of good intentions that ultimately led to his death. The story of David will form the first half of the show and then, in the second, we shall create a new piece in which Anselm shall portray the evil side of man.'

'Ah, I see,' nodded Buff, ardently hoping to be given something backstage in the moving scenery department, 'the duality of nature.'

Anselm got shakily to his feet. '*Entschuldigen Sie bitte, Direktor*, does that mean I have the main part? The evil man, he is the main part?'

'Oh, most certainly, Anselm,' agreed Frances.

Gina nodded. 'You will be the star of the show,' she declared and once again the cousins grinned at each other. This was fun.

Anselm made a slight choking sound and had to sit down.

'I say, chicken,' protested Alistair.

'Sit down, Alistair,' barked Gina with great relish. 'Now then, jobs,' she continued. 'Goran, I need you to get your camera. We will need photographs and a slide projector.'

'*Sigurno*,' answered Goran so enthusiastically that everyone took it as a Montenegrin yes.

231

'Buff,' ordered Frances, 'I want you to prepare the most beautiful food you have ever created. A buffet of beauty for the second half.'

Buff had never been spoken to so forcefully by a woman before and could hardly open his mouth. 'Right-o,' he stammered.

'Pito,' said Gina, consulting her notes, 'we shall need a small explosion, and do you think you could get hold of a gun and an old parachute harness?'

'*Certamente*,' barked the Capitán and practically saluted, for he understood orders better than any of them.

Frances stormed on. 'Madeleine, we shall need your engineering skills.'

'Yes.' Gina held up a pencil drawing. 'We want a chariot, but it needs to be sturdy. I've made some drawings of what I want. Who's next?' she asked Frances.

'Lila,' answered her cousin.

'Oh, yes, we need three kids to take part,' said Gina. 'Frances says you have no trouble talking to the locals so I shall leave that to you. And that leaves, ah . . .' Gina looked down at her notes. 'Margaret, unlikely as it seems, I think you will have to be the Virgin Mary.'

The rehearsals went well. Everyone was enthusiastic and excited, and it was impossible to leave that excitement at the door of the art studio. It was impossible, much as he tried, for Jack not to hear what was going on. He had avoided Frances since their last meeting in the garden but one night, at the end of class, he stopped her in the door.

'I need to speak to you,' he said.

Frances shook her head. 'Oh right, now you

need to speak to me. We'll just do everything on your terms, shall we? We'll talk when you want to. Well, maybe there's nothing to say.'

'Oh really? Well, maybe I have something to say about what you're planning to do with this play. Maybe I have something to say about your trying to destroy this town. Maybe I have something to say about your little charade where you take away the only precious thing these people have.'

'I am not trying to destroy this town. I am trying to save it. The whole place is based on a lie,' blazed Frances. 'Illusion and reality? Remember?' She felt hot, exhausted and, lately, in Jack's company, endlessly at a loss for words. She turned away in fury and went to breathe in some of the evening air from the open window. Jack came and stood beside her. The sun was setting in a tapestry of colour and for a moment they stood like visitors overwhelmed by a gallery's offerings.

Jack spoke quietly as they continued to look out at the natural art laid before them. 'Frances, if you have questions, why don't you ask Signora Fratelli?'

Frances shook her head. 'No. I can't. I mean, I don't have enough Italian and—'

Jack gently touched her arm so that she turned to look at him.

'I'll help you. Let me help you. Isn't it better than spending the rest of your life wondering what happened?'

Frances moved abruptly to the table in the centre of the room and began fiddling with the brushes. 'Yes, well, maybe, but not now. Now is not a good time. I have a lot to do and there is a mass of work to do with poor Goran who really hasn't

233

got a clue and—'

Frances turned to point an accusing camel-hair brush at her teacher but he had gone. The room was empty and she knew she stood at a crossroads. Stand and wait for him to return, or leave and never really know the truth. Frances felt panicked. Like a child running between the car and the house, uncertain whether she wished to leave on an adventure or stay safe at home. She had lived with uncertainty for so long that in a way it had become its own comfort. A blanket of ignorance that excused failure to move forward. Frances looked at her own bright red handprint imprinted on the wall. It stood out with more contrast against the whitewash than she had ever seen. It must be warm in here, she thought.

Jack did not take long. He was not a man to splash about in the shallow waters of indecision. Frances heard the slow, familiar shuffle of Signora Fratelli's slippers against the stone floor as he gently led her into the art room. He found a stool and gently helped her to be seated. The old lady smiled.

'*Mi mostri la sua ultima pittura, Giacomo.*'

'*Non siamo venuti qui per questo, cucciola.*'

'What does she want?' asked Frances.

Jack smiled. 'She likes me to show her what I am working on but I told her that is not what we have come for.'

Signora Fratelli reached out for Frances's hand.

'*Abbiamo atteso cosi lungo. Possiamo attendere un altro po'.*'

Jack nodded. 'She says you and she have waited this long. You can wait a bit more.'

Frances nodded. 'So show us.'

234

Jack shrugged and went into his room at the back of the studio. Inside, several canvases stood stacked against each other. He drew them out one by one and placed them on an easel. Each one was a portrait of a member of the class. They weren't exactly figurative, yet each captured the essence of the person. There was Goran in a fine cloud of dust, Madeleine drawn with mathematical precision, Fliss entirely composed of the greens of a golf course. They were wonderfully observed without any sense of unkindness.

Signora Fratelli clapped her hands at each new piece and tears coursed down her cheeks. Not for her the emotional constipation so beloved of the English. Without any preamble she began to speak.

'*Non sàpra' mai quanto l'amavano i suoi genitori,*' she said quietly.

Jack stood beside his work and quietly translated. 'Your parents loved you more than you will ever know. After you had gone, your mother was ill with grief until your father could bear it no longer. Before they left, your mother came to Signora Fratelli and spoke to her. She promised that one day the truth about what happened to Sophia would be told.'

'*L'hanno seguido, con l'intenzione di trovarla in Inghilterra.*'

'They left to go after you. They left for England but . . .' Jack stopped in his translation task. Tears were now streaming down the old puppy's face and he too was unashamedly crying. Jack put his arm round her and stroked her shoulder gently. 'Oh, Angeli, I'm so sorry. You know that they were killed in the car, here in Umbria. The police investigated and they found the brakes had failed.'

235

'It was an accident?'

'No. The brakes had been tampered with. There was an investigation and people were questioned.'

'Benito?'

'He was sent to the Vatican for some months and by the time he returned the matter had been buried in paperwork. No one really wanted to know. The whole town was afraid. He is their priest. It could not be.'

'Benito,' repeated Signora Fratelli quietly. She looked exhausted. Helped by Jack she stood and put her arms round Frances. The old lady was tiny but her hug was fierce. It was a hug across decades of uncertainty and pain and Frances, strong, capable Frances, dissolved.

Jack returned Signora Fratelli to her room. Frances sat in the art room taking deep breaths until he returned.

'Thank you,' she said. 'Please, Jack, you must see why I have to do this.'

'I think you are making a mistake,' he said.

Frances put up her hands. 'I have to do this for Sophia and my parents and Signora Fratelli. I can't just leave and pretend it's nothing to do with me.'

Jack sighed and nodded. 'Then you have to be careful. You have to play your cards like an Italian. Do you know about Scopa? It is the most common Italian card game. Rule number one in Scopa—always try to see your opponent's cards. If you are going to do what you believe is the right thing, then you have to make sure you are all playing the same game by the same rules. The English will tell you not to kick a man when he is down. I've been here long enough to know that the Italians would be bewildered by this. Why not kick a man when he is down? It is the ideal time. Don't kick him if he is old or strong enough to kick you back or there is a policeman around, but otherwise kick him. You have to accept that maybe the only person who is not happy with the way things are is you.'

Frances shook her head. Having Gina on her side had made her feel strong again. She would not listen to Jack. Not only would their second-act story of the Innocent Children and the wicked priest be dramatic, it would, once and for all, make sure everyone knew the truth about Benito.

When she returned to her room, Frances found a note from Alistair saying he had popped out to the café with Fliss and would she please join them? But Frances had a plan and drinking coffee was not part of it. Frances knew Alistair well and could detect warning signs. She was aware that he seemed to be spending more and more time with the Texan housewife, but she realised that she didn't really mind. Her old habit of jealousy appeared to have been packed away. Frances quickly changed into her Sister of Charity outfit. She hid her hair beneath the veil and, concealed in her black and white garb, even her nearest and dearest might have taken a moment to recognise her.

Finding Father Benito's house was no problem. Everyone in the town was more than happy to help the gentle nun who had arrived to meet the Innocent Woman. In the narrow lane outside the priest's house, three little girls were playing the ancient Italian game of Morra—a simple game involving guessing the total number of fingers held out behind the player's back. They blocked the door and Frances's determined march was halted for a moment. Every muscle of the participants' bodies was in play. There were no betraying movements of lips, no hint in the eye of what was intended as each child leant forward on one leg, one arm outstretched, the other held back in secret. It was a game that had been played for centuries. On Greek vases and in Etruscan sepulchral paintings, men are represented playing Morra. All part of the restless need through every civilisation for entertainment. A simple game, yet banned in parts of Italy because of the quarrels it so often led to. Such a quarrel seemed about to erupt when a voice called out from a window above their heads and further down the lane.

'*Madonnina! Madonnina!*' Little Madonna, a child's mother called and the game came to an end. The children looked up and saw Frances watching them. Instinctively they crossed themselves and dipped slightly at the knee. Frances raised her hand to remonstrate but this only caused them to bow their heads with respect at the nun who had appeared from nowhere. Their incipient quarrel forgotten, the girls exchanged hurried promises to meet again and ran off to separate homes and enterprises.

It could have been Francesca, Maria and Sophia from so many years ago. Playing in the shadow of the priest's house. Safe in the narrow confines of the town where each and every citizen was ever ready to stand, daggers drawn, around the bell tower against the threatening incomer. But the threat had not come from outside. It had come from within and it was time to face up to the consequences. Frances waited. It was nearly lunchtime and, if Gabriella was right, the Holy Father would be out for lunch.

Up two stone steps from the street, the wooden door to the priest's house had stood for generations. Long enough to have received a knock from the odd saint. The entrance was framed in brick laid with no particular thought to regularity. The red of the brick bled into the tessellated stones, some of which seemed freshly plucked from the hillside. One of the bricked-in doors of the dead was to the right of the main doorway. Several shadows of arched stone and brick showed it had been opened and closed at various times. Frances turned her attention to the entrance for the living. This door was made in two halves of oak, each wide enough to allow admission on its own. A large iron knocker hung high in the centre on the right-hand side, shaped like the head of an Egyptian sphinx, with a great swoop of metal suspended from its ears to bang upon the door. Frances found herself praying to God that Father Benito would not return. She raised her hand and knocked. The sound reverberated through the lane. A surprisingly loud noise from such a symbol of silence. It seemed to match the pounding in Frances's chest. Up and down the narrow street, heads appeared in doorways and windows. There was no one in town who would not know the priest's house had a visitor, but it was a holy woman and no one thought anything of it. Frances hoped to God Maria was ready for her bit of fun.

CHAPTER TWENTY

Art is a kind of illness.

Giacomo Puccini
Italian opera composer (1858–1924)

The night of the play Pito was on the door looking out for *portoghesi*—people claiming to have free theatre tickets. Centuries ago a gala performance given in Rome in honour of a Portuguese mission was swamped by Romans who entered saying they were Portuguese and entitled to free seats. The poor Portuguese had given their name to the practice ever since. The theatre of Montecastello was tiny. Only a handful of patrons could be accommodated and there had been a positive clamour for tickets. Margaret had tried to persuade Frances that they might even give a second performance but Frances had been insistent that this was a one-off for which they could charge unusually high prices.

Jack had helped Buff carry some of his creations backstage and he was just leaving when Gina and Frances emerged from the dressing room. Being busy with the play and not attending his classes, Gina had not really encountered Jack before, so she was surprised to see Frances so flustered.

'I'm Frances's cousin, Gina,' she announced brightly while Frances, embarrassed and uncertain, bent down to fuss over Auroch.

'Hello, boy.'

'So, *le vernissage*,' said Jack.

Frances looked up and smiled. 'Sorry?' She realised how much she loved his forays into the arcane areas of life.

'The French call it "varnishing day". It's when the paintings are hung but the critics have not yet arrived. I brought you some flowers. Here.' Jack reached into his sleeve and produced a bouquet by magic.

The women smiled. Jack handed them to Frances, who blushed. 'Are you nervous?' he asked.

'Not a bit,' smiled Gina. 'This is what we do. Nice to meet you.' Goran called out for help and Gina headed off.

'Jack, I—' began Frances.

'Frances!' Alistair called petulantly from the tiny dressing room. 'This costume still does not fit properly around the neck. I do not believe that St Michael would ever appear in something uncomfortable. I mean, he's an angel, for fuck's sake.' Alistair was always a bundle of nerves before any performance and it didn't improve his manner.

'I have to go.' Frances turned to leave and then turned back. 'I was wondering if we could . . .'

But Jack was gone. Auroch, however, ever a dog with a mind of his own, had stayed backstage. He found a pile of old theatre curtains, circled his body into a small nest and settled himself to wait for the performance. Frances was about to call after Jack and say the dog couldn't possibly stay when the pass door to the auditorium opened and Lila stood framed in the light. It was bright behind her and for a moment she looked darker than she had ever been.

'Frances, I just wanted you to meet my parents. I've never been in a play before so . . . anyway, they said they'd come,' she announced like a child in her first nativity. From behind her appeared a late middle-aged black couple. They were entirely black. Blacker than black. Not even a hint of white. Frances made a slight choking noise and managed to say, 'Your parents?'

Lila nodded.

'Right.' Frances tried to be professional. 'You'd better get ready, Lila,' she said with more kindness than she had ever shown the woman before.

Lila's parents headed for the public side of the theatre where a great stir had gone up among the gathered patrons. Cardinal Vacceccio from the Vatican City in his brilliant red papal colours and Signora Biche from the Italian Commission of Culture in an exquisite grey suit had arrived with Father Benito. Even the Father had made an effort and for once the white of his collar shone out against the shiny pressed black of his suit. Paolo was representing the town committee and almost falling over himself as he led the honoured guests to a box on the first floor facing directly on to the stage. This was what the families who had first funded this folly of a theatre had always dreamt of—dignitaries gracing their town, waiting to see what art Montecastello could produce. Sadly, no professional performance had taken to the stage since a touring company of *Tosca* had passed through for one night in 1987. It had not been a big success as the diva had been large, the stage small and the theatrical timbers less supportive than anyone could have predicted. Tonight that was forgotten and it seemed the entire town was dressed for the occasion. Certainly each member of the select and small audience had pulled out all the fashion stops as if they instinctively knew that they too were somehow part of the performance. There had been talk that the ticket-holders themselves might be photographed and the air was thick with the scent of hairspray and gel. Outside, in the small square beyond the front door, those unlucky enough not to secure tickets waited in whispering anticipation. They might not be able to see the show but they felt confident that somehow the waves of emotion generated inside would sweep out into the cobbled street.

The plush red stage curtains with their broad band of golden tassels had been carefully brushed down for the occasion. Imperiously they divided the excited throng from the art about to be revealed. Having found the tickets difficult to obtain in the first place and having dressed for the occasion, there was not one member of the audience who did not feel entitled to take as fulsome a part in the piece as possible. No Montecastellian intended to be one of the chosen ones and keep quiet about it. They called to each other in displays of effusive greeting, which also helped to highlight the precise location of their prized seat, the men kissed the hands of women they might ordinarily have ignored and almost every single individual found a reason to pop into Paolo's box just to say hello. The fact that a cardinal and a member of the Culture Commission were sitting there seemed to greet each new arrival as a complete surprise. Cheers went up in the house for the programme seller, there were 'hurrahs' for the young boy who was caught slipping in through an air vent and even Pito, on showing the last couple to their place, received a spontaneous burst of enthusiastic applause, which he accepted with a gracious wave to the entire house. In all Frances's and Gina's years in the theatre they had never opened before such an attentive and enthusiastic public.

The cousins stood in the wings waiting for the performance to commence.

'He's very cute,' said Gina.

'Who is?' asked Frances.

'Your art teacher.'

Frances blushed. 'Cute?'

'The flowers were cute,' said Gina.

'What are we suddenly—twelve?'

Gina grinned. 'Maybe. There was something of the giggling schoolgirl about you when he was here.'

Frances slapped Gina on the arm as Pito arrived to say that the front of house was ready and they could begin.

As soon as the curtains began to rustle towards opening, there was a great expiration of audible appreciation and even one or two early calls of 'bravo' just to prepare the dignitaries for the brilliance that was no doubt to come. Considering the curious nature of the cast, the first half went quite well. Goran appeared as *Povero Davide* and there was much nodding and murmuring. This was a local story and most people already knew it. They felt quite comfortable when David announced that it was foretold he should die for the sins of others just as Christ had done.

There was much whispering of 'That's true' and 'That's exactly what happened' or 'My aunt knew his mother.'

Much of the comment was done slightly too

loudly in the hope that the Cardinal himself would hear and realise the great capacity for faith that filled these Umbrian hills. Alistair's appearance as St Michael very nearly brought the house down. He looked stunning in his angelic outfit and gave a stellar performance. Here Alistair was a big professional fish in a small pond of amateurs and he swam his lengths with huge gusto. He was not a great actor but he had sufficient skill to make each individual feel as though every line was directed straight at them alone as he plucked their heartstrings and stirred the loins of men and women alike. So much wild applause greeted his final line that he came back on and did it all over again.

By the time Alistair finally retired to heaven, Goran was getting tired. His pointy hat was a tiny bit too tight and had given him a headache. Waiting for the Alistair love fest to finish had left him feeling a little confused. The main upshot of this was that all his carefully rehearsed lines began to leave him.

'This,' he said in a low voice, 'is . . . this is . . . well, I can't recall.'

'A sign of blood,' prompted Madeleine from the wings. She had rehearsed endlessly with her new love and felt she could have played the part herself.

Goran nodded and pointed to Madeleine who for once was wearing black and was thus entirely concealed from the sight of the audience.

'That's right,' he said. 'That's what it is. What she said.'

After the outstanding overacting of Alistair the audience was ready for a bit of light relief. There was appreciative laughter. No one felt anything was being spoiled. Rather Goran was enhancing the performance by adding the possible drama that he might not get through it. Even in his bewilderment Goran knew that this was supposed to be a serious moment in the piece. He was about to die and the laughter rather threw him.

He stepped forward and spoke to the giggling house. 'I have to die now,' he explained, 'so you have to be quiet.'

What he had not expected was that this breaking of the conventional 'fourth wall' of theatre meant the audience felt they had been invited into the possibility of a conversation.

'How?' someone called out from the back of the stalls.

'This is . . .' Goran's next line left his mind once again. The question had ruined his train of thought. 'How what?' he asked into the darkness.

'How are you going to die?' asked some other helpful soul in one of the boxes.

'I am going to be shot,' Goran explained patiently.

'I'm not in the least bit surprised,' someone else shouted and the place erupted into mirth. The man who called out the remark was an instant local hero and it took some moments of back-patting and cat-calling before order could be restored.

By now Goran had metaphorically and literally lost the plot. Anselm, a seasoned performer, decided to be helpful and appear early as *Povero Davide*'s brother. He strode on just as one of his lines suddenly occurred to Goran.

'God makes me a giant among men . . .' the tiny man declared as he turned and walked straight into

Anselm's chest. Anselm was indeed a giant beside Goran and pleasure rippled through the already over-excited audience. No doubt there would be tears before bedtime. If these two were brothers then clearly their mother must have played away from home.

'Everyone is tired and hungry, David,' boomed Anselm in a confident Teutonic tone, which possibly lost some sense of the despair he was meant to be feeling. 'Please let your people rest. Do not come down to Arcidosso for there are armed men waiting and you will surely die.'

'I fear nothing,' replied Goran.

'Good man,' yelled Paolo, who, despite the weight of his civic responsibilities, was beginning to be caught up in the drama.

Goran nodded in the direction of the box. 'Thank you.' He smiled at Paolo and kept nodding until Anselm tapped him on the arm to continue. 'Ah yes. My followers will not be hurt. I alone will be the victim. Come, let us depart. We shall descend . . .'

'Singing,' assisted Madeleine.

'Indeed, singing,' agreed Goran.

Well, this was marvellous news all round. Everyone was ready for a good tune and it was at this point that Margaret appeared as a Daughter of Song and began a chorus from *Carmen*, which was as close to a classical piece as she could manage. Everyone in the house knew the tune, and so almost without exception decided to join in. *Povero Davide* descended the mountain towards his death to a fairly raucous accompaniment. Margaret took several curtain calls and Anselm spent some time dissuading the audience from moving on to other hits by Bizet. Gina, aware that things had taken a slightly pantomimic turn, sent on Pito, who entered the stage carrying a gun.

'Halt. I am the Mayor of Arcidosso,' he declared, 'and I have nine *carabinieri* and an officer waiting.'

'Where?' shouted the bold man in the stalls whose part was growing by the minute.

Now Pito too broke the wall of consensual silence between the stage and the main house. 'They are in the wings,' he explained patiently. 'This is the theatre and I can have as many people in the wings as I wish.' It seemed perfectly reasonable to everyone and after some discussion the story was allowed to continue.

'I go forward in the name of Righteousness and of Christ our Lord and Judge,' declared Goran, building up to the interval. 'If you will have peace, I bring peace; if you will have mercy, have mercy; if you will have blood, here I am.'

He opened his arms dramatically and turned to face the hidden policemen.

'*Viva la Repubblica di Cristo,*' yelled Lila, suddenly remembering to appear as a Matron of Mary. This set the audience off again. They too began calling out '*Viva la Repubblica di Cristo*' and other invocations to the Lord. Lila's proud parents, who after all had come some distance for the performance, felt this stir had been caused by their beloved child and set off a round of applause. Pito, fed up with being interrupted, did what any self-respecting soldier would do: he aimed his gun and fired. It was quite a loud noise and Goran, who looked more shocked than anyone, took a moment to realise he was supposed to be hit.

Anselm gave him a shove and the small man dived to the floor where he remembered to writhe for a little before giving a final death rattle and passing out. Anselm stood over his brother's body and solemnly declared, *'L'uomo propone ma Dio dispone'*—'Man proposes but God disposes.' Then he picked Goran up and slowly carried him towards the back of the stage as the lights dimmed and the curtain descended. Pandemonium broke out. The clapping took on a kind of rhythmic mania and even Auroch took to a howling of approval. The scene had been a triumph and everyone knew it was now time for a drink. Never in all the years of the small theatre's existence had a crowd been so ecstatic.

By the time order and the audience were restored for the second half there was an air of great excitement. Drinks had been taken, flirting had been done, gossip exchanged and now more entertainment was to be presented. Surely this was a night that would be talked about for years. The curtain went up on a black stage. A large black-edged mirror stood on a stand beside a table covered by a black cloth. Images of a woman's face seemed to float in the air. She was beautiful but sometimes appeared to be black and sometimes white. Ethereal music played as Anselm strode on dressed as a priest. He wore the everyday garb of a Holy Father and seemed not to see the images that played around his head. He looked menacingly at the audience, who were quickly silenced.

'Pito, the Virgin Mary,' hissed Gina to the Capitán, who was standing in the wings entirely engrossed in the scene. Pito bowed a quick apology and reached for a stout rope. Above the stage,

Paolo's wife, the magnificent Margaret, hung suspended in an old parachute harness that Pito had procured from an Italian air-force chum. In addition, Margaret wore a pale-blue shift and veil intended to create the image of the Mother of God. Pito swung her gently into view above Anselm's head and she actually looked quite holy. She floated there for a second, but Anselm's priest did not see her and she swung away back into the flies. Holiness was all around the priest, but he was oblivious and had other things on his mind.

Anselm walked to the cloth-covered table. Someone in the audience coughed and he looked again at the house to demand total silence. Clearly this was not a man to be messed with. With the flourish of a magician, he pulled off the cloth in a single movement. On the table was revealed a display of food art which outdid anything Buff had created until then. Here was a dome of tiramisu in raw sienna and yellow ochre; a cake of zabaglione on which scarlet raspberries floated on a bed of deep cadmium yellow; there were Sicilian fig cookies with hearts of burnt umber; tortelli cake; zuppa inglese with fresh strawberries; Amaretti alla Piemontese; a white chocolate salami; crumiri biscuits and more.

A gasp of astonishment went up from the crowd. No one, even those who had been to great restaurants in Rome, had ever seen such a stunning gastronomic display. The priest began to eat. This was performance art that Anselm understood. He relished his part and dived headlong into the ultimate portrayal of gluttony. Using his hands, Anselm crammed the food into his mouth, allowing the cream and the custard to drip from his chin and down on to his vestments. By now the crowd too had become hungry. The interval drinks had sharpened the appetite and the food looked more delicious than anyone could bear. A slight murmur of dislike for the priest began to percolate through the throng. As he ate, the greedy man of God looked in the mirror and adjusted his hair. The floating faces disappeared and as they did so the priest glanced at something in the mirror. He turned upstage, where three small girls appeared.

The girls carried on a small piece of scenery representing a chapel and began to play a game. They were pretending to be saints. They were imagining what it would be like and what they might see. The priest, glistening and drizzled with food remnants, hid and listened. By now no one liked him. He was vain, he was secretive and he had failed to share his plate. As the girls continued their game, the audience slowly became restive. It seemed too familiar. Too like their own story of Sophia, Maria and Francesca to feel entirely comfortable. *Povero Davide* had been one thing. That too was a local story but it had happened across the valley. This, however, was their own tale. There were plenty in the audience who could still recall the fire in the chapel, the death of the Fratellis and then the Angellis. One by one the audience began to glance from the corner of their eyes to the box where Father Benito sat with the Cardinal. The dim emergency light at the back of the box showed the Father's face had become pale and taut.

Suddenly one of the girls fell to the floor, writhing and calling out to the Black Madonna.

Her friends ran for help as the priest leapt forward and picked up the little girl in his arms. He turned to the audience and displayed her like a trophy. Madeleine and Pito appeared as townsfolk with the remaining girls, one of whom was crying.

'It was just a game. There was no vision. Tell the truth,' she cried to the child in the priest's arms. At this, there was a general murmuring in the house and one or two even got to their feet. The sense of impending commotion spread out into the street where the waiting crowd could wait no longer. They poured up the stairs, through the entrance and filled every available space at the back of the theatre. By now the audience was in a three-ringed circus unsure where to look next. Their hearts and minds were transfixed by the stage, but more and more their eyes were glued to Father Benito. And Anselm was heady with his main part and playing it for all the evil available.

'You will not get in my way, child,' he boomed. He put the girl he was carrying down on the table among the food debris, and went to grab the girl who continued to call out about telling the truth. As he dragged her away, Madeleine and Pito tried to cling on to her. They were pulled behind the chapel scenery, whereupon Buff set off his small explosion and the child, Madeleine and Pito disappeared in a burst of flame. In the wings, Frances held Gina's hand almost unable to watch. They could hear that the place had erupted into a frenzy and knew it was too late to turn back. They were opening the can of worms once and for all.

Montecastello was a small town and there was no one who did not know the gossip about Father Benito. He might have been their leader but they

252

were not blind to his faults. Now everyone in the audience was torn. They wanted to watch the action but they were also keen to see the Holy Father's reaction. Even the Cardinal, who knew none of this, had turned to Benito when he had heard a deep intake of breath from the man. At last Benito could stand it no longer. He got to his feet and stumbled out into the foyer. Here he was met by a wall of his parishioners entirely focused on the drama. They didn't block his exit on purpose, it was simply that no one could conceive of his leaving at the height of the drama. Escape being impossible, Benito had nowhere to go but down towards the stage. Suddenly, in a moment of great clarity, he knew what he must do. He must stop this nonsense and speak to his people. He had moved them before and he would do so again. For an old man he moved quickly and the theatre was small, so he was up on the stage before anyone had a moment to think. At this point the greatest director in the world could not have controlled the ensuing stage activities.

Paolo, mortified that one of his principal guests seemed to be escaping, and mindful of the presence of the Cardinal, had also leapt to his feet. As the civic representative he felt honour-bound to do something but he could not think what, so he simply gave chase and was the next to appear in the stalls. Meanwhile Benito had timed his unscheduled appearance on the stage with the appearance of the Virgin Mary from above.

Frances and Gina stood frozen in the wings with horror. They'd had productions go wrong before but never quite to this degree. The play had been intended to expose Benito but not to have him take part. Meanwhile, Pito was busy congratulating Buff on his pyrotechnics and failed to realise that he was leaning on the rope from which Margaret was suspended. This resulted in Benito's untimed appearance coinciding with the equally unplanned reappearance of the Virgin Mary from above. Buff and Pito both grabbed for the rope but Margaret was a substantial weight and not easy to stabilise in mid-air. Despite both men frantically hanging on, the voluminous Virgin swung back down from the flies with surprising speed. Margaret, who had not rehearsed a second appearance, attempted to regain some balance by kicking out with her not inconsiderable feet. Father Benito's only thought was to stop the performance, so he was as ill-prepared for Margaret's entrance as everyone else and was flung with some force when her descending toe clipped him soundly on the ear. Margaret swung stage right out of view as the Holy Father rose unsteadily to his feet, only to be sent flying once again by the combined force of Pito and Buff who made a further unexpected appearance on stage, desperately swinging on the other end of the rope. Buff called out, 'Geronimo!' which Madeleine took as her cue to release the double doors at the back of the stage.

Out in the street, lit only by candles, the Innocent Woman, Maria herself, passed through the sight of the audience as if floating. She drifted in and out of their vision and then seemed to come towards them. She was dressed in pure white and, all around her, black-and-white images of the Virgin Mary were projected on the surrounding buildings. Unseen by the audience, the chariot she stood on was being worked by Goran. He smoothly carried his charge from her glide in the street on to the stage, where she stepped forward. Unfortunately Goran forgot to apply the brakes to his vehicle and slipped beneath it with a cry of pain. Madeleine, ever anxious about her beloved, cried out to Anselm who yelled, *'Mehre Licht,'* which was either a tribute to his beloved Goethe or a demand to see what was happening. Lila hit the lighting board with her hand and a great shaft of white light filled the stage. Undaunted and used to being the centre of attention, Maria walked towards the audience. When she reached the front of the stage she removed her customary veil and showed her thin face. Then she began to remove her white garments beneath which she wore the clothes of an ordinary woman. She reached out and cuddled the child on the table and turned to look accusingly at Anselm.

By now the entire crowd was on its feet, yelling and gasping with amazement. Roused by the noise, the dazed Father Benito once more tried to get to his feet but the noise had also stirred Auroch who, never a fan, leapt at the opportunity to grab the priest's ankle. He stood to shake the dog off, at which point Buff and Pito disappeared back into the wings with a deeply satisfying crash and Margaret, succumbing to the ultimate laws of physics, swung back into view. It was clear to anyone that while landing on Margaret might once have saved a life, having Margaret land on someone was never going to be anything but tragic. The vast flying woman, by now also chased by her husband from below, took no time to knock both the holy man and the dumb animal flying into the wings, where Auroch landed on the by now winded

Pito, who accidentally let the gun off again. To say it was an evening no one would ever forget was an understatement.

CHAPTER TWENTY-ONE

Quando finisce la partita, i pedoni, le torri,
i cavalli, i vescovi, I due re e le due regine
tutti vanno nella stessa scatola

When the chess game is over, the pawns,
rooks, knights, bishops, kings and queens
all go back in the same box

Father Benito was dead, Goran had tyre marks on
his ankle and Paolo had inadvertently been shot in
the arse. It was hard to say exactly what killed
Benito. It could have been the blow to the temple
with a size-eight sandal or it could have been the
rapid descent from above by the world's largest
virgin. Goran bore his marks with pride and
Madeleine took the opportunity of applying salve
finally to cement their love. As for Paolo, while the
shot had only been a blank it had been fired at
close enough proximity to cause a burn that would
be some time in healing. In truth, nothing had
quite turned out as planned. The play, far from
spoiling the story of the Innocent Woman had
merely enhanced it. It was, in the end, Frances's
inclusion of her old schoolfriend that had clinched
it. Illusion is a wonderful thing and Maria's
appearance had seemed so miraculous that
Madeleine never got the credit she deserved for
the chariot she had created to float the miracle
woman down the street. Goran's photographs had
been so well produced and projected that they too
were given a level of reality that was flattering but

unintended. Much to Alistair's chagrin, the first part of the play was entirely forgotten—and no one seemed to recall the denouncement of the visions. Indeed, the Cardinal concluded his visit by calling on Maria and blessing her. It was agreed that she would continue to live in the priest's house with Gabriella to care for her and a stipend from the Church for her needs. A doctor was called on the quiet and Maria's fits were found to be due to epilepsy for which medication was secretly prescribed.

On the whole, the town was content with this outcome and not wishing any further investigation they fell into agreement for Father Benito to be buried in Vatican City. It reflected well on the town and no one was immune to the irony of his resting at last in the place whose approval he had so craved. The papal offices had offered his body to the town but Paolo, on behalf of the committee, had graciously given up the honour to Rome. On the surface it looked extremely magnanimous, but in fact most Montecastellians were glad to be rid of the man.

The town was buzzing with excitement and the story of that night spread across the valleys until it grew beyond all proportion. The press arrived and soon Margaret was flooded with enquiries. Her dreams for I Gelosi were coming to fruition. Perhaps the world needed art after all. Even more pleasingly, Paolo was exactly where she wanted him—on the sofa in the hall, unable to do anything without her help.

Frances and Gina sat in Frances's room measuring time with the sun.

Gina smiled. 'I doubt we will ever be able to top

that performance.'

'No. It was quite something.'

'Did it help?' asked Gina.

Frances nodded. 'Thank you. I think so. I don't know what I was looking for—some truth or other. Jack said it didn't exist and it probably doesn't, but Maria will be safe now. I don't know what she saw and it doesn't matter any more. She's good for the town and it will be good to her.'

Gina stood and looked out across the valley. When she turned back into the room she spoke softly. 'I have to go home, Frances, and I think I need to stop working for a while. I haven't paid enough attention to the business since the kids were born and actually I don't want to. I need time with them. I think we should go out on the high of that great drama on that tiny stage.'

Frances was about to reply when there was a soft knock at the door. It was Jack.

'Sorry. Frances . . . Signora Fratelli, she . . .' He didn't need to finish. As if to set the seal on the story's conclusion, on the night of the play Signora Fratelli, Sophia's grandmother, had passed away in her sleep.

The workmen came and opened the door of the dead in the hall. At last, the door through which she had so longed to pass was unblocked and she left the world peacefully to her eternal rest.

And when she was gone Paolo, who now spent his days with his arse in the air on the hall sofa, declared, *'Tutto è bene quello che finisce bene'*—'All's well that ends well'—and it seemed right. The wall was plastered back into place and Jack arrived with his paintbrushes. Slowly and carefully he began to create a new *trompe l'oeil*—a false exit until the next time.

Gina went home, but she left without worrying too much about her cousin. Frances could have gone with her and wasn't sure why she stayed.

'I have some things to do,' she said, and Gina hugged her.

Once Gina had gone, Frances felt uncertain. She wandered down to the art studio and was surprised to find Fliss standing in the centre of the room.

'So no Bible centre, eh?' Frances remarked. 'I'm sorry things didn't work out for you, Fliss.'

Fliss nodded. She was standing before the last canvas she had been working on. 'What do you think, Frances?'

Frances had paid little attention to the work of the others during the lessons. Now she came and stood in front of the large piece of work. It was an impressionistic view of the landscape from the studio window and it was wonderful. Great sweeps of colour had been flung on to the canvas with such joyful abandon that it made you smile just to look at it. It was not a faithful representation of the view, yet it captured every emotion one might feel when standing looking out at the lush hills of Umbria.

'Dear God, it's brilliant, Fliss. I had no idea,' uttered Frances.

Fliss nodded. 'Frances, do you think it's possible that the good Lord was sending me a message about coming here but that I didn't hear it properly?'

'Well,' said Frances, 'none of us see that well, so I don't know why our hearing should be so damned good.'

260

The women laughed and for a brief moment Frances thought she had misjudged this housewife from Texas, that she had seen only the surface when she looked at her. Then Alistair appeared in the doorway carrying his bag.

'You ready, darling?'

'No,' began Frances; then she realised that it was Fliss he had addressed.

'Yes, honey, I am,' replied Fliss and moved to stand beside him.

'Sorry? Alistair? What's going on?' Frances asked, taken aback.

Alistair looked sheepish. 'Look, chicken, I meant to say. I love you. I always will. Fliss knows that. It's just that you seem quite, well, different now and I'm not at all sure that you need rescuing.'

Frances took in Fliss and Alistair standing beside each other. He looked like her toy boy but in truth he was probably nearer Fliss's age than he cared to think. She could see that he was ageing and it was not going to go brilliantly. Frances tried to summon up the feelings she had once had for this beautiful boy but they were, thank God, tucked away somewhere. She realised that in their time together they had seen what they held jointly in completely different lights. They had shared a passion but not a vision. For Frances, the relationship had been all-consuming and when, at forty, she had declared a need to stop work, it had been for him, to create an image of him in which he had proved to be uninterested. Alistair saw life as a place to idle, not contribute.

'Had a better offer?' she grinned.

Alistair did his best to look scandalised by the suggestion. It was a good try, except Fliss took his

261

arm and told him it was time to go.

Fliss smiled at Frances. 'The play was good, honey, but we're out of here. I don't think I'm ever going to be all that popular.'

Alistair kissed Frances on the cheek and whispered, 'Texas! You don't suppose I'll have to get on a horse, do you?'

'Alistair, you could ride anything you put your mind to.'

And with that he was gone.

*   *   *

It was a few days after their theatrical triumph and no one was in the mood for art class. Frances found Buff and Pito in the kitchen with Margaret.

'. . . and I see no reason why in the winter months we couldn't run cooking classes,' Buff was explaining enthusiastically.

'Yes, Buff he will cook and I will teach Italian,' enthused Pito.

'But where will you stay?' asked Margaret. 'I've had so many enquiries . . .'

Pito looked at Buff. 'I have . . . found us a little flat.'

'Us?' smiled Margaret.

Buff blushed. 'Do you think Paolo will mind? He's very . . . well, you know, religious.'

'My dear boys, Paolo will do as I say or being shot in the arse will be the least of his troubles.' Margaret shouted the last remark through the kitchen door and into the hall where her husband was heard to murmur, *'Lei è' la carta di briscola, lei è' la carta di briscola.'*

With the contrariness of human nature, now

262

that Frances was free to leave she wasn't at all sure she wanted to go. She said goodbye to Anselm and Lila. Lila's parents had departed and she was off to Berlin to learn performance art with the master. Anselm leant down to kiss Frances on the cheek.

'It was a work of genius, Madam Director. It will stay in my mind as a performance to be proud of. Anytime you are in Berlin and wish to see some real art I am usually in Alexanderplatz.'

'Thank you, Anselm.'

Frances went back to the theatre, kidding herself that she needed to check everything was in order, that props and costumes had been tidied away for another time. Sheets had been draped across the seats against the dust which gathers faster in theatres than in any other kind of building. It was the most extraordinary place. Even here, in the smallest theatre in the world, great dramas could be played out. The moral foundation of the human race could be discussed, affirmed or denied. Lit by the traditional single lamp on the stage, the place should have been still but wild shadows were playing across the back wall. Frances did not stay to investigate but it seemed that Madeleine and Goran had found another use for the parachute harness and there was no question that the neat little French woman had finally unlocked her wilder side.

Frances smiled and let herself out. She headed for one last circle of the town walls. It felt so familiar now that when she reached the gate into the garden of her childhood home, where she had first met Jack, she was not at all surprised to see him there. He was playing with Auroch, chucking a stick and making him bring it back. Jack looked up and saw Frances through the grille.

'Isn't that amazing?' he called.

'I don't know,' answered Frances, 'I've always found "fetch" a little over-rated as a game.'

'No, Angel, he can see. Auroch can see. He must have had a blow to the head in all that kerfuffle and he can see.'

So there had been a genuine miracle after all but it was small. It had happened to a dog and occupied no one's attention. After all, it had not been what they were looking for.

'I came to say goodbye,' she said.

Jack put the stick down and walked towards her. 'Why?' he asked.

Frances shrugged. 'There is nothing to keep me here.'

Jack nodded as if he understood. 'Alistair,' he said simply.

'No,' replied Frances. 'He left with Fliss. Something about her large property portfolio that I expect he found very sexy.'

'I'm sorry.'

'Please, don't be. It was time. Well, I'd better . . .' Frances moved to leave but Jack put out his hand.

'Mind if I show you something?' he asked and led her into the garden. They wandered over to the bench where they had first sat together. Frances took in the view and saw the vast fields of sunflowers content to spend their day turning slavishly towards the sun—*girasoli*. On the bench lay an artist's portfolio crammed with pieces of paper. Jack opened it and pulled one out. It was a glorious nude woman lying across a bed.

'Lila,' breathed Frances without really looking,

and turned to leave. Jack pulled her back.

'No. Look at the face, at the body. It's you. I tried to get Lila to model but all I could see was you.'

'Wait a second.' Frances paused. 'I saw Lila in your room—she was modelling for you?'

'Yes,' said Jack.

'That's all?' persisted Frances slowly, although her heart was beginning to increase its pace.

Jack spread his hands in a stance of honest innocence. 'Of course that's all.' He tried to reach for Frances's hand but she wasn't ready yet. They stood for a moment in the wild grass and breathed the fresh air.

'What does Francesca mean?' asked Jack at last.

'It means "free",' she said. 'And Jack?'

'It comes from an old word for "gracious".' Jack smiled. 'Gracious living. It has a nice ring to it.' He turned to view the dilapidated house in its overgrown garden. 'Isn't the place looking great, Angel? Look, the sun shining on the stable door, the smell of coffee coming from the kitchen where bougainvillaea is trailing over the window and over there, a little girl is playing . . .' Jack squinted. 'Maybe it's a boy, what do you think?'

'I think I have to go.'

'Frances . . .'

'Jack. I'm forty, I'm very English now and I have such a lot of feelings about this place. I don't know if I could ever start again.' She reached down to pat Auroch for the last time and turned towards the gate. She brushed through the long grasses, wondering what was next.

Jack called after her, 'There is something in art called *pentimento*.'

Frances stopped with her back to him. She had been utterly seduced by the art, by his lectures. Perhaps just one more.

Jack stood his ground and continued.

'It is when the artist changes his mind,' he explained, 'and paints over the work he has done. An artist can regret and change his mind. The picture doesn't have to stay the same. You can change whatever you want as long as you do it carefully enough.'

Frances turned to look at him. 'I was thinking,' she said, 'Lila's parents, they really were black, weren't they?'

'I know,' agreed Jack. 'You just can't tell anything by looking, can you?'